Charlie appeared at the doorw it. She dragged Ayesha's near butterfly tattoo she had there. Ay(hand off. The man in the hazmat ѕ coming towards her. Ayesha ran (Hazmat Man and the cries of Charlie for her to come back. She ran; the heels of her trainers squealing on the shiny floors as she rounded a corner and ran into two more hazmat clothed figures. An older man and a younger woman went to grab her.

"Who is she?" The man shouted at his female companion.

"Relative of one of the deceased nurses," the woman said back.

Ayesha put her head down and butted an opening between them both. With their plastic gloves on it was hard to keep hold of her hands. Ayesha ran on in search of her mother with three suited people in pursuit of her. She headed off down a well-lit interior corridor with doors on either side. A door banged open four yards further on, and a hazmat-suited person of indeterminable sex pulled a trolley out into the corridor through a plastic opening. The trolley squeaked as it was pulled through the doorway. It also yanked back the white plastic sheet covering the body of a dead person underneath.

Yet there was no face on the female corpse. Just hair and a gory mess where her skin and nose used to be. Ayesha screamed at the top of her lungs, fainting dead away just before her pursuers could catch her.

THE FLOOD

BOOK 1 OF THE END OF ALL FLESH

BY PETER MARK MAY

The end of all flesh is come before me; for the earth is filled with violence against them; and behold I will destroy them with the earth.
Genesis 6:13

I love War of the Worlds by H. G. Wells, the book, and musical audio drama, as it mentions Walton-on-Thames where I was born and the local area I knew so well. I always wanted to set something in real places, where local people could recognise and get the same thrill from as I did as a boy.

This is a fictional book, set in the real world, with a situation not beyond the stretch of the imagination. Nothing is scarier than that.

PMM

For

Richard Farren Barber

CHAPTER ONE

HEAVY WEATHER

Hannah Britton was already soaked through her school uniform into the back of her underwear, but that was the least of her worries. She had left the comparative dryness of the bus shelter five minutes ago, and she was already drenched. Hannah could not stand the barely whispered names for her, the catcalls, and the malicious rumours, twisted with schoolyard fiction. In the microcosmic world of St. Mary's Secondary School, she was number one in the gossip stakes. So she left the taunts and sniggers behind and let the rain engulf her. Her mood was not helped when ten steps away from the bus shelter, the heavens opened even wider and began chucking it down. The downpour was harder and faster than anything she had experienced in all her sixteen years on this earth. The rain was icy cold and penetrating to the core, but she could not turn back now. She would have to walk the forty-five minutes to the house she shared with her grandparents and younger sister. *A drowned rat*, her grandfather, would call her when she got in. The rain ran down the back of her bare legs under her skirt and into the sodden heels of her useless slip-ons.

She rounded the corner of the hill upon which her school and the church next door were built. Her head was down to keep the blinding rain from her eyes. Even then it bounced up high from hitting the pavement so hard. The edge where the road and pavement met, was a blurred river of down-coursing water. She nearly slipped as she reached a part of the road that undulated like a fabled sea-serpents back. She could see a massive lake of water milling across the entire road in the dip. She had to stop and hop, as one of her sodden shoes was left behind. It would have to be just then, that the bus she had waited so long for came haring around the bend. She saw the lights were on even though it was only the afternoon. She heard a wave of raucous noise and muffled music from her school-mates. Then the bow-wave of the front and back wheels speed-ing through the deep pond on the road hit her. The water shot up from the wheels at a forty-five-degree angle, going right up the skirt of her raised leg and soaking the only dry parts left on her body. She shivered and let out a shrill cry of chilled anger as she put her foot back in her waterlogged shoe.

The bus carried on down the ever winding round road until it was lost from sight. She was glad of that at least as the icy rain ran down her thighs. The toes in her left shoe were under-water. She began to cry in frustration, something she never did. Crying was for weak people, and she was no chavvy; my-little-pony, pink loving girl. She had grown up fast. Forced to, by circumstance rather than choice. Outgrowing her so-called school friends. So much so, she found their childish *X-Factor* and celebrity gossip chatter repugnant. She felt like an older woman trapped in the uniform of a child. She was *sixteen going on sixty,* her grandfather replied when she told him she wanted to become an archaeologist. She adored Mr. Davies's Geography class and had even dropped French to take Latin classes. She may dress like the rest of the woolly sheep at school, but she yearned for so much more than her friends' wishes to be foot-baller's WAGS or have fifteen minutes of reality TV fame.

Thunder rumbled so loudly and so close it made her jump in her squishy shoes. The sound of the pelting, head-stinging rain was loud enough as it was. So she didn't hear the car pull up beside her. It stopped, but then had to move off again to catch up with her. Only when it went ahead and stopped again, did she look up and notice it. A smile crossed her face for the first time today since Geography class. The dark car's passenger door was pushed open, and she rushed over to it. It was warm and dry inside. Then she saw him, in the motion of leaning back to the steering wheel after opening the door for her.

"Need a ride?" he asked giving his warm, confident smile he only reserved for her.

"Yes, cos I'm soaking wet," she said with a devilish smirk as she got into his car.

He smirked back, raising his eyebrows as she closed the door behind her and the dark car drove off down the hill.

Brita Mikkelson felt like she hadn't slept for a week, she was so tired. She had started her journey yesterday with a four-and-a-half-hour train journey from her hometown of Randers to Copenhagen, with a short walk carrying her life on her back to the airport. The cheapest flight she could get to London Gatwick was three-hundred-and-twenty Danish Krone, but she had to travel at one in the morning. The flight had only taken her an hour, but by the time she had got her backpack and gone through customs, it was three in the morning. No trains were running, so she had to wait at the near empty airport until just after five to catch a train to Clapham Junction. She had gotten confused at the station as it was so huge; with so many tracks she missed her first train and had to wait until six-forty-five for the next one.

She arrived at Thames Ditton station in the heart of Surrey commuter belt at ten past seven. It was the nearest station to her final destination. The train station was set up on a bank. The rain she hoped to leave behind in Denmark had followed her across the North Sea. She was sheltered until she exited the station after walking down a flight of steps. She adjusted the heavy pack on her back as she stared out at the hard rain from under the shelter of a nearby bridge. The station was the closest one to where her true love lived, but from here, the map on her mobile phone told her it was another fifteen-minute walk away. She tied up her shoulder length blonde hair into a ponytail and pulled a green cap from a zipped side pocket in her rucksack. Donning the hat, she took a deep breath and what felt like her first proper steps on English soil. She followed a line of railings for a while, which took her past a few roads lined with pleasant looking leafy-green cul-de-sacs and streets. It didn't conjure up the remote English villages she had in her mind, but it seemed a lovely place to live all the same. The road she walked parallel to was busy with cars, buses and vans going in either direction. After a while the pavement rose up like a quaint little bridge, white concrete with poles on the side served as a guard rail. She followed the road round to the left to reveal a high street of shops on either side. Dead ahead through the driving rain, was a pub set back from the road. The rows of twee shops with red brick sides and white wooden facades were tempting, but her phone was directing her right. She waited for a white van to pass, it hooted her and some man called out, "oi-oi," to her. She frowned, wiped the rain from her chin and crossed the road, ending up at the pub entrance. She knew it would be closed at this hour, but she wondered when it would be open and if it served hot food and coffee.

She looked up at a sign next to her swinging in the strong breeze. It was squeaking as it was blown backwards and forwards. It had the picture of a knight on a horse spearing a coiled dragon under-hoof, with a long lance. She did not understand the words at the top of the sign which she guessed were the name of the brewery that owned the place. Yet the words at the bottom were plain to see and work out: *The George & Dragon*. It looked a nice place to visit, on a sunnier summer's day. Maybe she could come here with her lover for her first taste of English beer.

Feeling cold and damp, even with her waterproof coat on she hitched up her backpack and headed off down the right-hand road towards her new life. She walked on, patting a red post box as she passed it. Then the road opened up to a mini-roundabout. To her left was a large, set apart white painted house, with a white picket fence. The road either carried on in front of her or turned sharply left. In the wide gap between the two roads was a vast playing field. Brita frowned and checked her bearing on the phone map again. Ahead of her was Giggs Hill Green. She wondered where it got its hill name from as it looked as flat as Holland to her. Yet her true love she met two months ago on holiday in Greece lived half-way down the left-hand road. She hurried along the wet pavement. Her DM boots splashing through ever larger puddles. The wet front of her jeans was rubbing up and down the cold flesh of her thighs. Thoughts of sizzling hot sunny days on the beaches rushed through her mind. Of cocktails, dancing close and romantic walks down the beach at night where they had first kissed. She ran, passed an old lady in a beige head to ankle Mac, with what looked like a clear plastic bonnet over her permed white hair. She had a yappy little dog with her, also attired in its own clear plastic coat to keep off the rain. She ignored the barks of the tiny dog and the pain in her shoulder, as she ran as fast as her backpack would allow.

Then she stopped. She was at her destination. Brita felt cold, wet and extremely nervous. A slight sloping drive led up to a large mock Tudor decorated house. She walked up the drive before she could lose her nerve. She had spent nearly all of her meagre waitress wages to get here today. She reached the three steps up to the green front door, glad to be under the cover of a small balcony above it. Her cold white right forefinger reached out and pushed the white bell button, encircled in green painted wood. She rocked her weight back a little and waited for the next part of her life to begin.

In Walton-on-Thames Selena Fenshaw-Wright drove through the gates into the private road where she lived. It was hissing it down. The wipers on her £66,000 grey *BMW Active Hybrid 7* hardly kept the windscreen clear of water. After three hundred yards, she turned left into her drive. Stopped, and waited for her own set of electric gates to pull across. Puccini's *Tosca* played softly from the surround speakers. Once her black metal gates were full open, she drove up her front drive to her large house.

She stopped parallel to the front door of her house. Even parked at the edge of her stone drive, it would be an eight foot dash to get under the cover of her front door. Yet she didn't move. Unless you counted the trembling of her hands on the wheel of her expensive car. Her shaking right hand turned the key in the ignition, killing Puccini and causing the internal lights to dim out to nothing. She turned over her trembling hands to look at her palms, and then raised them to her face to cover her eyes. But her hands could not hold back the floodtide of tears. They ran down her cheeks, down the wrist of her suit and blouse cuffs.

Outside the driving rain matched her.

"Stupid, stupid woman," she said bashing her steering wheel with her thin fists.

For the first time, since she had become an adult she had no idea what to do next. She always had a plan, plus a backup plan and third option. It came naturally to her. She had forgotten how many scowls she had made over the years listening to fat-bellied, over-egotistical men; waffling on when they had no clue. She always had a way and two outs, that was her mantra, her life motto. Anyone else who hadn't were some sub-human species that deserved all the shit life gave them.

She was struggling to find even a single way out of this with her reputation intact. The day had started so well, she had dismissed her court case by eleven due to lack of evidence. Having filled in some paperwork, she found she had the afternoon suddenly free. She called Mahesh, and he had booked a room in one of those cheap but clean hotel chains, where all the staff spoke with an Eastern-European twang. Mahesh had gotten her out of her staid clothes in moments. Eleven years her junior he was all energy and knew she would only cum through cunnilingus. Then she had said it. After the orgasm, after he had spilt his seed inside her, she said *she loved him*.

He dressed as quickly as he'd torn off her clothes. *He had a wife and baby to get home to.*

He had left her there stunned on the bed, lying in the wet patch crying. One hand over her eyes and one hand holding her hairless vagina. Her pits were always shaved clean and her hair dyed dark brown. How could she have been so stupid, she was acting like a girl twenty years younger, not like the respected judge she was. On the drive home from the Chertsey hotel, she thought up at least three ways to ruin Mahesh's up-and-coming law career. The rain, bad earlier in the day, had become torrential. The sky was as dark as sackcloth and visibility was low. She was angry at him and upset at herself for letting a man into her thoughts again after David. Yet she didn't slow down, nor did she see the cyclist until the bike bounced up over her expensive bonnet.

She stopped twenty yards down the deserted road. Opening her car door and in getting out, she was soaked in seconds. The bent bike had found its way halfway in a bush, only visible to someone walking by. She blinked out the rain from her eyes, but could see no sign of the rider anywhere. Then she spotted it, one ladies boot standing up against one of those green BT boxes. The top of the green box with thousands of telephone wires inside was slick with blood. As she watched, trying to catch her breath, the rain quickly washed the blood away.

She suddenly found herself getting back into the dry of the car, buckling up and driving off. Like it was some out-of-body experience. She was halfway through Weybridge town centre on the road home, before she realised what she had done. Run a woman over, and left her for dead in the pouring rain in the vain hope of what? That there had been no witnesses or CCTV cameras on that stretch of road. That the deluge would wash away any blood from the front left of her car.

She looked right at her front door, through the rain pelting on her side window. The very door her husband David had exited through five years ago, dragging a suitcase. His words, she laughed off, then when he'd found out about another young lawyer she had helped up the ladder for *reciprocal fucks*.

"One day Lena," he had thrust an angry finger at her. *"One day you'll run out of plans, back-ups and excuses and you'll be all alone, and nobody will be here to help you."*

Until now, she had not yearned so much as a moment for her ex-husband. They had met in Uni on a CND rally. He had taken her to a pub and bought her chips. For their first date, he didn't do the safe dinner; no, they went to see *Carter The Unstoppable Sex Machine* at a local polytechnic. She had slept with him that night back in his bedsit room. David had always loved her ginger hair wherever it grew. They had married four years later, he working at the local labour headquarters while trying to sell his paintings. She formed herself a steely reputation as the *Maggie Thatcher* of the law courts. The irony was not lost on them both.

She never wanted kids, and he accepted that. She didn't take his name when they got married, he had agreed to that. What he never agreed to was being taken advantage of over the years, or her belittling his art that made little impact on the household bills. What he couldn't accept in the end was her breaking his heart.

He lived on a narrowboat now, with a lady poet. They were poor but happy by all accounts. They had a son together called Byron who was coming up three years old, she heard. She rooted in her handbag as the rain drummed harder on the roof of her *Beamer*. She flicked through her contacts but found she had no number for him. She gripped the mobile in her left hand until it hurt.

"Oh, David… I've run out of plans."

The sound of the rain beating down on the conservatory roof was driving Ann Gables up the pole. Yes, she had been pleased when her hubby Tony had built it three years ago, only after six years of nagging. Yet in his wisdom, he'd taken away the french doors, to give the extended back living room a more open feel. This was all right except on days like these when it pissed down. The drumming sound on the plastic roof was deafening. She had to keep turning up the volume on the telly, to hear Loose Women she had *recorded* earlier.

She couldn't hear the washing machine in the kitchen when it finished. She was constantly up and down to check if the orange light was flashing, to show that the load was done. That brought her within close proximity of the kitchen cupboards and normally resulted in her returning back to the sofa with a couple of digestives; a Penguin or Cherry Bakewell. She knew the last thing she should be doing was snacking between lunch and the big dinner for when *Tone* got in. She looked at the skinny girl on a beach in a white bikini, with two kids from some advert; before appraising herself.

She had had two children, but she was no smiling skinny bint on the beach. She was a blob, and she didn't need Tony's constant reminders, to tell her. She looked up at her favourite picture on the mantelpiece. She had been twenty-four years younger then. In a one-piece holding a swimming medal standing next to a grinning David Wilkie. She had been toned and athletic back in those days, only her dampened down curly perm made her cringe a little.

Eighteen, not bad looking; with perky breasts and not the dumpy sacks of flour that spread under her arms. Then *Tone* had gotten her up the duff with their Mike, followed by marriage and then their Stacey. She had taken the kids swimming as youngsters, but when they reached a certain age and level of swimming they didn't want to go anymore. Well not with her at least. Each child had added a size to her body mass. When the kids stopped going swimming, so had she. Now over forty, she was eighteen stone somehow, not the eight when the David Wilkie pic was taken. The kids had grown up and gone, Stacey had two of her own. Ann Gables had been left alone, with her overbearing misogynistic hubby and a cupboard full of chocolate, biscuits, and cakes.

She didn't drive anymore because Tony had taken the piss and belittled her so much her confidence had melted away. She wasn't sure what she did anymore. Watch *crap* telly like it was the most important thing in the world, doted on her grandkids; wash, cook, clean, iron until *Big Tone* got home and started issuing his demands of her time.

"Fuck it," she spat at the telly, sending biscuit crumbs onto the floor. "Tomorrow I'm getting the bus to the leisure centre and having a swim."

It was always tomorrow for Ann, as the rain pelted down on her conservatory roof in Weston Green.

Ayesha Adebayo waited in the closed glass entrance of a shoe shop waiting for the rain to stop, or at least slow down. She hadn't brought a coat with her this morning as she had somehow dodged the intermittent showers. The heavens had opened over Surbiton, so she checked her mobile phone while she waited.

She only lived up the hill, in her mum's two-bedroom council flat. Her father had buggered off back to Nigeria years ago when she was only 18 months old. Her mother and her had not heard a dickie-bird from him since, nor received a penny for

Ayesha's upbringing. Her mother had not wanted another man since and saved herself years of frustration and disappointment. Then eight years ago Charlie (Charlotte) had come into their lives. It was odd at first to have two mums, but Ayesha soon got used to it. Her home life had always been full of love and Charlie shared her passion for shopping. Charlie and her mum had always dressed and treated her like their own princess. She always looked forward to going home after a hard day at the salon. Ayesha had started there as a Saturday Girl, five years ago, where's she washed the client's hair and made them tea and coffee. She had gone to college, after leaving school, to learn how to be a hairdresser. Sonia, her boss, had sent her on a tanning course a year ago, as that was a money-spinner these days. She had taken to it straight away. She was pleased because it was much easier than cutting hair and earned her and the salon more money, which meant more money for clothes, clubbing and the two holidays she saved up like mad to take each year.

Charlie and her mum were always banging on at her to save her cash for a deposit for a flat of her own. They were a lovely couple, but sometimes they did go on a bit like oldies do. She just wanted clothes, hols, and casual fun for the next six years of her life at least. She had plenty of time after that to take stock and see what her future held. She had none of her mother's tastes in men or women. She loved muscular men with tight blond hair; lots down below and not much in the brains department. She never stayed with them longer than a month at a time, which drove her two mothers to despair. They could never keep up with her love life, or approve of all the men she went through. They tried not to judge, because that was not their way but insisted she write her latest beau's name on the whiteboard in the kitchen to avoid embarrassment when they answered their home phone.

Ayesha rubbed her cold, wet exposed arms as she peeked out from the shelter of the shop doorway. Just in the nick of time to see her bus coming up Victoria Road. She ran as fast as her high heels allowed. Luckily other people in sensible coats and holding brollies wanted to get on before her, or she might have missed it. Even those fifteen seconds waiting to get partway onto the bus had soaked her down her right side. She felt her makeup running and the hairspray in her tall hairstyle flopping as she reached the bus driver.

"Had a fright luv?" the beer-bellied driver laughed at her.

Ayesha smiled without showing any teeth and paid her single fare. As she sat down on a seat next to an old biddy in her wet coat, she stared past her out the steamed-up window. The rain seemed to pause for a second, before hailstones the size of marbles began to pound the bus.

"Oh dear, my dog's out in the garden in this," the old lady said with a worried look at Ayesha.

Ayesha smiled again with fake concern. She was more concerned that the painful looking hailstones would not have stopped by the time the bus pulled up at the stop, near her flat.

CHAPTER TWO

IT NEVER RAINS, BUT IT POURS

Hannah Britton had just closed the front door of her grandparents' house when she sneezed three times in pistol-fast succession. Her grandmother bustled in at the sound, to find her on the welcome mat dripping rainwater everywhere.

"You're late," she said taking the sodden bag from her granddaughter's shoulder. "Got soaked I see, let's get you out of these wet clothes before you catch a chill, my girl."

"Sorry Gran, I stayed late to finish a project with Nina and then missed my next bus." Hannah lied as she let her gran tug her blazer down off her sodden arms. There was no project and Nina wasn't even her friend anymore. She recalled the last heated conversation had included the words *whore* and *slag* in them; all directed at Hannah. Not that Hannah really cared that much. Nina Alonso wasn't going to help get her degree or onto a summer dig site.

"Shoes!" her gran prompted.

Hannah kicked off her shoes. The bristles of the welcome mat tickled the underneath of her bare soles.

"Right, dinner is in forty-five minutes, so gives you plenty of time to go and have a shower and change into some dry clothes before you catch your death of cold." Her gran held the heavy wet jacket away from her pinny, to stop it dripping on her slippers.

Hannah nodded, sending water off her flattened fringe down her thin nose and onto the hall carpet. She grabbed her wet bag and trudged upstairs, as her gran bustled back into the boiler room (as her grandparents referred to it) to put the jacket in front of the fire to dry out. Hannah pushed open her bedroom door marked:

HANNAH'S ROOM. KEEP OUT

Each letter marked out in different colour sharpies on an A4 piece of print paper taped to her bedroom door. She dropped her bag on top of an old magazine she had finished reading and grabbed her dressing gown off the back hook of her door. Leaving a trail of drips, she padded into the bathroom and locked it behind her. Putting her white thick fluffy dressing gown on the heated towel rack, she began to undress. Her school blouse was plastered to her skin. Her numb fingers found it hard work getting the buttons undone at first. Even when it was unbuttoned, it was stuck to her skin so that it was near transparent. She got it off her shoulders, but tugging it off her wet arms took ages, and in the end, she had to stand on it, to pull her wrists out. Her bra was the easiest thing to take off. Her wet skirt followed, and she looked down to see she wasn't wearing her cotton briefs. She looked down at herself with a frown wondering what had happened to them.

She touched her cold thighs. Most of her body from the thighs down felt numb and raw. Then she remembered what had happened to them. She walked over her pile of wet clothes towards the shower to turn it on. She stepped into the hot water while outside the rain came down heavy like stair-rods.

Brita Mikkelson sat in the huge back kitchen of the house, with a towel around her neck and a bowl of steaming chicken soup on the table under her chin. The kitchen was so vast and open plan that Brita reckoned it was larger than her entire flat back in Denmark. She let the steam rise and warm her cold face. A half-eaten bread roll sat on a small plate between the yet unused soup spoon and the bowl.

"So, Eloise says you met on holiday and became fast friends?" Mrs. Chambers said just to make conversation. She was in her mid-forties, dressed in long white trousers and long sleeved warm looking white and cream patterned cardigan. She was an older, slightly lined version of her daughter. She leant her small behind on the back of a work surface where she stood cradling a cup of half-drunk coffee in her crossed arms.

"Yes in Skiathos town, on the front by the boats," Brita said in a dreamy voice recalling the time they had first met.

Ellie, as Brita called her had been sitting on a large iron post, which the larger ships moored up too. She had been wearing high white shorts over a pink one-piece bikini. She had only one flip-flop on, and the other was nowhere to be seen. Her long brown hair was down covering her face as the sun set on it making it shine like gold. Her head was bowed, and Brita could tell the poor girl was crying.

Both young women were alone on the busy port side. Brita waited, but no friends or relatives came to comfort her. Brita, a confirmed loner, walked up around the front of the woman and knelt down to look up at her face. Her assumptions had been right; the poor girl was or had been crying.

"Er du okay?" she asked in Danish first.

"Sorry what?" the girl replied in polite crisp English. She swept back her long hair as she turned to look at Brita. A tear wobbled, very unattractively on the end of her nose.

"I said are you okay huni?" Brita put her left hand on the sitting girl's bare right knee and was rewarded with the tear from the English's girl's nose dripping on her hand.

"Yes. No. Not really," she said, moving her hands quickly to gently wipe her tear off the back of Brita's hand. She looked in her twenties, maybe a couple of years younger than Brita. "Sorry about that."

"It's okay, I needed hydrating after sunbathing all afternoon," Brita laughed, which brought a trembling smile on the plump natural lips of the English girl.

"Plenty more where that came from I'm afraid," the girl replied in a slightly less timid voice.

"That's good to know..." Brita let the sentence hang, hoping the cute English girl under her sad face and tears, would fill in the blanks. Brita was close enough to smell the coconut fragrance of the suntan

lotion the much paler girl had been using.

"Eloise but my friends call me Ellie," the English girl said, looking down at their hands that were still pressed together.

"My name is Brita, and I hopefully will be permitted to call you Ellie."

Ellie Chambers smiled down at Brita and nodded. "I could use a friend Brita; I'm here on my own, you see."

"Do you want to go get some beers or shots and get shit-faced with me Ellie? I have no friends here on the island either." Brita stood up still holding onto Ellie's hand.

"I've lost my other flip-flop in the sea," Ellie said in a sad voice, sticking out her bottom lip.

"I have a spare pair in my backpack you can wear," Brita said pulling the sad English girl to her feet.

"That would be most kind," Ellie forced a smile. "And I'll get the first two rounds in as a reward."

"Sounds good to me Ellie," Brita said tugging her dusty old pair of flip-flops from the mess in her backpack. She handed them over to Ellie. The English girl looked down at her lone cleaner flip-flop, looked around and then kicked it off over the side of the dock to float away on the sea. She dropped Brita's borrowed ones on the dock and kicked them on. Then she offered her arm to Brita, who shifted her bag on her other shoulder.

"Shall we go?"

"Yes," Brita said. She took her new friend's arm. "I know a great place not far from here. Nice food and cheap spirits."

"Sounds like my holiday is about to start proper," Ellie smiled at her.

"And mine," Brita nodded and led her up a rising side street to a little-known back alley bar, most tourists didn't know about.

"You must be a miracle worker. She was so depressed after Matt and her broke up. That holiday did her the world of good and she came back a happier, different person, Brita. I think that was all down to you, you know." Mrs. Chambers sipped her coffee again. "You can stay here as long as you like, as far as I'm concerned."

Brita looked up at Ellie's mother and smiled. *So far, so good.*

Just then the front door opened, and the sound of someone coming in could be heard but not seen in the back kitchen.

"Eloise is that you dear?" Mrs. Chambers called smiling wickedly at Brita. "We're in the kitchen; I've got a nice surprise waiting for you."

"Really?" It was Ellie's voice from the long hallway, making Brita's heart pound in her chest.

Mrs. Chambers moved next to the table where Brita sat expectantly waiting for her true love to come through the half-closed door. "You know without you I don't think she and Matt would have got back together again," Mrs. Chambers said as Eloise walked through the door rubbing at her wet hair.

"Brita," Ellie said stopping dead in shock.

Not as much shock as there was on Brita's face as she saw the large engagement ring on her lover's third finger of her left hand.

Selena Fenshaw-Wright had hidden the car in the garage and covered it with a tarpaulin sheet to hide the damage. The blood had been washed away by the torrential rain, but the dents to the bonnet, roof and the broken front left light were a dead give-away. At least she had her other car she could use, her jazzy new mini in pillow box red. She bought it on a whim, thinking she and Mahesh could take it to the coast and fuck in the back with the roof down. It never happened of course, so the mini hardly got a run out. She suddenly slapped the top of her Beamer with the flat of her left hand. The tarpaulin took a little of the impact out of it, but her hand stung with pain for a few seconds. The pain felt good, and she missed it when it was absent. She collected her martini from a shelf next to the door that led inside to her utility room. She took a swig and then stepped up out of the twin garage. Her extra fridge freezer greeted her and her line of other white goods in a row.

A half-open door led back into the small pantry areas off her vast, underused kitchen. While to her left down past the tumble-dryer was a door that led out into the garden. A couple of pairs of her flowery wellies lay where she had kicked them off last time she'd forayed into her vegetable patch. She took another gulp of martini and made a bee-line for the back door. She unlocked the deadbolts, pushed the door open and stepped out into the freezing rain. Leaving her Barber, wellies and the warmth of her huge home behind, she walked out in her £200 shoes into the mini-lakes forming on the flagstones. She skirted the tall rhododendron bushes, taking three stone steps up to the vast lawn. The solar lamps in the bushes were giving off only useless dim glows as she walked further along the sodden lawn. Her expensive heels were sinking into the turf. She moved her glass to her lips to find it was ninety percent rainwater. She threw the glass towards the rose bushes to her right. It didn't make the beds, bouncing once unbroken on the saturated lawn.

Overhead a rumble of thunder echoed across her expensive part of North Surrey. She looked up at the dark sky, the rain pelting down so hard she had to close her eyes to slits. She was soaked through already. Her jacket was hanging off the back of a chair at the breakfast table in her kitchen. Her blouse was plastered to her cold skin, and she could feel the water running down under the waistband of her knee length skirt. Her shoes were sinking into the lawn so she kicked them off. Then as the rumbles of thunder grew nearer, she decided to rip off her blouse, sending buttons everywhere. Her bra, skirt and thong she wore as an illusion that she was still young and sexy all followed. Lightning flashed deep in her retinas, somewhere up and to her left. She opened her arms wide, tilted her head to the sky. Selena urged nature to do the decent thing and strike her down dead. She had become everything the socialist teen at Uni had hated to the core. It was time for karma to do her bitchiest best.

In the dark heavens, the lightning flashed even closer.

Luckily for Ann the sound of her husband's work van pulling up on their pea-shingle drive always gave her enough time to hop up from the well she was making in the seat cushions of the sofa and waddle off to the kitchen. She turned the extractor fan and oven on high and grabbed two pans with lids from a cupboard to place on the hobs, just as the front door opened.

Ann hurried over to the chopping block and began to dice a nearby carrot for no good cookery reason. She had nodded off in front of the telly again. It was becoming a bad habit in the afternoon lately. Her friend Rachel said it might be *the change* coming on or even Type Two diabetes. Her friend loved to read up online about every medical thing she could find and try and diagnose all-in-sundry with rare medical ailments. Rachel was a laugh after a few Sambucas, but a pain in the bum if you had even the slightest sniffle.

"Fucking cunting weather." Tony's grumbles from the hallway shook her from her daydreaming and stopped her from slicing deep into her left thumb. She gripped the knife hard and then forced herself to put it down on the wooden chopping board. She heard him take off his coat and kick off his boots before he headed up the hallway to the kitchen.

"What's for dinner?" Was his entrance speech he'd said thousands of times entering the kitchen. No *hello*, or *hi luv*, or even *how was your day dear*? No, she never got one of those.

"Shit and sugar pie," she responded with one of her over-used replies.

Tony grunted at her, but it nearly forced a smile out of his large chubby face. Her husband was a built like a brick shit-house. He would immediately make a ballroom feel cramped just by entering it. He was six-four, with a shaven skullcap of black on his large head. He was English through-and-through down to his union flag boxer shorts and the bulldog with a flag on this thick right bicep. Yet his skin had a slight olive tone to it. His nose was big, his mouth was large, and his ears increasing in size as he got older. Two of her hands made one of his, and she often wondered how he did the delicate electrical parts of his job, as a gas boiler fitter. He wasn't that fat, though, just big-built. He had a beer belly on that he loved to tan up on their fortnight holidays to Tenerife each year. But he wasn't overly obese; he was just large in all proportions—like those trolls in that *Hobbit* film. Ann used to love him for his large portions. The weight of him on top of her on their Sunday morning sessions left her feeling like a used condom afterwards: flat and full of sperm.

"So how was your day then?" she asked without any real conviction. She just wanted him out of the kitchen so she could stop with the charade of the pretend dinner and cook some ready-meals from the freezer. A few potatoes and some frozen veg would sort him out, if she smothered enough thick gravy on it.

"Interesting to say the least. They've replaced Jay with some young bird right out of university. I give her a fucking week." Tony said leaning against the doorframe, as he wiped raindrops from his face.

"Really? Well, Jay had been off for three months with stress, they needed someone in there doing that role." Ann stepped sidewards, opened the fridge door and leaned over to pull a cold lager out for her husband. She closed it with her left knee and offered the can of beer across to her husband.

"Yeah, but not a bloody woman," he said taking the can with a nod. "Cheers."

"Can't be any worse than Jay or that Asian bloke you had before him, he only lasted four months. That supervisor role should come with a government health warning luv."

"It's cos they always get weak pricks in that know nothing about gas boilers or how long jobs take. What does some posh bint know about fucking boilers I ask you? Bet she don't know one end of a fucking screwdriver from the other, stupid cunt." Tony pulled the ring of his can and downed a third of the lager inside in one go.

"So is she pretty then?" Ann asked with a slight raise of her eyebrows.

"Blonde, thin and nil-tits, but Joe reckons he's going to slip her one by the end of the month. We even put a tenner on it." Tony's smiled, and he drank some more of his beer.

Ann was glad his mood since coming in, had improved a little. She never knew with Tony, he could be placid for months, then fly into a rage over something really minor. "Well, why don't you sit your fat arse down in the front room and watch the news or this dinner will never get cooked."

"You can fucking talk," he said moving forwards to grab and squeeze her bum. He kissed her cheek, though, before wandering off into the front room.

Ann sighed in relief. Then rushed around the kitchen like a cat on crack, trying to get the dinner on fast.

Ayesha stared out of her dark bedroom window. She was watching the rain run down the hill like a river on either side of the road. She was knees-up on her bed in her tiger onesie. She'd eaten a lamb casserole Mum had cooked, as she chatted to Charlie about the torrential rain they were having. It had rained a bit yesterday, but it was like some natural disaster you saw on the news from the Philippines or something.

Her bedroom overlooked the road going down the hill to . It was set back with some grass and trees, but the road was always a bit noisy. Friday and Saturday nights you could hear all the drunks come up the hill from the pub or the high-as-a-kite clubbers who had decided to walk home from Kingston. It didn't bother her much these days as it had, as she was normally one of those pubbers or clubbers. She preferred going up town with her mates. The train station was only five minutes' walk away, and the trains only took thirty minutes to get to Waterloo.

She used some cotton wool pads to cleanse her face and get rid of her makeup. Her elbows sat on the cold windowsill as she peered through the drops of rain on the glass to the yellow street-lamp lit world below. She had promised to go round her friend Carly's house but had blown her out due to the inclement weather. She needed a car really but was too tight to pay for lessons. Her mum didn't drive, but Charlie, who worked for Surrey County Council did. She had given Ayesha a few lessons at night in the car park at the back of Waitrose. She enjoyed it, but she couldn't afford proper lessons or a car anyway. As she lived only ten minutes' walk from work, she didn't really see the need much. Only on dark, damp nights like these. Or if she and her mates had a fancy to drive down to Brighton on the weekend, when or if, they got a summer. What she really needed was some rich sugar daddy to drive her around or some fit young Chelsea footballer.

She threw the used pad in the pink bin at the end of her bed and looked out at the rain again. Lightning flashed dazzling her eyes. When she opened them again, all hell had broken loose on the road outside. A large burning branch lay across the dented bonnets of two parked cars. Both sets of lights were flashing, and alarms were wailing into the wet night.

"Fuck-in-hell," Ayesha stated. Then she jumped off her bed, bounded out of her room to fetch her mum and Charlie. They were curled up in each other's arms on the sofa watching a programme about new-born babies. She still had blue blobs in front of her eyes as she spoke. "Hey you two, a branch got hit by lightning and has come down and busted up some cars outside on the road."

"Not my car I hope," Charlie said jumping up off the sofa. Ayesha's mum slowly pushed herself up after her wife.

"Nah, out my side. Come and 'ave a look." Ayesha urged and led them both off to her room. They hurried after her, all in furry slippers. All three women knelt on Ayesha's bed making the mattress groan under the extra weight.

There was a man outside with a coat over his head, looking at the damage done to the car on the left. The burning branch's flames had been put out, only red embers where the bolt had split it from the tree above.

"Bleedin hell," Ayesha's mum Pam muttered.

"Hope he's got insurance," Charlie added.

Ayesha was in the middle of her two mums, watching the man hopping around in the rain in a right old rage. Maybe car ownership was not for her after all; as the rain continued to fall outside.

CHAPTER THREE

NO CALM AFTER THE STORM

Hannah's gran had called her four times, but it was her granddad coming into her room to physically shake her that finally woke her up.

"You'll be bloody late for school at this rate girl," he said in his rumbling voice, as her eyes finally flickered half-open from under her duvet. He slammed her bedroom door hard on the way out, which forced her eyes wide open in shock at the loud bang.

"Not another school day," she groaned putting her right forearm over her tired eyes. "I was sure it was Saturday."

Exhaling hard, she pushed down her duvet with both arms and swung her bare legs out of bed as she sat up. She made a pained face as she leant over and pulled her bed shorts out of her crack. She wiped some drool from the left corner of her mouth and rubbed her midriff. She felt hungry. That gnawing early morning hunger that made you feel a little bit sick. She stood up. Her blue painted bedroom spun a little, and she seemed to lose gravity for a second. She sat back down on her bed with a bouncing squeal of her mattress. Big black blobs of dark exploded in front of her eyes for a second and then were gone.

"That was weird," she muttered, rubbing at her closed eyelids. When she opened them again, her vision was normal again. She grabbed her headboard as she stood up this time, but there were no stars or loss of balance. "Need breakie."

She looked in the long mirror attached to the centre of her

double wardrobe. She could see the reflection of the rain drumming on her bedroom window. She looked left to take it in. It looked like it hadn't stopped all night when she had been sleeping. Her frown turned to a slight smile, as she saw her gran had laid out clean, dry school clothes over the swivel chair in front of her desk. She blew on her bottom lip and ran her fingers through the tangled mess that was her hair. Yesterday's torrential rain and a towel dry when she got home had not left it in a good state. She pulled up her cami-top to reveal her taut abdomen and thin waist. She held her top up to her chest and pinched at the tight skin around her middle.

"Maybe I'll skip breakfast," she said to the mirror. Grabbing her thin dressing gown, she headed off for a shower.

Breakfast was in full flow when she eventually made it downstairs to the kitchen. Her gran was in full cooked breakfast mode. Her grandfather and nine-year-old sister were tucking into a full English breakfast. Hayley had enough baby fat for two already, their gran's frequent fry-ups wouldn't help her lose the extra weight she carried. They were sitting at the breakfast table in an extension her grandfather and father had built themselves ten years ago. The sight of their plates swimming with grease and the brown sauce turned her stomach.

"Up at last eh," her grandfather grunted as he chewed his sausage, before washing it down with a mug of builder's tea.

"Lazybones, lazybones," her sister sang.

Hannah retreated to the kitchen to maybe grab a slice of toast or at least a cup of tea. She hoped it would settle her sickly stomach down. But going into the open plan kitchen didn't help either. She stared at the open smoke alarm set in the middle of the ceiling. It had been like that for years, covered in grease and dust. The battery hanging down by the wires, one end disconnected, as the constant noise of it going off had driven the household to distraction.

She made for the toaster, but it was too near to the smells of the eggs her gran was frying up. "One egg or two luvvy?" her gran asked her.

That was enough for Hannah. Clamping her right hand over her mouth, she ran as fast as she could to the downstairs loo and threw up. The door was half open; Hannah had her elbows on the black seat spitting bits of last night's lasagne from her teeth. Her gran bustled in and held her hair back as her stomach muscles tighten into knots again, and she threw up one more time. Hannah coughed and spat into the brown water below her.

At least I've guaranteed myself a Friday off school, she thought as her gran made soothing sounds above her.

Brita Mikkelson woke up in a strange single bed, but not the bed she dreamt of sleeping in last night. She was in the Chambers' spare box room. A bare magnolia painted room, with an old wardrobe, dressing table, with pushed up stool and dried dusty flowers on top. The curtains were thin and did not keep out the morning light. Not that there was much of it. The rain from yesterday continued on into today. It matched Brita's mood precisely. Her top mauve pillow was still damp from where she had silently cried herself to sleep. She had long gotten used to crying without making a sound in the orphanage where she had spent four years of her life. She had been four when her junkie mother had overdosed on some bad drugs her junkie boyfriend had gotten her. He hadn't been Brita's father, her mother had told her he had been a soldier, but told her little more. Nothing that Brita could remember into her adult life. Four years without any real life had taught her to take care of herself and guard her feelings. When she finally was adopted, it was by a childless couple who owned a dairy farm outside Randers.

They worked her hard, but not cruelly. They gave her as much love as they deemed suitable. Her adoptive father doted on her. He had taught her to ski, swim, shoot and all about farming. Her adopted mother taught her how to cook for pleasure, rather than survival. She had been an Olympic archer and taught her how to use a bow. Her adopted parents had been in their mid-forties when she arrived. They died when a snowplough lost control at an icy junction and crushed their car to half its width.

Brita had not been there. She had been away doing her National Service. She came back to put them in the ground and put the farm up for sale. She had no real love for farming, only her adopted parents. In the army, she found comfort in the arms of another female soldier. It wasn't love, but sex and passion to forget her woes. After she had left the army, she worked in a gay bar in Copenhagen for a while. Drifting from one one-night-stand to the next. Not wanting to put down any roots or give away any love. If she loved someone, they usually left her in some manner, and that hurt too much. So she stopped doing it and stopped getting hurt. She drew comics for fun but was too scared to show them to anyone. So she went travelling, and in Greece only a month ago, fell in love breaking all her guarded firewalls. She had shown Ellie her drawings when they had laid naked on her holiday white sheeted bed. The shutters had been open and the curtains moving slightly on a warm breeze.

She had kissed Ellie and said the L-word and smiling happily back at her new love had repeated those very same words. Those twelve hot day and nights had been the best of Brita's life. They had parted at the airport in floods of tears, going back to different countries. Brita should have stuck then, but she gave her heart away for the first time ever and twisted. Losing the game of hearts the moment she stepped onto the train to leave her flat in Randers to come to England.

The rain hit the bedroom window hard and ran down the panes in rivulets. Brita did the same, but without the noise. She wiped her eyes with the back of her hand and decided then-and-there to pack her stuff and leave. She would get a waitress job in a bar to try and get enough money for a ferry to Holland, and then hitchhike home. Her thoughts were interrupted by the sounds of soft footfalls on the landing carpet outside her bedroom door. Brita checked her watch, it was just a little after half-six in the morning.

The door opened, and Ellie appeared in the doorway. She was wearing a girly pyjama set with cute bears, and she had a sheepish look on her face. "May I come in?"

"It is your house," Brita replied sternly. She tried not to see how lovely Ellie looked but stared at her engagement ring instead.

"We need to talk before my parents wake up," Ellie said in a soft voice.

The sound of it made Brita want to retch. The well-to-do

English princess had had her fun, had gone back to her arsehole of a man, as soon as she got home.

"I thought that ring means we have nothing left to say." Brita pointed to Ellie's left hand.

"I thought it did too until I saw you yesterday in my kitchen. I thought Skiathos was some dream, a fantasy. When I got home, reality hit me, life hit me." Ellie moved closer to the bed unbuttoning her pyjama top. "I was a coward Brita."

"What are you doing?" Brita scratched her nose and retreated to the far side of the bed until her behind touched the cold magnolia wall.

"I want to say I'm sorry," Ellie said letting her top drop to the floor.

"But you forgot about me, you hurt me," Brita replied trying not to look at Ellie as she kicked off her pyjama bottoms.

"I'll never hurt you again I promise, I'm so sorry Brita, I want this. I want you, not Matt," Ellie pulled back the cover to find Brita was as naked as her.

Brita jumped up and grabbed Ellie painfully by the upper arms.

"Stop, you're hurting me," Ellie looked shocked at Brita's actions.

"And you think licking my pussy stops my hurt do you. You don't understand me or what it is to be me, Ellie. I love you, and you fucking came home and forgot me. That is hurt."

"Sssh, you'll wake my parents," Ellie looked towards the door.

"Wouldn't want to find their daughter naked in another woman's arms would we. Wouldn't want them to know their precious Eloise is a fucking rug-muncher would we," Brita yelled into Ellie's face.

Ellie began to cry. Brita could see the tears working up the cheek muscles of her pale face to her eyelids, where tears overflowed like the torrential rain outside. "I'm in love with you Brita. I'm so sorry I was too weak, I let you down...I let myself down." She sobbed, but never once looked away from her lover's eyes.

Brita went to say something harsh and cruel, but instead

pulled Ellie into a tight embrace. They cried naked tears into each other's necks. Ellie pulled away first and mashed her salty lips against Britas'. She resisted for a second and then gave into the kiss.

"I'll pack a bag now," Ellie said pulling back and grabbing Brita's hair in her hands, her white-blond hair combing through her splayed fingers. "I have savings; we could run away to Greece again and spend the rest of our lives together."

"No," Brita said solemnly shaking her head.

Ellie looked crestfallen.

"We stay here; we do not run. You have three days' grace to let your fiancé and parents know about us. If you do, we will plan a proper life together. If you don't, I will pack my shit, and you'll never hear from me again." It was Brita's turn to grab Ellie's neck under her ears and hair.

"Brita," Ellie said looking scared and confused.

"Love is not running away or two weeks fun in Greece. My love is for a lifetime, and you have to decide if you want that Ellie or go back to being your parents' and boyfriend's Eloise."

Selena Fenshaw-Wright called in sick for the first time in about six years. She leant against the breakfast bar of her vast white and chrome kitchen, hugging a half drunk coffee to her right bosom. The rain was still lashing down outside, as she watched through her french windows. It wasn't cold in or out, so she wore her green Japanese kimono dressing gown and nothing else. Her short-styled dyed locks were a mess of bed-hair, but she wasn't in the mood to wash it. The sandstone patio paving directly outside had turned into a mini-lake. She wondered how many days of rain it would take for the water to rise up over the step and under the french windows. If she stayed here long enough, how long would it take to drown? She tried to work it out but gave up when the local news came on the television above her wine chiller. She put down her lukewarm coffee and snatched up the remote to increase the volume five bars.

She watched the five-minute bulletin intensely, but no mention was given to a fatal hit-and-run accident. She wasn't sure where she had left her mobile, so she fired up the laptop next to the coffee maker, to check the local news online. Still nothing. Thunder cracked suddenly like it was right above her house making her jump. She could not remember thunder ever making her react that way before. She had always enjoyed storms as a child. Her father always told her it was the Thunder Gods waging war in the heavens. They used to watch from the upstairs window of their house in Guildford that overlooked fields to the left and a cricket pitch to the right. What she wouldn't give for him to be alive to hug her close and comfort her.

But he was long in his grave. He died on her thirteenth birthday, at her party right before her and her friend's eyes. Aneurysm, the autopsy said. The effect of losing the most important person in her whole life sent a cold dagger of ice into her heart that day. A cold heart that had served her well in her chosen career, but not in her relationships. She turned and looked at the torrential rain again, wondering if the body was still out there maybe lying unnoticed in a water-swollen ditch. All the while friends and relatives would be going out of their minds with worry. Selena began with a hitch and then a loud mewling sob. As the floodgates of her tears burst, she sunk down the side of her kitchen cupboards. The cord around her waist caught as her small behind hit the tiled floor, pulling her kimono open to reveal her flat stomach and most of her left thigh.

Above her, the main news gave out flood warnings for Chertsey, Walton-on-Thames, Hersham and other locations along the rivers Thames & Mole.

"Fucking 'ell Tone, have a look at the pond," Ann said over her shoulder to her dressing husband. She was at their front bedroom window which overlooked the large pond on the green where they lived. Someone she couldn't remember had told her that the pond had only been around since1941. Some German bomber had dropped a thousand-pound bomb there, trying to hit one of the many nearby reservoirs. She wasn't sure if it was a true tale or a load of old bollocks, but she kind of liked it. She had told her kids when they were young about it, like a local fable.

"What!" Tony moaned from his side of the bed where he

was dressing. "I'm trying to pull me cacks up?"

"Looks like it's risen over three feet overnight." Ann wiped at the condensation her breath had made on the window pane. She moved her head back a little, the rain was still with them. She felt the heavy weight of her husband on the creaking floorboards before she felt him tower over her from behind. He had to pull back the net curtains at a higher angle to get a look down at the pond.

"Fucking hell, you're right," Tony conceded. "Another couple of feet and it will be up over the bleeding road."

"We don't have to worry about flooding do we Tone?" Ann looked from the edge of the road to her front drive, wondering how long the water might take to reach them.

"Silly moo, it ain't going to get that high. If it does, I have boards and sands bags in the shed still from when I did the conservatory." Tony had one last look, exhaled into Ann's hair and headed off to the bathroom. "Looks like another shitty day to drive the van, hope the rain keeps all the stupid women drivers at home."

Ann let the comment go, as she always did. The rain and swollen pond interested her more. She felt goose bumps rise up her bare arms for some reason, even though it wasn't that cold out. Once Tony had gone to work, she would check out his shed herself to make sure about the bags of sand. She wouldn't dare enter his little kingdom filled with *Dolly Bird* calendars and packs of beers if he was there. Tony's house might be his castle, but the shed was his only little keep.

A loud, long act of flatulence erupted from the bathroom, as Tony, as usual, had not bothered to close the door since the kids had left home. Ann shook her head and wrinkled her nose up in disgust as she made her way across the landing. She made it downstairs before any stink hit her and made for the kitchen to put the kettle on. Ann was just getting the bacon on when the landline on the kitchen wall rang. She turned the gas down under the frying pan and reached over to grab it.

"Mum, can you take Madison today, her schools been closed because of a leaky bleedin' roof." There were no hellos or a please from her daughter Stacey. Only a presumption that she would take her youngest grandchild without any thought that she might be busy today.

"I was going to go swimming," Ann said in a feeble defeated voice.

"You can do that any day Mum, or take Maddy with you. I'll bring her swimming cosy and a towel in a bag if you like. But it's wet enough to swim outside as it is. The river Mole is really rising around here. Her daughter lived in Hersham in a block of flats that backed onto the river there. Ann could hear Maddy singing some pop song in the background, then Jayden her other grandchild shouting how he'd be late for school soon if she didn't hurry herself. "*Shut up Jay, I'm on the phone to your gran.* So will you take her? The manager will kill me if I take time off work again."

"Okay then, drop her off luv," Ann finally gave in.

"Love you, Mum, you're a fucking star. Seeya in about twenty mins or so." The line went dead. Ann pressed her lips together and exhaled. She put down the phone, as Tony came downstairs and returned to her bacon.

"Who was that?" Tony entered the kitchen zipping up his work overalls.

"Stace. Maddy's school has sprung a leak, and she is dropping her off in a bit." Ann flipped the bacon, making sure the rind was crispy like her husband liked it.

"Give you something to do eh," Tony said picking up the tea she had earlier made for him. "Might lose some of that lard off your arse chasing after her all day."

Ann didn't need to turn round to see his smirk, she could almost hear it in his voice before he slurped at his tea. She said nothing and let his bacon char a little instead. She couldn't wait for him to leave for work.

Ayesha only had her cropped denim jacket on but had brought her brolly with her. She wore boots today and a tight leather-look Lycra skirt that nearly touched the tops of her knees. It was long for her.

Ayesha decided to walk down the hill today. She normally did as it was much easier walking down, than coming back up after work. Today, she also wanted to see if there was any more storm damage along her route to the salon. She hurried across the road, just beating an old white Escort as it bore down on her. She won the moral victory, until the puddle it sped through splashed up her skirt and legs. The male driver blew her a kiss as he drove off down St. Mark's Hill. She gave his shitty retreating car a two finger salute. She was soon distracted by the churchyard anyway. A tree had fallen sometime overnight. It lay across the tombstones, with only the bushy leaves sticking out onto the path. Ayesha had to walk on the edge of the pavement to get around it. There didn't seem to be any other damage on her walk down the hill. The sewer grates appeared to be struggling with the rivers of water running down the hill on each side of the road, but that was about it.

An alarm was ringing inside a closed estate agents as she got to the bottom of the hill, but apart from the numerous umbrellas, it was a typical working day in the heart of suburbia. The queue in and outside Cafe Nero was horrendous, but she had to get her latte fix in the morning or she was a crank until she ate lunch. Her skirt and legs were still wet from the spray of the white Escort man. It felt horrible running down the backs of her thighs. The quashed up queue and the humid insides of the coffee shop weren't helping her mood either.

Only when the fit young guy served her did she break a smile. Out in the world again she put up her brolly and held her coffee under it like it was some holy relic that could not get damp. Trinny was already in before setting up the front hairdressing part of the salon, so all Ayesha had to worry about was the tanning booths in the back. She put her brolly next to Trinny's on the matt inside the staff entrance at the rear, before taking her first slug of latte. She could move bottles, towels and the paper underwear with one hand anyway. She was set up with fifteen minutes to spare before they opened at nine.

Time for a quick gossip with Kylie the stylist, when she turned up shaking off her wet coat. There wasn't any gossip to be had, so in age-old British tradition, they talked about the weather. On the radio, *Cupilul* gave out flood warnings all over the south of England. Ayesha had just finished her coffee seconds before the shop front door was open. A large chubby couple, with bright orange hair and the whitest skin Ayesha had ever seen were her first clients of the day. They were giggly newlyweds wanting a tan before heading off to Spain for their honeymoon. The man wasn't too bad, she just joined the dots of his freckled skin, but the wife was almost blue-white of skin and needed three goes to get up to a stage a lot of people are like before the session begins.

For once Ayesha praised her mother's choice of baby-daddy, giving her perfect all rounded skin that people would pay hundreds of pounds for. She just hoped the couple's tan wasn't washed off by the rain before they made it to Gatwick.

CHAPTER FOUR

FALLING APART

Hannah felt fine but didn't want to burden her grandparents with such news. She nibbled on a digestive from her hidden stash in her knicker drawer. This only helped to make her tummy rumble even louder, but she didn't have a second one, worried she might throw up again. So she lay back on her bed, with the duvet kicked down to the end to form a pillow for her feet. Her bedtime shirt was pulled up to just under her breasts and her knickers pushed down to obscene celebrity levels. Her left arm was bent back under her head, while she absently rubbed at her exposed empty belly, because she liked the feeling of comfort it gave. Her mobile was next to her but switched off. She stared at the darkened window of her bedroom and watched the rain bounce off it. The constant rhythm of the pelting rain was soothing in a way. The wind whipped up, causing the intermittent cessation of the rain now and again. She was also glad of her *puking fit* this morning. It at least kept her away from school and getting a soaking twice in one day. Her grandparents had driven her younger sister to school and were then heading out into town to buy some *wellies* or something. She wasn't sure, she wasn't really listening. Sighing loudly, she pulled her left arm from behind her head as it was getting numb and picked up her mobile phone. A loud rumble of thunder overhead turned her attention from it to her bedroom window. Hannah turned on her mobile but left it behind on the edge of her bed. She swung her bare legs off the bed and tip-toed over to pull back her net curtains and look into the garden. It looked like a lake in places. Her grandfather's immaculately tended lawn had taken as much water as it could. She heard that some people who live too close to the river were being evacuated because of the rising water levels. Her mobile chirped several times. She turned and looked at it. The tight skin of her forehead creased in three distinct lines. She wondered how many abusive messages she'd gotten this morning. Or if any of her silenced friends would bother sticking up for her. She walked back to the bed, with a resigned slowness, expecting bad news. She ignored Facebook and went straight to her emails.

There was one from him.

Her thumb covered the face of her mobile screen for a second. Then she gave in and opened the message.

Where are you today? I miss looking at you. I miss staring at your beautiful eyes and recalling our special times together.

I tear rolled down her left cheek and dropped off her jaw and onto her purple bedroom carpet. She didn't know why she was crying; she was better than that. Stronger than that. She also felt an uncharacteristic surge of anger course through her body. Lightning flashed outside as she began to type her reply. Thunder exploded overhead as she finished and sent the message back in response.

I got morning sickness, she typed to wind him up.

Never a truer word was typed in jest.

Brita and Ellie ate breakfast in a subdued manner. Mainly to do with the fact that Mrs. Chambers was fussing over them at the breakfast table. She was enjoying having another woman guest in the house to take care of. Both girls would rather have the house to themselves so they could talk more. But Ellie's mum, stuck close like they were sisters forming a pop trio.

All Ellie and Brita could do was stare across the toast and marmalade at each other. Trying to converse, with smiles, mouthed words of love and eye contact. Brita snorted as Ellie made two o-shapes with her thumbs and forefingers and rubbed them together. A beep of her mobile and her mother putting down a fresh pot of tea quickly ended that. Brita looked at the white teapot, with a red/green floral design and wished for coffee. Apparently none of the Chambers touched the stuff outside the odd Starbuck's visit as there was none in the house.

"Is it from Matt?" Ellie's mother enquired, stopping to clear up some miniscule crumbs from the kitchen breakfast, close to her daughter's left-hand side. Brita could see she was trying to peek at what her daughter was looking at.

Ellie angled her phone to the right in response to this. "Yes, just texting to say he has been landed with two hours' extracurricular stuff at school and has tons of marking to catch up so won't be round tonight."

Ellie and Brita exchanged glances of relief that her mother did not pick up on.

"Aw, that's a shame. Well, I'm sure he'll get to meet the lovely Brita here tomorrow night," Mrs. Chambers said walking back to the sink to do some washing up. "But could be a blessing in disguise Eloise, he might fall in love with our pretty house guest." Mrs. Chambers gave out her little long laugh; the one she did when she thought she had said something witty.

"Thanks, Mother," Ellie said, glancing from the sink back to Brita's clear eyes. "Everyone falls in love with Brita."

"Yes," Mrs. Chambers laughed again. "We are the loveliest looking ladies in the whole of Thames Ditton."

With her mother's back turned Ellie reached past the jam to grab Brita's nearest hand and gave it a quick squeeze. Brita smiled back at her lover, appreciating the words and touch of Ellie's slender fingers.

"So what are you two girls going to do today?" Mrs. Chambers said peering out onto the rainy back garden. "It's raining cats and dogs outside, again, though."

"Not sure, we could head up to London on the train, show Brita the rainy streets of London and its shops and culture. Or stay in and have a good old catch up." Ellie gave Brita's hand another squeeze and then pulled her hand back to pour herself some more tea.

"Wish I didn't have to go out today in this weather, rather be spending time with my favourite two girls."

"You-you're off out today then, Mum?" Ellie inquired with a

quick raise of her thin eyebrows at their house guest.

"Wish I wasn't." Mrs. Chambers clinked two plates together in the soapy water. "I've got to take your grandfather shopping for underwear. I've had enough of those holey rags he wears. I know he'll moan about shopping, spending his pension money and this god-awful rain, but it has to be done."

"What time are you leaving?" Ellie asked as coolly as she could. Her imagination was working overtime on what she and Brita could get up to while she was out.

"About eleven. Give him time to get up and turn his grumpy dial down a tad by then. Will you two girls be okay on your own?"

"Mum, we're not five you know."

"Oh, you'll always be my little baby girl." Mrs. Chambers dried her hands and walked over to kiss her daughter on the crown of her head. "You take care of my baby, Brita, when I'm out." She said giving her daughter a squeezing embarrassing parent cuddle.

"I will, Mrs. Chambers, for sure." Brita nodded with a little-curved smile.

Selena was on her third triple Glenfiddich of the morning on an empty stomach. She was watching a TV show where very common speaking people came to sort out their complicated lives by shouting their deepest secrets at their supposed-loved-ones in front of the nation. At first, it made her feel superior to them, but the realisation sunk in. They maybe thieving, cheating Chavs with low IQ's but at least they hadn't murdered someone and left them to die like a yellow-spined coward. They weren't hiding from their world in a two-million-pound mansion, drinking expensive twelve-year-old reserve whiskey. Selena stood up and threw the drained glass into the dried Pampas Grass in a white vase that sat in her cold marble fireplace. She clicked off the television and went to the kitchen to get some food inside her.

The rain was still threatening to come in through her french windows. The paddling pool outside had become a lake and was only centimetres from overrunning the bottom of the doors to come flooding into her expensively Italian tiled floor. Even though hunger gnawed at her tight flat stomach, she couldn't face the act of cooking herself something. A new resolve took over her thoughts and some of her old strength of will returned to her thin frame. She instead headed up her large staircase to her walk-in closet. There she got dressed in her sharpest court-room suit. She tied her unruly dyed hair in a ponytail behind her. She was going to walk into her garage, get in her murder weapon car and drive to the nearest police station and tell them everything. She may lose her reputation, house, and liberty, but she might be able to look at herself in the mirror again.

Only when she sat down at her dressing table to put on some blusher, eyeliner and lipstick did her resolve quiver. She rushed into her en-suite bathroom, her hand over her mouth and threw up in the sink. She knew she wouldn't make it to the toilet in time to get the lid open. She threw up again until there was just drool and stomach lining coming out. She turned and slid down her cold white underground tunnel-style tiles and sat on the bathroom floor sobbing. Her blouse and jacket were splattered with her own sick. That made her stomach muscles clench twice in revulsion, but she had nothing more to bring up.

"Got to get cleaned up," she said to herself as she pushed herself up the tiles to a standing position. Her high black leather shoes clicked loudly on the bathroom floor as she walked into her shower and turned on the water as hot as she could stand it. She knew she wasn't going anywhere fast today. Not to the police station at least. Not today, maybe never. She wasn't the brave woman she always fronted up to being. She was like every-one else underneath, cold, cowardly and afraid. She resolved to take at least three weeks off work. Maybe go somewhere where the sun was shining and get some perspective. The thought of flight seemed the wisest choice. Maybe a lonely Greek island that you could only get to by boat. She and David had boat-hopped across the Aegean Sea in their late teens before her career became more important than love and beauty to her. She could get a place up in the hills, maybe take in ten or more stray cats and shout at anyone who dared come on her property.

The mad cat lady daydream did not appeal, but getting away

did. She stripped in the bathroom, leaving her hair to drip dry;
Selena pulled on her warm winter dressing gown and headed
downstairs to her home office. She would fire up her laptop and
book a flight out of this rainy hell tonight. There was a horrid
taste of bile in her mouth so she decided to head via the kitchen
to grab a gold-coloured coke from the fridge first.

"Oh, fucking hell."

Water from the garden was pouring through the bottom of
her french windows and was slowly annexing her kitchen floor.
Her matte grey-blue tiles were turning a slick, shiny colour as
the flood waters spread out heading for the closest kitchen cabinets to hide under. Selena grabbed five tea towels from a drawer
and hurried over to throw them under the door frames of the
french windows. The water underfoot felt cold and gritty on
her bare feet. She soon gave up and retreated to dry land. Her
feet leaving dirty wet footprints on the dry tiles. She rushed
upstairs and grabbed every spare towel she could from her air-
ing cupboard. She carried the thick, soft bundle down into the
kitchen. She started to make a defensive ring to stop the water
spreading out from the kitchen into the breakfast area, hall and
utility room. She was cold, and her damp hair clung to her neck
like a wet noose. Yet she'd forgotten her troubles for the time
being at least, as the flooding water from the garden edged
towards her towel barrier. All thoughts of the police, and escaping the country left her. She needed to defend her house against
the flood waters, and that was her immediate focus.

Selena then tip-toed through the cold water, opening low
cupboards and drawers. She hurriedly took everything out of
them and piled the contents high on her kitchen counters. Her
feet got used to the cold water. So by the time she was finished
the waters covered her toes and expanded out to reach her
towel dam. Shivering she exited the water and hopped over the
towels. She sprayed her dirty, grimy feet with Dettol spray and
then dried them with kitchen roll. The rain was still coming
down heavily outside, so she moved into the breakfast area and
put all her chairs on the table and anything low and valuable.
She bustled off to the utility room to fetch a pair of green Barber
wellies she kept there to find it being two inches lower than the

kitchen was already flooded from the back door and from under the garage door. Selena bent down, gripped the doorframe and leant out across the scummy water to grab her wellies. She just managed to drag them back.

Selena hurried back to the kitchen to spray and dry her boots so she could head around the ground floor of her house, without leaving dirty trails. Her towels were soaking up the water, but they wouldn't last too much longer. She stripped off her towelling dressing gown and added that to the dam. She must look a sight with her damp hair, and no clothes on except her green Wellington boots. But there was no one to witness her battle with nature. She forgot everything, the only thing she was focusing on was holding back the water like a female King Canute. She hurried naked from room to room moving valuable items and placing them up one side of her large stairs. She put law textbooks, nice and thick under her furniture to lift it four inches off the carpet.

Two hours later she found herself lying up on her carpeted staircase, exhausted and panting. A line of possessions ran up beside her, and many other things were gathered in her spare bedrooms. She was still naked and covered in a sheen of cold sweat. She was hungry like no other time she could remember in her adult life. Hungry and empty.

Outside the rain fell heavily still.

Inside the water invading her house appeared under the door from the kitchen, into the hallway.

"Nanny, why is there a sea outside your house now?" Ann's granddaughter was standing up on the back of her granddad's armchair her head under the net curtains staring into the front garden.

"What did you say, Maddy?" Ann was sitting on the sofa. Coffee to the left of her, biscuits to the right.

"There is a big sea in your front garden Nanny, come look cos it weren'ted there when Mummy brought me." Maddy had the same stern turn to her voice as her mother.

Ann exhaled hard and on the third rock, managed to boost herself from the sofa. She waddled around the left-hand side of the armchair under the window. She fluffed out the net curtain with her hands, so she could stand next to her granddaughter to peer outside. The rain was still coming down, even heavier than earlier. Then she saw what her granddaughter was on about. Facebook was already awash with horror tales of the Rivers Ember and the Thames had burst their banks, and Ann's house was in-between both. This brought it home.

The pond and green across the way were gone. Swallowed up by a sea of water. The road was gone, three inches underwater and creeping halfway up her drive. The pocket handkerchief of grass on the right might soak some of the water up, but it was sodden already. The rain did not look like it would abate at any time. The clouds covering the sky were dark, brooding and filled with precipitation.

"Oh fuck," Ann said out loud, forgetting about the five-year-old next to her.

"Nanny did a bad swear." Maddy put her fingers to her mouth and giggled. "Can I put on my boots and go outside to splash nanny, can I?"

"Think we both will have to put our boots on luvee," Ann said turning to kiss Maddy's cheek. "Come on, you wanna help Nanny Ann build a dam to stop the water?"

"Yay," Maddy clapped excitedly. "Nanny, what's a dam?"

Maddy waited by the front door, out of the rain, with her raincoat and pink *Lazy Town* wellingtons on. Ann's hooded coat was already glistening with rain. She put Tony's fishing waders on over her jogging bottoms. Her thick jumper, with a rainmac she got at Worthing one rainy English summer holiday. She pulled some rubber gardening gloves on and was already regretting putting the jumper on. She was hot already, toiling around the side of the house with planks of wood and then a wheelbarrow with four sandbags in.

"Can I come out now and splash, Nanny, can I?" Maddy continued to plead from the dryness of the hallway.

"Okay, okay," Ann gave in. Madison's voice was as relentless as the driving rain. "But promise me you'll stay in the front garden, not near the road."

"Yes, Nanny of course. You're the best Nanny around,"

Maddy said, jumping feet together off the second doorstep into the puddles on the small lawn.

Ann grunted putting down one long wide board to cover the open drive between the gaps in the low brick wall. She used two sand bags at one end, one of the other on the right-hand side near the grass and one in the middle. She used a garden fork in the grass against the end of the board to help secure it. She hurried back around the house with the wheelbarrow. She piled in four more of the small heavy sandbags, plus two of the floor sheets Tony used when decorating. She was going to shove the floor sheets along the bottom of the boards to plug the gaps then cover with more bags of sand.

Ann came back to find Maddy astride the one board hopping from one splashing foot to the other, singing some pop tune Ann vaguely recognised. She looked happy, but the water was splashing up over her boots and up her leggings. Ann would have to give her a hot bath after this before her mother came home and created.

"Look, Nanny splashy puddles." Even though it was dark as dusk, raining hard, Ann smiled in spite of it looking at her granddaughter's happy face.

"Back in the garden Maddy, Nanny needs to finish this dam before grumpy granddad comes home from work."

"Okay," Maddy said with one last double splash. Ann held her hand to steady her as she pulled her right leg over. Her Wellington had other ideas. It slipped off her straightened foot and floated three feet away before getting wedged under the left front wheel of next door's parked car.

"Don't put your feet in the water."

But it was too late, Maddy put her foot down in the inch of water next to the board barrier.

"It's dirty," Ann finished with a sigh.

"Ow," Maddy said hopping towards the front step. "Something bited me."

Ann was already over the barrier on the two inches of water that was the pavement, trying to not topple over while retrieving her granddaughter's wayward welly. "You take off your boot on the step and go inside, Nanny will look in a minute hunny."

Ann threw the boot onto the dry part of the drive and continued to build up the dam against the rising water. Once it was done, she put the remaining sandbags up against the french windows of the rain-drumming conservatory. Stripped off her and Maddy's wet coats and hung them to dry in the downstairs loo. While Maddy was watching cartoons, Ann ran her a hot bath. The bath looked very inviting, as Ann was aching from head to foot. Her breaths were coming like she had run a mile and she was hot, cold and clammy all at the same time.

"Bath time," Ann called down the stairs.

Maddy didn't reply, but Ann was rewarded with the sound of tiny pounding feet up the stairs three seconds later. "I like your bath Nanny, we only have a shower, and it's not as fun." Maddy ran into the steamy bathroom and was tugging off her clothes as quickly as she was able.

Give it a couple of years, Ann thought, *and getting her in the bath wouldn't be so easy. Add a few more years and getting her out of the bathroom would be the problem.*

Ann helped Maddy with her leggings which were wet through from the knees downwards. Her granddaughter giggled as she sat on the loo, and Ann tugged the sodden things off at last. On the inside of Maddy's left leg, just above the ankle was a red bite mark.

"That where you got bit hunny-bunny?" Ann pointed, as Maddy hopped off the loo seat with a squeak of bum-cheek against plastic.

"Yeah," Maddy replied getting into the bath. She sat down with a bump, causing bubbles to float up and tickle the end of Ann's nose. Both she and Maddy giggled.

"Does it hurt?"

"Bit itchy that's all," Maddy replied grabbing the three different sized rubber ducks from their usual repose in the corner of the bath.

"I'll put some special cream on it when you've finished in here, okay?"

Maddy nodded. "Why do you have ducks in your bath Nanny, you're a grown-up?"

"Your granddad plays with them," Ann said tapping her nose, "our secret."

Maddy giggled again. Her laughter was infectious, causing Ann to smile until the creases in the side of her mouth hurt. She forgot all about the rain for a while and was so very glad that she had spent the day with her only granddaughter. It made her feel useful for once.

Maddy was sleepy after her bath, so she put her down in her mother's old bedroom. Ann went down to put the kettle on and check her hastily put together flood defences. She opened her front door to constant rain. The boards and sandbags seemed to be holding back the rising waters, but she wondered how Tony would park when he got home tonight. The water looked a foot deep on the road surface and must be even more on the green and pond, which had turned into a vast lake as far as the eye could see.

Some swans were paddling about in the centre of the water, having the time of their lives and loving the new flash lake that appeared. Feeling cold, she rubbed her bare arms and went inside to brew that cuppa.

Ayesha felt like she was fighting a losing battle. The rear of the shop lead out into a sunken concrete jungle. There was an old bike out there, some old out of date stock still in its cardboard packaging. Tina, her boss, used it as her smoking bolt-hole. It only got the sun for two hours a day during the summer and none in the winter months. It was like a deep brick well and sometimes Ayesha leant against the wall and took in the summer rays. Lucy, a stylist, used to sunbathe topless out there until Tina got tired of her attitude and larger, firmer breasts and sacked her.

Today there was no sun. Only waterfalls of rain from the overburdened drains, gutters from all the nearby shops in the row. It poured into the concrete laid back space and was soon flooding in through the back of the shop. It began coming down the back wall, but all three sides were leaking rain water, like there was no tomorrow.

Towels, mops, and buckets could not stop it. Tina closed

down the tanning side of the business by two o'clock. The health and safety fears of its touching anything electrical like the dry-ers and clippers etcetera forced Tina to close the whole shop by half-three. They spent the next hour moving all the stock, electrical equipment onto the seats and shelves of the salon. Tina called up her builder boyfriend in floods of tears to come help her and sent Ayesha and the rest of the staff home two hours early. She promised to ring them each first in the morning if it was worth them bothering to come in.

Even though it was raining hard, and her umbrella wasn't keeping her legs dry Ayesha walked back up the hill with a beaming smile on her face. Free paid time off, was still free paid time off; whatever the weather. The amount of water running down the road reminded Ayesha of a huge waterslide. The cars going downhill were taking it slow, fearing any braking at speed, would send them aquaplaning into the side of a bus. Thoughts of waterslides soon turned to thoughts of holiday slides in the sunshine, with the hot sun on her skin. She looked down at her soaking wet legs and wondered if her credit card could take another holiday hit.

CHAPTER FIVE

SINKING FEELING

Hannah, feeling more like her old self, went downstairs to have some toast and strong tea. She managed to keep it down, so she ate some crisps, two *French Fancies* and then a packet of *Twiglets* as she craved something savoury after the sugary sweet cakes. She did the washing up, put the washing away and put some bath towels in to wash. All for a quiet life when her grandparents finally returned home from their long shopping trip.

She got a can of *diet coke* from the fridge, popped the ring pull and moved over to the front living room window to peer out into the gloomy world outside. The rain was still falling heavily over Hersham. Her grandparent's house was close to the River Mole, separated only by a dead end road and a high stone wall. Nobody was out, no cars were driving down the road, only the water moved. She double-checked the kitchen was neat and tidy, up to her grandparent's standards and headed back up to her bedroom. She'd got a book about South American archaeological digs off Amazon last week, and this seemed the best time to dive into it. It wasn't a subject she was interested in, but she knew she needed at least an overview of other cultures where her knowledge was lacking.

She grabbed the new large book off her *Future Line of Work* bookshelf, as she dubbed it, and flung herself backwards onto her bed. Her mobile chimed a message after only half a page. With a teenage grunt of annoyance, she used her left forefinger as a bookmark and picked her upside down phone up from just under her pillow.

There were eleven frantic messages on her phone; from *him.* She left it upstairs while she'd been eating and clearing up. They started off caring; moved to concerned, to angry, slightly abusive, back to soppy and pleading again. She read them all with raised eyebrows, wondering if he really was his age or just texted like a lovelorn twelve-year-old girl still into Barbie.

He wanted, needed, demanded to meet up to discuss her bombshell text.

Hannah stared at the rain drumming at her window, wondering who the adult was in this relationship after all. She wasn't in the mood for any heavy shit tonight, nor going out in the pissing rain. She texted back; thanking him for his concern, which was sweet of him, but it was all a bit of a false alarm. She put three kisses and then, deleted two, realising for the first time she was really the one who called the shots in their odd relationship.

But I really need to see you xxxxxxx

She looked at the text; a wicked smile crossing her lips. *You will, at school on Monday,* she texted back. Then she switched it off for a while as he was getting too needy and she grabbed a book she really wanted to read.

Outside the river rose to levels that had only been seen twice in the last fifty years. The river swelled by the rain and surges from the Thames broke its banks and reached the bottom of the defensive flood wall.

Brita and Ellie made love on her double bed for ages. Then shared a hot shower together to clean up and cool down, but it didn't really work.

They lay in bed together with damp hair mingling together on the pillow, holding hands under their chin and facing each other. They kissed and stared into each other's eyes. Brita could see only love there, a rare thing for her to share. She stroked Ellie's back and kissed her again, just for the happy hell of it. She never felt so exposed and so safe at the same time.

"I suppose we should get up soon," Brita said. She didn't

want her close time with Ellie to end, but her mother might come back at any time.

"Don't want to," Ellie said in a childish voice sticking out her bottom lip. "I want to do this," she said and then kissed Brita softly on the lips. "And this," she said moving down to kiss Brita's exposed right nipple. Then Ellie kissed down lower and lower and any thoughts of Brita arguing the toss went out the window.

Brita turned onto her back and lifted up her right leg. Ellie just kissed down to somewhere interesting, when there was an almighty crash outside the bedroom window. Both women jumped out of bed and hurried naked over to the net curtains. They did not have to pull them to see the problem. Overburdened with rust, age and water of the past week or so, one of the gutters was hanging down at a forty-five-degree angle, spewing torrents of water over the front porch.

"Oh crap," Ellie said as she reached over to her chair to pull on her blouse.

"Fun time over then," Brita shrugged, staring at the spilling water.

"Yep," Ellie said pulling on her underwear and searching around for a pair of old jeans to wear.

"You any good with repairs?" Brita said pointing at the hanging gutter outside.

"Of course not, I'll ring dad," Ellie said pulling on some trainer socks. "Will you get dressed."

"Am I distracting you, then my love?" Brita bent over Ellie's dresser and wiggled her bare behind at her lover.

"Yesss," she said with fake annoyance. She kicked on her trainers and gave Brita a playful slap on her left buttock cheek. "Now come on, let's go out and check for any more damage."

"Okies," she said turning around to plonk herself on the side of the bed. She scanned the floor, trying to figure out what Ellie had done with her underwear.

They couldn't open the window far as the downed gutter blocked both side windows and the middle window only opened at the top. Brita, borrowing Mrs. Chambers' wellingtons and Mr. Chambers' wax jacket, then joined her lover to inspect the damage from outside. The gutter was pointing down at the little porch above the front door, causing a waterfall of water to run down its left-hand side. The rain was heavier than ever and hurt Brita's head, under her old army cap. A metal creak was all the warning they got. But it was enough time for Brita to grab Ellie and pull her back under the open front doorway as the gutter gave up and crashed down. It skimmed the top of the porch and then came to rest in the muddy rose beds nearby.

Ellie kissed Brita on the lips, just as the old lady with the jacket wearing dog walked past. "Thanks, hun," Ellie moved into the house, getting her mobile from her coat pocket. "I'm calling Dad."

Brita watched the old lady give her a shocked look, before carrying on taking her dog for less of a walk and more of a paddle. Brita looked at Ellie, who was in the hallway talking to her father and oblivious to the situation. She peered up at the dark heavens and wondered if it ever stopped raining in England.

Selena gave up the good fight. She sat on her cream carpeted stairs, watching the water slowly creep along the polished wooden floorboards of her hallway. She watched the invading water, drinking a large glass of her favourite Merlot and tucking into a big bag of very overpriced, sea salt and balsamic vinegar crisps.

The welcome mats she stuffed under the hallway door that led into the kitchen had been a futile effort to stop the water. They were dark and sodden, letting the water pass in huge trickles. The flood water reached her standing table, upon which her vintage Steampunk looking old phone sat. She wondered how long it would take for the water to get in the wiring and the plugholes dotted around the skirting boards. She had enough sense to turn off the downstairs power switches before she lost the battle to save the kitchen. She always loved the landscaped slope that ran down from the rear of her garden to the Italian sunken one under her kitchen window. It always made the one hundred and fifty-foot-long garden look even bigger as it sloped up to a set of trees bordering the next property along. The aesthetically pleasing rolling lawns and vistas didn't mean much as the water blitzkrieged itself from the rear to the front of her home.

"Maybe God is trying to drown my sins away," she said to the lip of her wine glass before drinking. This made her atheist self laugh. She was half-cut and laughing her head off, as water crept up the hallway after her. Maybe the floodwaters were sending her a message, get out, go to the police and confess, confess, confess. She drank the rest of her wine and stuffed some more of her overpriced stale tasting crisps into her mouth.

She chewed until all the bits of potato that weren't stuck in the gaps of her whitened teeth were small enough to swallow down. She poured herself another full glass of wine and wished she had rescued more from the kitchen before she abandoned it to nature. She took a sip and raised her glass in a toast. "Here's to you David. You were bloody right all along. I live alone in a rapidly sinking house, while you have your family around you on your boathouse, barge thingy. Yes, members of the jury, I feel pretty fucking dense now." She toasted the creeping waters once more as they rounded the foot of the stairs and drank deeply from her glass again.

Ann wasn't sure if it was the sound of the front door banging open or her husband's angry grunts as he came in, that woke her up.

Ann was up and out of her side of the sofa quicker than any time in the last few years. She was into the hallway a second later, to see Tony was in a foul mood from his body language. He was wearing his company's green sweatshirt with the firm's logo emblazoned on his right breast. The top was soaked down to the side pockets and his thick legs from the knees down were sodden.

"Fucking bollocking weather," he stated, arms wide on the doormat just shaking with rage, not sure what to take off first.

Ann glanced up at the cuckoo clock her grandfather procured from a German officer's house in 1945 at the dog end of that war. It only read just after two o'clock. Tony was back home very early.

"Well don't just stand there like a fucking lemon woman,

help me get this clobber off." Tony didn't move. He was soaked to the skin, wet through, but still expected her to get wet undressing him.

"You going to put the wood in the hole then first," Ann bit back pointing to the open front door. "Don't want half the street seeing your white arse."

Tony just grunted and kicked the door shut with a back heel of his boot. "You do that out front?"

"Who bloody else do you think did it, the fucking water fairy," she said kneeling down in supplication to untie his mushy wet laces.

"Oi, don't fucking push your luck, Ann, I've had a shitty day. Could hardly get to any of my jobs because of flooding, *and* I had to park the van round the bleeding corner. Bet some workshy tea-leaf will have a go at it tonight. Cunts!"

Ann let her husband rage on. He could be handy with his fists if the mood took him, normally after a few drinks though first. But she knew he wouldn't hit her while she wasn't looking. Tony liked to look her deep in the eyes and share the rage inside before giving her a backhander.

His last yell was so loud; her thoughts went to Maddy sleeping upstairs. And sure enough, she was awake crying for her Nan.

"Nannnnnnny," Maddy yelled long and hard. Both grandparents forgot their anger. There were tears, pain, and fear in that shrill voice. "Nannnnnnny," Maddy screamed this time. Ann stood up, exchanged a worried glance with her husband and then turned to run upstairs. Ann took the carpeted steps two at a time with Tony lumbering after her. They bundled into their daughter's old bedroom. Ann was breathing hard just from running upstairs, while Tony's smoker's wheeze was coming on.

Maddy was sitting up in bed with tears streaming down her pained face. She wore an old *My Little Pony* top that was a little short for her and underwear. The bedsheets were thrown back and stained red. At first, Ann thought she must have dropped a Ribena drink on the inside of the covers, but realised she never left Madison a drink earlier. Then she saw her granddaughter's left leg and let out a horrified gasp of shock. Madison's leg left from the sole of her foot to just under her knees was a raging red wound. The skin seemed to have dissolved, leaving only seeping red sores and a darker red puss.

Both Ann and Tony were frozen on the spot. Maddy looked down at her leg and screamed again. Ann moved forwards and knelt down to hug her granddaughter. Tony looked at the viscous wound on Madison's leg. "How and when did this happen?"

"I dunno," Ann said pulling her in-pain granddaughter into her neck to gently rock her. "It was fine when I put her to bed."

"It looks like someone's thrown acid on her bloody leg woman, what's going on?"

"Sssh Tone, you'll scare her. Do something useful and call a fucking ambulance."

"No ambulance is going to get down here Annie, we need to put one of my coats over her and take her in my van, it'll be quicker."

"You pick her up Ton, I'll get my wellies and coat on." Ann pulled back and grabbed Madison under the chin with both hands. "You're going to be alright Maddy, Nanny and Grandad will take you to the hospital, and the doctors will sort this out in no time."

Maddy was crying so hard and grinding her teeth with the pain she hardly heard anything Ann said to her. Tony lifted her from the bed, his strong left arm under her thighs so as not to touch the seeping wound. Ann let her husband carry Madison downstairs while she followed anxiously after. She pulled on her old wellies from under the stair cupboard and tugged on her waterproof winter coat. Then she grabbed one of Tony's monstrously large coat's and gently pulled it under, round and over Madison to cover her up against the cold and rain. Tony held her close as she did this, not speaking a word. Both of them were in shock and running on pure protective adrenalin. Ann opened the door. She stepped out and around the side of the house to let Tony out. The rain made her blink quickly, washing away her concerned tears for her granddaughter. As Tony paddled down the ever increasing flood water towards her barricade, she hurriedly closed the front door and followed after him.

"Which hospital is quicker to get too, Chertsey or Kingston?" she asked as she put one leg after another over the dam she'd built earlier.

"Kingston is nearest," Tony said wading down their street, with the precious bundle whimpering under the coat he held. "Chertsey is like bloody Atlantis at the moment, we'd never get there."

Ann rubbed at his wet back, as they hurried as fast as their overweight and unfit bodies would allow. Her husband at times of crisis like this was always at his best. He was calm and strong, while she was faltering and just wanted to collapse in tears. She tolerated him most of the time, hated him and her life a lot of the time; but if somebody needed help, he always came through.

They hurried on through the driving rain. Round the corner and up the road to a broadway of shops. Tony's company van was parked outside the bookies there, tyres inches deep in standing water. Tony fumbled his keys out of his zipped sweatshirt pocket and unlocked the van with a double beep. The passenger side was next to the pavement, so Ann opened the door.

"You get in first," he urged in a commanding, but not his usual foul-mouthed bullying, way. In a crisis, he still could be the man she fell in love with years and many dress sizes ago. She hurried in, glad to be out of the driving cold rain. With gentle grace, belying his frame he lifted Madison into her waiting arms. Ann gathered in the wet coat, soaking any dry spots left. The passenger seat was wide, and she kept Madison's feet away from the door as Tony closed it. She uncovered Madison's face. The poor girl was white as a sheet and just lay in Ann's arms with her eyes closed, her lips moving slightly.

Tony jumped in beside her and started up the van. He drove off down the broadway, turned out on the road heading for the *Silly Isles* roundabout. None of them put a seatbelt on. Ann imagined a policeman trying to stop her Tony taking Maddy to hospital: he'd kill the poor bugger.

"How is she?" Tony asked in a low, concerned voice as they

turned left onto the Portsmouth Road heading for Kingston.

Ann swallowed hard and opened up the lower ends of the large coat Madison was wrapped in. The red wound that seemed to be eating the top layer of Madison's skin had spread to cover her foot and knee.

"Hurry Tony please," she croaked out, just barely audible over the windscreen wipers.

Both of her mothers were still out at work. Ayesha took the time to light some scented candles, put on some music and have a long soak in a warm bubble bath. The cold rain was forgotten, and she eased under the water. She stopped as her small delicate chin hit the bubbles floating on the deep water. The flat may be old, and a little cramped for three, but the bath was old, deep and lovely for a nice soak. She didn't bother tying up her hair, she wasn't going out tonight so would let it get wet and as frizzy as it liked. She would spend some quality time with her mums; maybe chocolate, *Baileys* and a good rom-com on Netflix. It would be good to catch up on all their gossip. Ayesha eased her head under the water, letting the warm water envelope her like she was back in her mother's womb.

Her head broke the surface of the bath again. She wiped the excess water from her eyes and nostrils. She had a couple of hours alone time in the flat, so she would make the most of it. Her mum and Charlie both worked in nearby Kingston-Upon-Thames, but not close to each other. Her mum was a paediatrics' nurse at the hospital at the edge of town, and Charlie worked at County Hall not too far from the river.

Ayesha was lying on the sofa watching the music channels on Sky when Charlie came through the door of the flat shaking off her long dark blue mac. Ayesha checked the time on the info screen of the television; it was only just past five.

"You're back early," Ayesha called through the open doorway into the long hallway.

Charlie shivered as she came into the living room, pulling her right hand through her lank wet hair. "Flexi. Anyway, you can talk, looks like you've been in a while, Ash."

Ayesha smiled stretched out turning on her back, hands

behind her head on all the three sofas' cushions. 'Ash' was the shortened pet name Charlie had for her. Her other mum had called her Ashia for the first two weeks when she started dating her mother. Ayesha had been too polite at that age to correct her at first. Then after two weeks of calling her the wrong name, Pamela (Ayesha's mum) had heard her say it and they had all had a good laugh about the situation. Charlie still liked to call her Ash sometimes, mainly when Pam wasn't about.

"Water flooded the salon, got sent home early and paid hols for me until it's all fixed," Ayesha smiled at her other mum and bit her bottom lip in warm delight.

"You lucky fuck," Charlie said sitting on the edge of the sofa next to Ayesha's feet. "Budge up, you."

Ayesha pulled herself up into a sitting position against the cushions, her bare legs still across two of the three-seater sofa. "You not picking Mum up tonight then. Raining hard, shitty bus ride home, what are you like?" Ayesha tutted.

"She sent a text half an hour before I left work, they've got a rush on with these floods and lots of road accidents. They need her to stay on until eight, so you are stuck with me kiddo." Charlie said walking her fingers up Ayesha's bare left leg stopping at the knee.

"So are you cooking then?" Ayesha asked. Charlie was funny, bright and a shopaholic, but she was no Nigella Lawson in the kitchen, unlike Ayesha's mum.

"Cheeky bitch," Charlie said tickling Ayesha's bare feet as she stood up. "I was going to have a warm bath and order in pizza, guess you won't be wanting that then?" Her other mum let the words hang as she left the living room to run her bath.

"Good luck with having any hot water," Ayesha whispered with a cheeky grin and stretched back down into the full length of the sofa to watch the telly again.

CHAPTER SIX

UNDER THE WEATHER

"Hannah, give us a hand with the bloody shopping will you," her grandfather called up the stairs from the hall. His shout had woken her from a nap. She felt groggy and worse for it, as she stumbled out of her bedroom onto the landing. She hadn't had a nap like that since she was five.

"How you feeling now luvee?" her grandmother called up coming through the front door laden down with glossy wet shopping bags.

"Sod how she feels, come down here and give us a hand taking this shopping through to the kitchen.

Hannah exhaled and trudged downstairs wondering what time it was. Then her sister hurried in through the open front door, her wet weather coat on with the hood up and drawstrings pulled tight. Her fringe was soaking wet, and she did not seem a happy bunny at all.

It must be later than I realised, Hannah thought to herself. If her sister was back from school, it must be after half-three at least. Hayley went to a school only ten minutes slow walk away in Hersham, while Hannah still went to school where they used to live in Woking. She had decided she still wanted to go there rather than transfer and lose all her friends. *Friends, that was a laugh.* She missed her old house in Woking, missed her old larger bedroom and her dead parents.

She shook her head, trying to get thoughts of her late mother and father from her mind. She picked up two bags that her grandfather had dumped on the hallway carpet before he'd gone back out into the rain to collect more bags from the back of his Skoda. A breeze curled around her ankles as she peered outside. What she first thought was rainwater covered the road, but it was too deep. The river across the road must have burst its banks. The whole street looked like a mini-lake. Her grandfather's red car, with its boot raised high was parked in the sloping drive above the water level. Hayley shook off her coat next to Hannah, sending droplets of water all over her arms and neck.

"Hey, watch what you are doing you stupid cow," Hannah spat out with only the venom a teenage voice could manage.

"Well move out the way then," Hayley shot back in an equally annoying pre-teen way.

"Move out of the way then," Hannah mocked, knowing repeating back people's stupid words, really did wind them up.

"Gran, she's being mean," Hayley said playing the trump younger child card like siblings had done for centuries.

"Be nice to your sister and bring those bags into the kitchen Hannah," her gran barked from the dining room that lead round to the kitchen at the back of the house.

Hannah grunted and carried the heavy wet bags through to dump them on the kitchen floor. She wheeled around, wiping raindrops from her neck to see her grandmother still standing at the far end of the dining room. Hannah moved back towards the tiny hallway, but her grandmother stopped her, putting her cold, wet palms over Hannah's warm cheeks. "You look much perkier now luvee, must have been something you ate eh?"

"Probably," Hannah muttered in reply.

"Coming through," her grandfather barked. Hannah and her gran retreated right against the dining table to let her grandfather through holding three bags in each hand.

"Got a lot of shopping today?" Hannah observed.

"Got to be prepared. We were here when the Mole last broke its banks back in sixty-eight, flooded all the downstairs rooms and right across the road to do the same to Aunty Sue's house," Her gran said, letting her hands drop down to rub Hannah's shoulders.

"Dad was born in nineteen-sixty-eight," she said with a sad smile.

"Yes, he was, in this very house during those floods. Your grandfather couldn't get me to the hospital, not that we could afford a car back then." Her gran's wet face softened, and she hugged Hannah to her ample bosom. "Do you miss them luvee?"

"I miss my dad every day." Hannah normally resisted such shows of affection, but today she needed a big warm hug.

"And your mother?"

Hannah wiped a single stray tear from the corner of her left eye. "Better get this shopping in before the water floods us out." She hurried out of her gran's embrace back to the draughty hallway. The less she thought about her late mother, the better. She stared outside. The rain and wind making her toes feel icy cold. Her grandfather's car was closed and locked. The floodwaters had left the pavement and were inching up the drive that sloped up to their raised front door. She rubbed at the one-inch scar under her clothes on her upper left shoulder. It ached suddenly like a stabbing pain. Maybe it was the wet weather on her old wound, or maybe some psychosomatic reaction of thinking about her dead mother.

Hannah slammed the front door shut. Closing out the rain and shutting down her terrible memories. She picked up the last very heavy wet bag, which dripped down onto her bare feet and carried it back into the kitchen to help unpack the shopping.

Ellie's parents both turned up in separate cars, from separate directions within thirty seconds of each other. Ellie and Brita were both outside with coats on when they arrived. The green seemed like a lake, with only tufts of higher grass showing as little islands. They were close to the Thames, but far enough away to be safe. Those houses right by the river or on Thames Ditton Island were starting to flood already. Some families had moved out to stay with relatives, and others moved to the local church hall to lie on army cots.

Ellie pushed open the door as both her parents rushed inside under her father's large golfing umbrella from the boot of his Jag. Once his wife was escorted inside, Mr. Chambers stepped back into the rain to survey the damage. He was dressed in his business suit, with matching charcoal grey waistcoat. His shoes and trouser bottoms were soaked, but he wasn't a man who minded about such things. He gave a long whistle, as he looked along the broken guttering and then hurried under the porch. He shook off his brolly and left it leaning outside as he followed his wife indoors.

Brita noticed that Mrs. Chambers was sporting a new and expensive looking pair of dark green Wellington Boots. One still had the tag attached to the back which read: *Le Chameau*. Mr. Chambers closed the front door and walked over to the home phone to call a trusted workman they always used over the years.

"Who fancies a nice cup of tea then?" Mrs. Chambers said clapping her hands together. "Or would you prefer coffee, Brita?"

"No, tea would be nice Mrs. Chambers," Brita replied feeling slightly more at home in England than yesterday. Ellie's mother seemed very welcoming, and Mr. Chambers seemed nice enough, for a man.

"Call me Helen please," Ellie's mother said shrugging off her wet coat and hanging it up. "Being called Mrs. Chambers in one's home sounds far too much like *Downton Abbey* to me. Come on girls, let's leave the man to do all the hard work eh, who fancies a few of my macaroons I baked yesterday?" Mrs. Chambers took each of the girl's arms and led them back into the house's large kitchen. "Then you can tell me all about what you too have got up-to, today."

Brita heard Ellie clear her throat at that remark. She smiled to herself as Mrs. Chambers moved over to fill the kettle with cold water from the tap.

"I see you've been shopping, Mum," Ellie said walking over to stand next to Brita.

Brita felt Ellie's hand quickly caress her backside through her jeans and then pull her hand back as her mother turned to face them. Even though she wanted Ellie to tell her parents and fiancé soon, her lover's furtive touches were a little bit of a turn-on.

"Oh you know me Ellie dear," Mrs. Chambers said turning

the kettle on. "Any excuse to buy some new clothes or footwear. So who wants one of my macaroons then?"

"Me," Ellie and Brita said together, both raising their left hands at the same time.

"Good," Mrs. Chambers said turning her back on the two young women to open a cupboard to grab a cake tin.

"I'm going to tell them tonight," Ellie whispered softly in Brita's left ear, before giving the lobe a little lick.

It was music to Brita's ears.

"Macaroon?" Mrs. Chambers asked straight-faced, offering the tin to her daughter and guest.

Both women burst out into fits of laughter, bemusing Ellie's mother, who joined in to be polite.

"What so funny?" Mr. Chambers said walking into the kitchen. "That gutter's going to cost five hundred pounds to replace."

The women of the house just laughed at him. Mr. Chambers turned around and headed for the haven that was his home office. "Women," he muttered as he walked down the hallway. "Even more expensive and unreliable than guttering." He shut himself in his office and went to the oak sideboard to pour himself a triple, single malt whisky aged twenty years. Down the road, the swelling river Thames was outgrowing its banks; flooding two pubs and many rows of houses right up to the church graveyard. It was the worst anyone had seen down by that stretch of the river in living memory.

Selena couldn't really believe what she was seeing. She wasn't that close to the river, even though she lived in Walton-on-Thames. It seemed to her that a river was running through her house, from the back door and out under the front one. The whole of her newly built luxury home was under a foot of dirty looking water.

She just sat in the middle of her stairs watching the wonders of nature unfold under her very roof. She expected David Attenborough to wander in any second and give a lecture on the fish life that lived above the flooded Italian tiles of her kitchen. She had dressed in a pair of jeans she found at the back of her wardrobe. They must have been eight years old, but she could still get into them.

Thank god for small mercies, she thought, I'm still a slim bitch.

The water turning her ground floor into a river had lowered the temperature somewhat. She only had the heating on upstairs and wondered how long that would last if the water got into the electrics. She had wellies on over her jeans, an old red check shirt her husband had left behind and she had used for some office fancy dress party. Over that was a fleece she sometimes wore to do the gardening.

"All dressed down and nowhere to swim to."

She had an urgent need to pee. Instead of going upstairs to one of the three bathrooms, she trotted downstairs. Pulled her jeans down to her knees and squatted down to piss in the dirty water two inches over her hall carpet. "Might as well add to the water levels," she said as she eventually finished. Pulling up her jeans and fastening them, she waded over to the front door. The water was flowing freely through her house. Selena wondered where her alcohol saturated urine might end up. She unlocked and opened her front door, hoping she would be able to get it shut again afterwards.

Just in time to see the vehicle with flashing emergency lights on top park in the deep puddle outside her electric gate. She watched as two uniformed men jumped out and beckoned her over.

It didn't take them long to be seen by the triage nurse. She called a paediatrician over to see them in their enclosed cubicle right away. Ann was glad that neither she nor Tony had to go into *angry-shouty-grandparent mode* to get something done. The nurse was very good with them, seeing the tension and worry on their concerned faces.

Tony stood rigid next to her, arms like a vice around her waist. She was holding Maddy's left hand trying to comfort her as best she could. The nurse and Doctor both gasped as they lifted the blanket off her leg, Ann felt a cold fear creep up from her guts.

"This started as a bite you say?" The young doctor with

glasses and a stethoscope around his purple shirt collar sounded rather sceptical, to say the least.

"Yes, we were trying to stop the flood water coming into our house and she got a tiny tick like bite on her leg. She wasn't well so I put her to bed, what's wrong with her doctor?" Ann explained. The nurse was holding the cover up so they could not see her leg.

"And you put nothing on the bite, nothing corrosive or bleach or ammonia?" the doctor pressed.

"Cause she bloody didn't," Tony's red anger was starting to rise. He let go of Ann to move round to look at what they could see. Ann felt dizzy, and her head spun for a second. She felt cold inside like she was going to throw-up for a second, but after blinking fast three times, the equilibrium seemed to return to her head. She leant on the examination table and felt her granddaughter's head: it was burning up. Maddy moaned turning her head left and right in pain, her eyes screwed tight shut.

"Oh God," she heard her husband whisper in the softest tones she ever heard issue from his harsh lips.

"Nurse, ring the Paeds Ward see if they have a single room for this patient, failing that, call ICU and see what they have got. I'll page the on-call consultant," the doctor said to the nurse who hurried off with a whisk of curtains.

"What's wrong with her, doctor?" Ann moved around the end of the examination table and saw what was wrong with Madison. She had no skin on her bitten leg at all, just red oozing mess with yellow running sores. It had moved up to her buttocks and was also on the ankle of her other leg.

"I'm not sure until we get upstairs and run some tests." That was all Ann heard before her vision went blank and she fainted against the foot of the table and her husband's shins.

Ayesha's maternal mum was still not home when she left Charlie snoozing on the sofa. They had polished off a bottle of *Blue Nunn* while eating pizza and watching some Cameron Diaz action film that was on. It was only just gone half-ten, and Ayesha was already yawning. That was not like her, her Friday nights normally only just got going by now. She had a pee and checked her texts and Facebook pages on her mobile.

She replied the word *bored*, to her friends Jasmine on her Facebook page. Checking through her other messages, she found one from *The H*, or Harvey as his mum still called him. They had hooked up last year for a couple weeks of fun. The H ran his own gym out of an old refurbished church in Southall. He used to live with his mum in Kingston before his luxury flat above the gym was completed. She hadn't seen or heard from him in nine months.

His text was succinct and to the point as always: *In ya area for da nite, wanna fuck?*

The tiredness suddenly left her, and she realised she hadn't had sex for nearly three weeks—which seemed like a lifetime to her. She closed her eyes and remembered his muscles, well one muscle in particular. The boy had no social skills, was a narcissist and the IQ of an amoeba; just what Ayesha loved in her fuck-toys.

Pick me up in 15, she texted back. She half-stood, wiped and went into her room, not bothering to replace her underwear. It would not be required tonight. She chose a tight black skirt; a crop top, with added zip up knee-length boots and her thick long coat were the order of the night. She stuck a bright orange post-it note on the empty wine bottle on the table for Charlie and her mum to not wait up for her. She left the flat, loving the freedom of no panties between her legs. She was soaked in seconds running from the lit communal doorway to the blurred black BMW by the curb *The H* was waiting for her in.

She shivered and shook her wet hair about as she slid into the passenger seat next to The H.

"Hey, I had a shower before I came out," The H complained as the side of his neck was spattered with rainwater.

"Gotta get wet, to get wet," she purred leaning over to lick his cheek and rub his groin at the same time.

"I get it," he nodded. *He really didn't.* "So where you wanna go?"

"Somewhere close, dark and quiet where I can fuck you," she said in her cat like tones that her sex partners loved to hear.

"I hear that," The H said pulling away from the curb as fast as the coursing water would allow.

CHAPTER SEVEN

FLOODS OF TEARS

Hannah had ignored his messages, voicemails, Snapchats, rantings for her to contact him. It had been interfering with her sleep so she turned her mobile off at eleven. She read a book about the Sutton Hoo, Anglo-Saxon burial mound find. It had been a lady landowner who discovered it, she noted. Hannah dreamed of such things for herself, finding artifacts long-lost of such importance. Girls in her year dreamed of going to Ibiza and Kavos, to party all night. She would go to the same places, but try and find local archaeological digs that she could help out with.

She was asleep by eleven thirty. Her angle posed lamp over her bed still on, the Sutton Hoo book still open on top of her pushed down duvet. She woke at six am. Turning over, her arms had felt cold, and she hiked up the duvet to her chin in her sleep. This sent the thick hardback slipping to the floor to wake her up with a bang.

Hannah sat up on her arm and pulled her long hair out of her face. She grabbed her mobile, wondering why it was off in her darkened bedroom. It was still raining hard outside, she could hear. Her phone slowly chirped into life revealing tons more texts and messages until two in the morning from him. She saw the time, the tone of the texts and exhaled deeply. Even though she was sixteen, she was mature enough to know she had to kick her older guy into touch before he wrecked her adult life even before it got started.

She felt the pressing need to pee. She kicked on her slippers and padded to the bathroom next door. She had only got a step outside her bedroom door when a sudden wave of nausea hit her. She managed to close the bathroom door and get the loo seat up before throwing up once into the bowl.

After two more dry heaves, she closed the toilet seat and leant her hot face against the cool plastic. "What the hell is the matter with me," she asked the darkness.

Throwing up had seemed to have cured the sick feeling she had. She pulled herself up to sit on the toilet seat sidewards and use the eco-flush. No one came running to see how she was from any other two bedrooms. She washed her face, rinsed the taste from her tongue with minty mouthwash and headed back to bed. Another new text appeared begging her to contact him, or he would knock on her front door in an hour's time and damn the consequences.

We need to talk. Park at the far end of Waitrose car park at 9 am. She typed a few more things but then deleted them before sending. She turned off her phone again and her bedside lamp. She needed to break up with him, end this mess before it got even messier, but she had a nagging feeling it was already too late for that. She grabbed a teddy bear from the shelf above her that her father had bought her for her third birthday. It was a little dusty, but she hugged it tight to her chest and wished to all the stars in heaven that her father was still alive.

Brita and Ellie's night did not go according to plan. Mr. Chambers had gone out right after dinner. He had gotten a call from the local golf club where he was serving as Captain at the moment. The nineteenth hole clubhouse had flooded and partly collapsed. So it was all hands to the clubs, to clean the rest of the building of cups, pictures, booze and golf equipment. He hadn't gotten back until eleven, had a warm bath, with a double whisky on the side and went straight to bed.

Brita lay awake and sadly still alone in the spare bedroom. She thought back to the events of the night before. With Mr. Chambers out, Ellie said it would be easier to tell her mother first anyway. Brita had agreed, maybe this was the best approach. They had both been wrong. Mrs. Chambers' words echoed around Brita's brain in both English and her native Danish.

"Don't be silly Eloise you are no more a dyke than I am. Even I dabbled or is it diddled with my roommate in Loughborough. It's like smoking a bit of weed or bum sex, we all give it a go, but then realise it's all silly nonsense, and we have to settle down, get married and raise children." She had smiled at them both after Ellie had told her she was a lesbian.

Brita closed her eyes and saw them both with wine glasses in their hands. Not that dissimilar in features apart from the age gap. Mother and daughter: one laughing and one crying.

"It's not a fad or some crisis I'm going through; I'm gay, and I love Brita. I'll call Matt tomorrow and call the engagement off. I'm serious," Ellie had shouted at the mocking look on her mother's over-powdered face.

"Serious, oh yes this is serious. You are engaged to a nice man, with prospects, you will have a lovely life together, get a house, Daddy and I will help you there and have babies. This is just a fling, something young girls do." Mrs. Chambers tilted her head on one side and put down her wine glass on the coffee table.

"I'm not a little girl anymore, Mother. I can choose who I love and make love too and who I want to spend the rest of my life with. If it's not here with your blessing, then we'll live in Denmark without it." Brita had winced at the sound of her love, shouting so loudly and so passionately.

She hated conflict like this within families. That's why she was such a loner usually, to avoid such confrontations.

"Look," Mrs. Chambers had said grabbing Ellie's arms lightly. "You and Brita can have all the fun you want, but when she goes home, you'll stay here and marry Matt, how does that sound?"

"How does that sound? Like patronising crap, Mother. Brita and I want to be together forever either here, or not here, it doesn't matter to me. The only thing that matters is her and us being a couple." Brita had been so proud of Ellie then when she shrugged off her mother and sat on the arm of the chair Brita had been rooted too. Ellie had taken her hand in hers and kissed her fingers. "Nothing can split us apart."

"Rubbish she'll be bored of you in a month," Mrs. Chambers

*sneered, her eyes the same shade as Ellie, bored into Brita's with malice
and resentment.*

"Never, we are in love," Ellie had said back.

*"You were in love with Matt before she turned up." Mrs. Chambers
grabbed the half-filled bottle of red wine from the coffee table and made
for the living room door. "I'm off to bed, and you two better go to
yours—separately."*

Brita didn't want to get up. She rubbed her palms up her
cheeks and over her moist eyes, into her hairline. She stared at
the dim grey morning showing around the edges of the curtains and sighed. She wondered again if it would ever stop raining in England. She pulled the covers up to her neck and tried
to look at her nails in the gloom. They were short, natural, bitten
down and painted a dark aubergine colour. She had always bitten them as long as she could remember.

A creak of a door on the landing outside made her turn
her head towards the guest room door. She held her breath
and hoped. She suddenly realised that her right hand had sub-
consciously moved under the covers to cup her left breast. She
checked her wristwatch to see it was only just after six in the
morning. She parted her lips and remembered to breathe as
feminine footfalls approached her door. She readied a smile for
her lover as the door handle slowly moved downwards, and the
door was pushed in towards her.

Even in the gloom she could see that it was not her Ellie,
but the shape of another woman. Grey natural light from the
landing windows revealed Mrs. Chambers was standing in
the doorway wearing nothing but a revealing black baby doll
nightie and a lustful smile. Brita sat up in bed in shock, forgetting she wore nothing on her top half. Mrs. Chambers moved
into the guest bedroom and closed the door with her near naked
behind.

"Mrs. Chambers I think you are in the wrong room," Brita
said covering her breasts with her right arm.

"I don't think so dear," she replied pulling down the shoulder straps of her nightie and letting the rest wriggle down her
body to the floor. Then she moved over to the bed and grabbed
the covers.

Selena used to have pride in the house her career had bought. She always knew that she could quiet any socialist qualms she had about being well-off, by knowing she had made her own way in life. She'd done it all on her own. No rich parents, not even her husband had made much of a financial contribution when he was around. She had been house proud but now look at her. She leant over the balcony on the landing, looking down at her submerged hallway. Her eyes danced from the native African zebra skin she had bought on a working holiday in Zaire, along the paintings and hangings on her beige walls and hardly blinked at all.

The downstairs was awash with water up to two feet in places. The fire crew that turned up yesterday to check on the entire road pumped out a lot of water, but it had come back overnight. Rushing through, around and over the long blue plastics sandbags, they had put down at the front and back. She had refused their offers of a place at the local church hall for the night. A camper bed and a mug of builder's tea wasn't going to fix her woes in a hurry. At least she had slept well, through exhaustion, she guessed from trying to save her downstairs turning into her own indoor pool. The smell wafting up from the dirty water lapping over her bottom step and halfway up to the second; was rank.

She had hoped it was the police that were coming for her. She had been resigned to that. Yet, also, she felt ashamedly relieved to be free for another day. The local constabulary were probably inundated with calls, looters and the flood waters at the moment. Only when the flood waters subsided in a week or so would the body be found. She knew from experience, a week or two in a watery ditch would degrade any evidence against her. She could easily buy another car, keep the old Beemer in the garage under wraps for two years and then sell it on the cheap. Or even torch it on wasteland.

Selena shook her head left and right vigorously to expel such criminal thoughts from her mind. The rain was still dancing on her bedroom window as she rounded her bed to put on the coffeemaker that had permanent residence on her bedside cabinet. One boon of a single life was she had two free bedside cabinets. One for books, work papers and her reading glasses and the other for the coffeemaker. It would be her second cup of the morning. Her tightly knotted stomach grumbled loudly for food, but she overruled its pleas.

She drank her coffee and watched the rain hitting her windows. She had also come-on this morning. That ever familiar coppery smell emanating from the toilet bowl as she peed; when she first got up. At least she wasn't pregnant to add insult to injury. Selena reached under her top and rubbed at her cold flat belly and suddenly wished she wasn't alone in the bedroom anymore. She knew she had to leave the house today or even turn on the TV to find out what was happening in the world. Was it downing like she was in self-pity?

In the end, she turned on the radio attached to the coffeemaker and listened as the Home Counties drowned.

Ann Gable woke to find herself alone in a strange room. Rough synthetic fibre itched her cheek, ear and around her right eye where she was laying. Her left hand was tucked up to her face, and she felt a blanket over the core of her body. She sat up from the three armless blue patterned chairs she had slept across and looked around the room. Posters for hand washing; catching sneezes and flu-jabs lined the blue-grey walls. She rubbed at her cheek as the family room door opened letting in the sounds of a busy ICU ward and her sobbing daughter. She was being comforted by Steve her other half and her brother Mike who had turned up.

Ann was up in an instant. Throwing aside the blanket she rushed over to take her only daughter in her arms. Trembling from head to toe, her sobbing daughter looked up with red-rimmed eyes. "She's gone, Mum, my little Maddy is gone."

Her vision dimmed for a second, and she thought she might faint again. But motherly instinct was stronger, and she took her grieving daughter into her embrace. Too stunned to cry herself, she stroked Stacey's hair and looked to Steve and Tony for answers. "What happened?"

"Something in the bite infected her with some waterborne

bacteria," Steve said repeating what he could remember the doctors saying.

"Some bloody flesh eating bug in the water Ann, it...it," Tony a giant of a man cried for the first time since he'd stopped wearing short trousers.

Just then not one, but three worried looking doctors entered the room.

"I'm Mister Cunningham, a Dermatological Consultant from The Royal London Hospital in London, this is Doctor Khan head of Tropical Diseases University College London and this is Doctor Grainger, who you know. I wish to pass on mine and my colleague's condolences at this tragic time." Mr. Cunningham was tall and thin, with a hawk of a nose and bald apart from a thin line of grey shaven hair connecting his ears around the back of his head. He wore a Saville Row suit instead of a white coat, unlike his companions. Doctor Grainger the ICU consultant they knew from last night. Plus, a much shorter tubbier Asian doctor they had not seen before.

"Doctor Grainger tried to explain what happened to Maddy, but we couldn't take it in," Mike said, as the rest of the family was too choked up to speak.

"What caused her skin to go like that?" Tony managed to croak, wiping away his tears.

"Well we still need to do some more tests," Doctor Khan said, only stopped by Tony's large raised hand.

"Tests, my granddaughter is dead, what use are bloody tests?" Grief had turned his voice to anger. A more usual tone for him.

"Well to find out the cause," Khan continued, shrinking back a little from the huge man before him.

"What Doctor Khan is trying to say is we can rule out certain things as Madison did not respond to the usual treatments. Antibiotics, Hyperbaric Oxygen Treatment, and invasive surgical procedures did nothing to stop this infection. So we can already rule out some sort of Streptococcus Pyogenos infection." Mr. Cunningham tried to explain, but his long words only brought confused looks to the grieving family. "We know it is not cholera or typhoid, but some form of Necrotizing Fasciitis acting in the same manner."

"In plain English please Doctor?" Ann managed to say, still not really taking in the fact that her little Maddy was gone from them.

Mr. Cunningham—who disliked being called a mere doctor or talking to grieving relatives—shrugged back his shoulder and stared down his beaky nose at her. "We think at this time, bacteria in the dirty flood water entered through an insect bite and caused her flesh to destroy itself. As we are not sure how these bacteria are transmitted you will all have to stay here for tests in an isolation ward, for the time being."

Mr. Cunningham was looking at Ann, so didn't see the punch coming from his left until it connected with his nose; breaking it in two places.

Ayesha woke lying on top of her own bedcovers, still dressed in what little clothes she had sneaked out in. She was drooling and turned over to find her bed was a little damp from last night's soaked clothes. She winced from a twinge of soreness between her legs. She had forgotten how well-endowed *The H* was in the trouser-snake department. She swung her legs off her bed, looking with annoyance at the rip in her skirt and dried silver stains across it. It had been a fun night, and she had soon forgotten about the awful weather riding in *The H's* ride. He wasn't much of a romantic conversationalist, but what he was good at, she liked a lot. She stripped off her dirty clothes and pulled on her soft, thick cotton dressing gown. Kicking on her furry slippers, she padded out of her room towards the bathroom.

"Pam is that you?" came Charlie's sleepy muffled voice from the master bedroom.

"She not back yet?" Ayesha replied, her hand on the handle of the bathroom door next to her two mum's bedroom.

"Not yet," Charlie replied opening the door a crack to talk to Ayesha.

Ayesha could see that Charlie had only just got out of bed, where she nearly always slept in the buff.

"Any messages on your mobile?"

"Nope, you?"

"It's back in my purse," Ayesha said thumbing back to her bedroom door. "Want me to go and check?"

"Nah, I'll check the home phone first, see if she's left a message on that, eh."

"Okies." Ayesha nodded.

"You going to be in there long?"

"Why?" Ayesha yawned letting go of the bathroom door handle.

"Cos I'm bursting for a piss, Ash," Charlie said, hopping from one foot to the next behind the door.

"Go on then," Ayesha said retreating to the wall, covering her eyes with her hand as Charlie's white body dashed past her into the loo.

"Thanks, hun," Charlie called from behind the closed bathroom door, followed by the fast tinkle of pee on water.

"Hmmm," Ayesha said and padded off to the living room to check the answer phone and put the kettle on.

Ayesha pulled the curtains to dismiss the hanging darkness of the living room, but even with the curtains open, it was still gloomy and grey inside. Little light could penetrate the dark rain clouds and driving rain. She stared out at the water swept world outside and shivered. Rubbing her arms, she turned to the home phone sitting on a small triangular table next to the settee. She was relieved to see it was flashing red, with two messages waiting to be heard. She pushed the play button and then crossed the silent room to the open kitchen beyond. She had just made it around the counter onto the lino of the kitchen proper when her mother's tired voice spoke from the answering machine.

"Morning my darlings, it's just after two a-m here and the place has gone mad with the influx of patients. Lots of people getting ill because of contaminated water (long yawn), so you and Charlie stay out of that crap if you can. Should be back home sometime after eight, love ya both, bye. You lucky people who get to sleep (kiss sound)."

"Okay, Mum," Ayesha said emptying the kettle of that's night's water into the sink. She managed to fill it up again before the second message chimed in.

"Hey....so I may be late again after all. This place has gone mad this evening. Erm...lots of people coming in some red rashes on their skin because of the contaminated flood water. Boil all the water before you drink it. (Long exhale of breath) I might be some time here...they need all hands on deck. Got to go, call you when I can...I love you both so very much. Stay out of the flood water, (sob) a child has died. Bye."

Ayesha turned on the kettle, but her eyes were fixed on the LED red 2 next to the phone. In the first message her mother had just sounded tired, a state Ayesha had heard her in many times over the years. But the second message was different. She wasn't tired, she sounded worried and upset by something. Maybe the death of the child had taken its toll on her, but Ayesha just couldn't take her eyes off the phone, she was concerned. The noise of the kettle slowly boiling behind her, the background to her worry.

The spell was only broken by Charlie coming into the front room, in the silky kimono she wore in the mornings. "Any news from your mum?"

Ayesha blinked. Her eyes were wet. She wasn't sure if it was from staring too long at the phone, or other reasons. "Huh?"

"Any news from your mum, Ash?" Charlie asked again, moving around the settee to see the two messages on the answer phone.

"Yeah," Ayesha said pointing at the home phone. "I'm worried about her."

"Why honey?" Charlie moved away from the phone over to Ayesha and rubbed her arm. "What's wrong?"

"It's hard to explain. Listen to the messages. I've just got this terrible feeling I'm never going to see her again."

"Don't be silly." Charlie gathered Ayesha into her arms and hugged her tight. Ash was the nearest thing she would ever have to a daughter, and she loved her just as much as Pam. "If she doesn't walk through that door soon, if not we'll drive up to the hospital ourselves and put all your fears at rest."

Ayesha felt empty inside. Like her stomach acid had turned to ice. Charlie always gave good advice and her words had been comforting over the years she and her mum had been together. But not this morning. Ayesha began to sob uncontrollably into Charlie's neck, her blurred vision never leaving the red number 2 on the answer phone. It took a long while for her second mum to calm her down.

CHAPTER EIGHT

THE DEAD RIVER

Hannah's grandparents were always, annoyingly, up with the lark every morning. Even though they were both retired. Long years of hard work had programmed them to get up early, even though they could spend all Saturday in bed and the world would not end because of it. Hannah wished she could stay in bed all day, but *he needed* to see her. In a way, she needed to see him too, to put this unprofessional and illegal relationship to bed once and for all.

She washed her face only, before getting dressed in the warmest clothes she could find. She tied her manky looking bed hair back into a French plait, knowing it would get wet soon anyway. She hurried downstairs at just after eight to find the household alive and full of busy activity. Even her younger sister was up and dressed. She had her coat and wellies on, not slumped in front of children's telly as she was most Saturday mornings. In fact, her grandparents were also dressed; her grandfather looked soaked already.

"What's going on?" She said jumping down the last two steps into the tiny, crowded hallway. Her remaining family was halfway between the hall and the dining room.

"The River has overrun the whole bloody street. It's only a foot away from our front door, Hannah, we need to take precautions because it will be coming into the house by the end of the day, mark my words."

"Oh Bill don't you'll scare the girls. It won't come to that surely," her grandmother tried to reassure Hannah and her sister, but her words were less than convincing.

"It will girl, you mark my words," her grandfather repeated himself. "We need to fill bags up with dirt from the garden and make a flood barrier in front of the front step. I've only got five heavy garden sacks, though; I'll need to buy some more."

"I'll do that," Hannah volunteered quickly.

"You sure Hannah, your granddad doesn't mind going, the water is bad out there." Hannah's grandmother said.

"She'll be fine love, stop fussing. Will give me time to get started with the bags we do have. I still have some sand somewhere in the shed from when I re-laid the patio two years ago." Hannah felt a warm feeling inside as her grandfather gave her a proud little smile. She didn't blame him for being the grumpy-old-sod he was. He and her grandmother had only just retired, when they were forced to take her and Hayley in. Bang went their dreams of a trip around America, no cruises for them or buying that cottage in Bournemouth. They had been forced into becoming parents again, even though they had done their time. After Hannah and Hayley had become orphans, their choices had been stark, either they took their son's kids in or see them disappear into the care system.

"You'll have to change your boots love," her grandmother pointed to the scuffed-up footwear she had on.

"What's wrong with these?" Hannah said looking down at her brown ankle high boots as she grabbed a waterproof coat that she hadn't donned in two years.

Her grandfather strode past her and opened the front door, and Hannah could see why. Half the sloping upwards front drive and the garden was submerged in flood water.

"You haven't got a boat in that shed of yours have you grand-dad?" Hannah asked as she pulled on her coat and zipped it up against the cold coming through the open front door.

"No, but I do have a pair of your dad's old waders when he went through his fishing stage. That should get you through to the shops," he said, putting two hands on her shoulders.

"Do you think Waitrose will be open?"

"Should be Han, but that car park might be a bit busy and flooded, so watch your step."

"I will," Hannah replied.

Hannah felt like Bear Grylls as she waded through the worst of the floodwater from the River Mole. With her waterproofs, waders, gloves and hood up, she looked, if not felt like an explorer. Down on street level, the water nearly went up to her thighs on occasions. But it soon dropped away as she made her way down the street. Her family was watching from the front garden, and she gave them a cheery wave, before pressing on. Further down the road where the water had already gushed into their houses, people were moving out. Other neighbours were trying to build barriers across their drives and front gardens to stop the flood waters ruining their homes.

Hannah, though, was just counting the dead things floating in the flood waters. She counted the remains of a fox, two cats and four birds by the time she made it through the rain, to less waterlogged streets. Hannah kept telling herself not to fall into the water with her mouth open. There was no telling what diseases were in the muddy waters. She took the longer route to the shops, nearer the bypass. The flood waters were creeping towards it but had not touched the four lane roads yet. The constant heavy rain made it look like a river. There weren't as many cars about as usual today and the ones driving were doing it at reduced speeds.

The garage was closed due to flooding. It had chains across its forecourt and a rain-splashed sign up to that effect. The flooding hadn't reached this far yet, and Hannah felt sweaty with exertion in her all-weather gear and waders. She only saw two people out in the rain anyway, on the way to the supermarket car park and both of them were dressed much like her. The car park was still quite full, she had fifteen minutes to go before nine so went into Waitrose, where people were buying up bottled water and tins like it was doomsday. Luckily for her, they were not so interested in garden waste sacks, and she bought three lots. The tills were jam packed with shoppers and the place looked a little understaffed. Lucky for her she was third in line when a manager opened up a far till. It still took her right up to nine to get served and out of the steamy-windowed warm shop and back into the rain.

She checked her mobile. No less than seven messages from him, begging her to come today and the last one saying: *'I'm here, far right-hand corner of the car park.'* She didn't bother replying as she would have to take off her gloves. Winding the Waitrose bag up in her left hand to keep out the driving rain, she headed for the end of the car park. As she walked up through the rain, she saw that the far top left of the car park had been cordoned off with upturned trolleys, yellow warning signs, and cones.

Hannah smiled as she saw two of the cones turning around in the flood water beyond like they were pirouetting dancers from *Strictly Cone Dancing*. At last, she spotted his car. The windows were steaming up, and she wasn't in her normal male fantasy schoolgirl uniform. He liked it if she kept most of it on as they made love, as it *turned him on big time*.

A wipe of the inside of his window and he finally spotted her just in front of the bonnet of his car. He smiled, that smile that had won her heart and got her out of her knickers and beckoned her inside. Hannah was damp, cold and sick of the rain. She probably would have gotten into the car if the devil himself was inside as long as it was warm and dry.

The inside of his car was warmer than she expected, so quickly pulled back her hood and unzipped her blue waterproof coat.

"I wasn't sure you would come, but I'm glad you did," he said leaning forwards to aim his lips at hers.

Hannah pulled back, so he could not achieve his objective.

"Hey, what's wrong Han?"

"What do you think is wrong Mister Davies?" she asked in a cold voice to match the weather. He was on the back foot right away, seeing the stare she was giving him.

"What's with all the Mister Davies shit Hannah, we aren't at school now," he said with a frown, putting his right hand on the steering wheel. His seat squeaked like a fart as he raised his left knee to turn to face her without twisting his back.

"I think we should break up," Hannah simply said looking down at the wet plastic bag resting on her lap. She didn't really know what to expect from her adult lover, or what he would say. She expected begging, maybe or angry threats. What she didn't expect, was him to burst into tears.

"But I love you," he said between sniffs and sobs.

Hannah looked at the man beside her who had taken an interest in her interests and then her virginity and couldn't help but laugh at the pathetic man sitting beside her. It wasn't when his hard cock had slipped inside her vagina when she became a woman, but this very moment in the car park. She was in charge of the destiny of their lives, she had to be strong, and she was the more adult of the two. She'd needed to be rid of him but had to make sure of something first.

"Matt, I need you to do something for me right now," she said in her new adult voice.

"Anything," he said sniffing up his tears through his nose. "Cos I love you so, so much."

"I need you to go and buy me a plastic jug or a bowl and a pregnancy tester." Hannah reached out to give some comfort to her ex-lover as he looked up at her with wide questioning eyes. She didn't keep his gaze. She looked around wondering if the windows were steamy enough for her to pee in the back of the car without anyone noticing. "Oh and some chocolate," she added.

Breakfast had been a cold sobering affair at the Chambers' household. Ellie had crept into Brita's room only to find her mother in the nude, trying to force her way into the guest bed. The silence was so loud and a mortified-looking Mrs. Chambers put on the telly in the kitchen to watch the news.

Brita felt like she was in some Anders Thomas Jensen's film this morning. Her engaged girlfriend's mother had tried to force herself onto her, while the man of the house was oblivious to the rising tide of lesbianism going on in his own home. Much like the rising flood waters in this part of England according to the aerial pictures coming from the TV news. Whole swathes of Southern England near rivers were suffering flooding to homes that had never been flooded before. A helicopter-mounted camera showed the River Thames, with its burst banks on either side and flood water running into people's homes ruining their daily lives. Then the news report took a sadder tone, a picture of a pretty little girl in a red coat appeared on screen. She had been playing out in the flood waters yesterday and died overnight due to some complications of being in contaminated water. Details, it seemed, were sketchy at best from the female reporter outside a rain swept Kingston Hospital.

"Oh-my-god that is so terrible," Ellie said breaking the silence.

"What were her parents thinking about, letting her play in dirty flood water," Mrs. Chambers said reaching for a very early glass of Pinot.

"I'm sure they did not realise the dangers," Brita said reaching under the kitchen table to squeeze Ellie's cold delicate hand.

"You still here," Mrs. Chambers almost snorted the words out as she poured her first of many wines of the day.

"Not for fucking much longer, Mother!" Ellie screeched back as she hastily shot up from the table, sending her chair falling backwards onto the tiled floor with a bang.

"Eloise June Chambers!" Mrs. Chambers' eyebrows were threatening to touch the end of her greying fringe.

"Come on Brita, let's go upstairs and pack. Let's hope Denmark will be more welcoming than Surrey, eh," Ellie shouted grabbing Brita's hand and nearly pulling her out of her chair. Brita followed her, but could not resist a winning smirk back over her shoulder.

"You wouldn't dare go, you're too much like your weak-willed father in that respect," Mrs. Chambers catcalled as the young lovers hurried towards the stairs.

"Are you sure about this, what about your fiancé?" Brita had to hurry to keep up with the long strides of her determined lover or else be dragged to her knees.

"Never been more sure of anything in my life," Ellie said stopping at the foot of the stairs to spin round. Her hands rose to Brita's cheeks as she planted an angry, but passionate kiss on her girlfriend's soft lips. Brita kissed her back, full of unbridled joy, her hands lost in Ellie's long brown hair. When they parted, they were both grinning like fools and crying like widows. Brita let Ellie take her hand in hers again, wrapping her long slender fingers into an interlocking bond of love. They started up the wide staircase together just as Mr. Chambers came into view at the bend in the staircase; skiing down three steps, but managing somehow to keep an unsteady upright gait. He was sweating all over his portly face, and the pit of his recently put on shirt was already stained with wet circles. His hands though were the terrible thing, each a red raw bloody mess, like something from the back of a butcher's shop. Mr. Chambers stumbled against the wall, leaving a bloody handprint behind, like something Brita once did as an infant at her first school.

"Oh-my-god Daddy what have you done to yourself?" Ellie asked through the fingers of her left hand that covered her shocked open mouth.

"Eloise, help me," her father croaked before his left knee gave way and he toppled forwards down the stairs. Brita and Ellie had to shake off each other's grip quickly and jump back down to the side of the stairs as Mr. Chambers fell heavily onto the last step where they had stood together only half a second ago. He landed with a splat of red bloodied hands on the cream hall carpet, bringing a scream from Eloise's frightened lips. Mr. Chambers was out cold.

His wife ran into join the screaming, forming a Chambers lady duet with her daughter. It was left to Brita to pull her mobile phone from her pocket, wondering what number it was to dial for an ambulance here in England. It was 112 back home, but she was sure it was different here in the UK.

"What is the ambulance number?" Brita shouted at the two Chambers women, who were still standing over Mr. Chambers in frozen shock.

"Nine-nine-nine," they turned and cried at her as one.

Brita nodded and dialled the number. She saw that Mr. Chambers right sleeve had pulled up as he fell, the button alone on the third step. It looked like a scene from a *Hellraiser* film, like all the flesh of his arm had been stripped away, leaving oozing veins and red tissues and muscles underneath.

"What service do you require?" A female voice spoke calmly in her ear.

"Ambulance please," she replied, knowing that she and Ellie

were not leaving England anytime in the near future.

Selena sat right back against her expensive, but bloody uncomfortable headboard. She was on her fourth coffee of the morning. The radio blared out next to her. Spewing out the woes of the wet world that threatened to swallow her home. Some words snapped her out of her blank thoughts, as she stared at herself in the wardrobe mirror.

She inhaled and exhaled loudly, riding a slight cramp in the core of her womb. She inclined her head towards the radio; found a sweet point on the headboard to rest her head. "*...The Environment Agency and the local Water companies are increasingly becoming worried about the possible contamination of one of their Surrey drinking water reservoirs. The Island Barn Reservoir located between Esher and West Molesey is under threat from the rising water levels of three surrounding rivers nearby that have burst their banks and flood plains. The rivers Mole, Ember and the ominously named Dead River, surround the reservoir on all sides. A spokesman for Thames Water says that there is no threat to the public water supply, and they had contingency plans for such an occurrence. Nearby homes have been evacuated and actually reaching the site to access it by road has become impossible since yesterday. In other news, the little girl killed by contaminated water yesterday has been named as Madi—*"

Selena switched the radio off. She had had her fill of death for the moment. Her stomach grumbled for breakfast, and her mind urged her to find some chocolate to eat. She pulled herself down the bed, the sheets ruffling up under her backside. She stood facing the mirror and lifted up her tight grey top. Her flat stomach and what she always thought was ugly belly button was reflected. Dull pain emanated from deep inside her as she sucked in her breath. Then made a fist and with a snarl punched herself hard just above her waistline. She doubled up winded, her other hand going flat against the cold mirror to hold her up. As the first shock of pain left her, she stood to breathe in again and tensed her stomach muscles. Then punched herself even harder than the time before. Her knees gave way this time, and she collapsed onto them, her hand making a horrible squeal as it rubbed down the length of the mirror. Sobbing, she looked up to see her glinting eyes. Wondering what punishment would be enough to take her guilt away. Then she thought of the kitchen and the razor sharp knives in their ordered wooden block.

She stood up on shaking legs and slightly bent over, made for the bedroom door. Her Wellington boots sat next to the balcony, where her damp jeans hung. She pulled her jeans on ignoring the red stain at the centre of the crotch of her knickers. Then without socks on, pulled on the wellingtons and went down stairs holding the rail tighter than she normally would. The water seemed to have risen to near the tops of her expensive green wellies. She frowned and went back upstairs to one of the spare bedrooms where she dumped lots of out of season clothes, and other things she could not find a home for downstairs. An old sewing machine she bought on a whim stood on top of a mahogany dresser that was ancient and out of keeping with the rest of the decor. It had belonged to her late mother. She never found anywhere to show it off in any of the flats or houses she had owned over the years, but she was loathed to throw it out. She pulled out the nearest top drawer and with only a cursory look banged it shut again. The next drawer along held the thing she was after. A role of brown parcel tape, which she used to wrap around and around where her wellingtons met just underneath the knees of her jeans. When she was done, there was little of the brown tape left on its large spool. She tossed it on the bed behind her and left the room.

The stench of the dirty water making a lake inside her house assaulted her nostrils as soon as she moved onto the balcony. The water levels seemed higher than when she had gone to bed last night. She trudged downstairs, trying to remember how high the fuse box was off the floor in the cupboard under the stairs. She wondered how long the rain could possibly keep coming down: *forty days and forty nights maybe?*

The third step was underwater, which hadn't been the case last night. She wondered how long she could realistically keep living here before she got ill. That brightened her glumness. Catching typhoid or something was maybe her just desserts for what she had done. She walked down the watery steps and let out a quivering near silent hiss as the icy water went up over her taped up wellies. It didn't stop until it was halfway up her inner thighs, making her open and close her mouth like a caught fish, as the coldness assaulted her. Wading through it was even worse. Her movement made ripples, waves and then splashes up into her crotch making her shiver. She used the top of the covered radiator to help her keep her balance, not wanting to fall into the dirty water. The kitchen door was closed, not that it made any difference to the flood waters.

This is getting ridiculous, she thought as her hand grabbed the door handle, *I need to move out to a warm, dry hotel, preferably in Bermuda.* Selena wrenched the door open towards her causing a bow wave that splashed against the zip of her jeans, causing her mouth to form a silent-O against the icy water. She looked up from her soaked jeans to come eye-to-eye with a dishevelled looking bearded man who was standing under one of her open food cupboards and was munching away at her expensive roast chicken and rosemary crisps.

All Ann Gable could see through tear blurred eyes was plastic. It covered the former geriatrics ward, now the hospital's emergency isolation area. The elderly patients had been shipped off to hospices and other hospitals, as the doctors had begun emergency protocols to contain any possible spread of the mystery infection that killed Maddy.

Clear plastic, white plastic, and yellow were everywhere on the ward. A sterile and bleak world to match her void of grief. To add to her misery, her entire immediate family was here. Tony was strapped down, and a little sedated, she guessed, to stop him trying to leave and assault any more members of staff. He was the lucky one. She wished she was out of it, dulled by some injection so she could not bear the waking grief she felt.

Mike was opposite her, and her daughter Stacey was to her left, sedated as well. Her remaining grandchild Jayden was lying flat on a bed next to his mother. Each separated by their own cocoon of clear plastic. She didn't mind where she was at the moment, she would feel drawn and lost at home; but at least she could hug someone. She was sat up on three pillows, in a paper nightie and wired up to a machine monitoring her body's every function. She looked around through the slight distortion of the clear plastic. The doctors and nurses in green gowns, masks and gloves were treating a patient at the far end of the ward. Ann could tell it was a woman, and she had the same red marks on her arms as Maddy had on her legs. Ann tried to summon the compassion to feel sorry for her pain, but she was numb. She sat on her bed, arms crossed just waiting. She knew she would never fully get over this and blamed herself for letting Maddy play in the flood water.

"Nurse fetch Mister Cunningham right away, we are losing her," called one of the doctors in a panicky voice. One of the gowned figures unzipped the plastic cocoon that all the patients were trapped inside and ran for the double zipped exit. Ann watched her body ripple as she watched through different angles and depths of clear plastic. Distorting the figure into nearly a ghost like apperition, as she exited the sterile area.

Ann watched on like a disengaged passenger in a car passing a crash on the other side of the motorway barriers. A witness to the pain and suffering of another human being. She saw a red stain hand reach out as the poor woman convulsed, extending her belly off the bed in agony. Then her frame collapsed like a marionette with its strings cut. A buzzer on a machine sounded; followed by a constant soulless beep that was chimes of death for the poor woman.

"She's gone," sobbed one of the female nurses.

"Shit," the doctor stated. "Time of death ten-forty-nine am."

Ann closed her eyes and tried to picture Jayden, but all she got was flashes of Maddy with her amputated legs bandaged up, moments before she passed away in the early hours of the morning. Ann felt useless but kept her eyes closed.

So she did not see the medical staff wheel in the metal trolley and body bag.

A&E was packed to over-capacity. It took Ayesha and Charlie ten minutes before they saw a nurse they recognised.

"Hey Julia, have you seen Pam?" Charlie asked, catching

the attention of a sister with her head buried in a brown folder as she rushed past.

"What...oh hi, you won't find her here I'm afraid. Big infection thing going on, they have nicked half my staff to run the place," Julia replied, finally recognising who they were.

"Where did they send her?" Ayesha asked, trying to keep a lid on her low patience threshold.

"Miller Ward; old block fourth floor, take the main lifts and head left a lot, you can't miss it. Tell her we miss her down here," Julia said, as Charlie and Ayesha hurried off to the lifts.

"We will, thanks," Charlie called back.

When the lift arrived they headed off to the old block, which was attached to the newer hospital buildings with a glass walkway over the road that led to the staff car parks. The place was silent and empty, and both women felt a rising sense of unease like they were trespassing. A rippled old sign showed them they were on the right course, pushing through three sets of closed double doors they could see lights and hospital staff at last. Charlie and Ayesha exchanged relieved smiles, as they parted the last set of doors only to be confronted by two burly hospital security guards.

"How did you get in here?" The wider of the two asked from behind a mask that both men were wearing. Ayesha saw that they were wearing blue surgical gloves and clear bags over their black DMs.

"I'm here to see my mum; she's a nurse on duty here." Ayesha stepped forwards as she had enough cleavage on show to bamboozle these two monosyllabic meatheads.

Security men Numbers One and Two were struggling to keep eye contact with her. *Men were so easy to manipulate if you had the right weapons on show.*

"Who's she then?" Security number Two barked at Charlie.

Charlie stepped forwards to give them a feminist vent of epic proportions, but Ayesha stepped closer between the towering guards so they could get even more of an eyeful as she bent her back a little. "She's my mum's *lesbian* lover." Ayesha finished by biting her bottom lip seductively. "So can we go find her?"

"You shouldn't be here really, it's restricted to hospital staff, patients, and family members." Security One said with less gravel to his voice.

"We are family," Ayesha said, quickly grabbing Charlie's arm. "We'll sit over on those chairs while one of you men can find my mom. We'll be ever soooooo good." Ayesha's eyes batted like they might help her take flight.

Two looked at One. Both shrugged.

"Okay then," Two gave in. "But wait over there and put on masks and wash your hands with the sanitising gloop."

"Here," One said handing them a mask each from a box on a nearby desk while pointing to the sanitising gel on the wall next to the set of six fixed waiting chairs. They had only washed their hands and sat down with their masks when they spotted a familiar looking nurse walk up to the empty reception area. She had a mass of dark auburn hair tied and braided up under her hat. She wore green scrubs and green plastic bags over her green rubber crocs. She pulled down her mask to let out an anguished sob. She had not spotted them sitting there, tears rolled down her freckled cheeks onto the counter. The two security men took one look at the emotional nurse and found distant doors to secure and guard.

"Siobhan?" Charlie rose from her seat clutching her mask in her long delicate fingers. "Are you alright?"

"Charlie!" Then the Irish-born nurse saw who else was sitting behind her. "Ayesha, how did you get here so fast, did one of the doctors call you earlier?" Siobhan blinked at the tears caught in her lashes while grabbing a tissue from a box on the desk.

"No, why should they? Pam left us some messages that she had to work on, she seemed a little upset. So we decided to come and find her when she finished work. Has something happened hun?" Charlie had to take a step back to keep her balance as Siobhan suddenly hugged her tight.

"She's gone Charlie, she died only fifteen minutes ago," Siobhan sobbed over her right shoulder, looking with red-rimmed eyes at Ayesha.

Ayesha stood up, but her knees did not have the strength to lock. She sat down again with a bump on the hard waiting chairs. No tears came, nor could she draw breath as a ball of painful loss wedged in her throat, making the edges of her world crumble into darkness at the edges. Charlie did not cry either, she wailed at the sudden loss of her wife.

Ayesha looked around the corridors, trying to catch sight of her mother, not believing she could be gone. The proper entrance doors to the ward opened and four men in Hazmat suits entered and began spraying every surface, ignoring the protests of the two security men.

CHAPTER NINE

THE BEGINNING OF THE END

Thames Water has advised all residents living in the Elmbridge and Spelthorne areas to boil all tap water before drinking for the foreseeable future, as flood water has gotten into the drinking water supply. If you have bottled water at home, drink that first. An official statement from the Department of Health states that they are working very hard with the local water companies to get this situation rectified as soon as…

Hannah turned off the car radio as Matt re-entered the car sending droplets of rain over her right arm and leg. "Sorry it took so long; it was a bloody madhouse in there. People clearing the shelves like some biblical flood was coming."

Matt unzipped his coat, sending more rain over Hannah. She frowned, rolling her eyes up at the roof of the car, but said nothing. Out of the warm confines of his coat, he pulled a Pyrex glass measuring jug, two chocolate bars and two different pregnancy tester boxes. He handed them over to Hannah, who held them in her lap and looked at them. She breathed in a few times, feeling Matt become more and more impatient beside her.

"Are you going to do it in the front or find a bush?"

"A bush!" she mocked him with a teenage sneer. "I'm not finding out if we are with-child behind a fucking bush. It's raining outside remember."

Matt tried to touch her arm to placate her, but she violently shrugged it off. She turned in her seat and scrambled over the handbrake into the back seats. She was glad the windows were steamed up in the back as she began to pull down her waders and unbutton her jeans. She remembered the nights she had done the same in the back of Matt's car that had got her into this position in the first place. She pulled down her waders, jeans, and underwear to her knees, then edged her cold bare behind to the end of the back seat. Grabbing the measuring jug, she opened her thighs as much as her pulled down clothes would allow. Hannah positioned the jug as best as she could and tried to relax. Her bladder was full, but peeing in the backseat of a car with her older lover trying to sneakily peek in his rear-view mirror was slightly off-putting. Hannah closed her eyes and tried as hard as she could to imagine she was at home in the loo. The sounds of a couple running past to their nearby car did not help her pee flow either. Just when she thought her bladder might explode inside her, a jet of pee came out and then stopped. Hannah relaxed and held her breath. After a twinge of pain, she started to pee freely. Thankfully the pain of hold-it-in ebbed away as the jug began to fill up. After fifteen seconds, she panicked that she might not be able to stop, and the jug would overflow all over the back of Matt's car. Then she had to stifle a giggle, *that wouldn't be such a bad thing really.*

Thankfully she stopped urinating at the three-quarters full mark. She carefully tried to put it down on the floor, but still had spots of pee on her hands. She wiped them on the upholstery as she tugged up her underwear, jeans and then waders. She grabbed a blue pregnancy test packet, tore the box open and pulled a single tester out. She had to lean near the window to read the instructions twice over, but they seemed simple enough. Stick in piss, wait for the happy or unhappy result: depending on your situation. Licking the inside of her cheek, she picked up the jug of her urine and put the end of the tester in it. She took it out after the desired amount of time and laid the tester on her lap. Opening the door slightly, and letting in the buffeting rain, she poured out her pee.

"So, we wait," Matt said unhelpfully from the front.

Hannah closed the door and laid the jug by her feet. She had a sudden maternal urge for the result to be positive for some reason she could not fathom. Having a baby now would fuck her life up forever, and she'd never be able to go to university and become an archaeologist.

"It *must* be ready by now?" Matt asked, twisted around in the driver's seat.

Hannah blinked and went to rub an imagined itch at the corner of her left eye. Then she remembered her pee splashed hands and stopped, just as the result appeared in the little white box on the tester. Hannah did one of those giggle like sneezes spitting on the back of Matt's passenger seat. Then it came rising up from her belly like a volcano. Hannah Britton began to laugh, louder and louder until tears ran down her cheeks and she beat at the seats where their baby was conceived.

"*What?* Is it good news?" Matt was smiling, sure that laughter meant a negative result.

"Oh, we are so fucked," she laughed on hysterically.

She was gasping for air between the laughter, trying to stop it but she couldn't. She grabbed her bag of bin liners and opened the car door wide. A blast of rain swept wind flew down her open mouth shutting her up completely.

"Hey, where you going?" Matt called from inside the warm, dry car. "We have to talk about this, and you know... an abortion."

Hannah let the water wake her from her childhood into the cold, bleak world of adulthood. She did up her coat and headed away from Matt and his baby making car towards the exit.

"I could lose my job," he shouted after her as he got out of his car.

"I've just lost my life," she said, bowing her head against the driving rain as she headed back home.

Ellie's mother went in the ambulance with her husband, while Brita drove Ellie's car, following on behind. Ellie was in no fit state, so had to blub and point the way after they lost the ambulance at a set of red traffic lights heading towards Kingston hospital. Brita was okay driving past a vast park on both sides, but when the traffic and the buildings grew denser, she began to panic a little.

She swore, Ellie swore. Mainly out of concern for her ill

father. Finally, after two illegal U-turns, they made it to the large hospital car park. Only then was luck on their side. Somebody pulled out just in front of them, leaving a space free in the packed parking pay-and-display area. Brita parked as best as she could. She unbuckled, and rested her head on the steering wheel and let off a huge sigh of relief.

"...get a ticket," she half caught Ellie's soft words as she left the car in search of a place to pay for the parking. Brita looked up a little, resting her chin on the top of the steering wheel. The bottom part of the wheel was pressing into her middle, hurting her ribs. She sat back in the driver's seat and scanned the rows of parked car to search for her girlfriend. She could not see her anywhere. She wished Mr. Chambers no ill at all, as she hardly knew the man, but his timing sucked.

Brita wished she had taken notice of which direction Ellie had taken to get a parking ticket. She had a sudden craving for a cigarette, even though she hadn't smoked since she had finished her National Service. She scanned ahead and to the left, but still could not see Ellie.

"Where are you baby?" she muttered to herself.

A loud rap on the driver's side window made her jump out of her skin, and she passed wind with a squeaky escape of fear. Ellie was there, already pulling the door open, thrusting a printed white ticket at her nose.

"Put it on the dash, come on," Ellie urged on the verge of rudeness. Brita took it and placed it on the dashboard in front of the steering wheel and exited the car as Ellie was already turning to leave without her. Brita shut and locked the car and hurried after her girlfriend through the lines of parked cars towards the hospital's A&E. Ellie ran, not caring about cars trundling towards her. Brita had to stop twice to let them pass, then sprint to catch up with Ellie just as she ran into the chaos that was A&E.

There seemed to be noise and people everywhere. There were people laid out on chairs, on gurneys up and down corridors: half of them looked ill, the other half scared out of their wits with worry. The main reception area was swamped with a wall two people deep; braying for help and answers. Ellie slowly reached out a hand, and Brita grabbed it and led her into the crowds of sick people and worried looking relatives. All the nurses and other staff had white masks over their noses and mouths, Brita noticed.

Brita looked around the manic scene noticing that all members of staff had those purplish rubber gloves on too, to stave off infection. The main reception was packed with angry, loud and scared-looking people, berating the poor women behind the desk for answers that they could not give. Brita stopped a cleaner in a mask and burgundy scrub top, near the toilets with a mop. She grabbed Ellie's arm and pulled her over to the man. He looked up from where he was changing the hand sanitiser spray bottle on the wall.

"I can't help you," he said in African-accented English.

"Of course, yes," Brita fluffed up her hair. "We just want to know where the ambulances drop off their patients, please. Where do they go next?"

The cleaner frowned and jerked a thumb behind him down a corridor with two sets of double doors. "That way," he said, putting the empty bottle in his cleaner's cart, ignoring the two women again.

"Thank you," Brita whispered before Ellie dragged her off towards the double doors.

"You won't," the man muttered and began to rub at a red mark he had not noticed before on the underside of his left wrist. He looked up to see two army Red Cross vans pull up right outside the A&E entrance, blocking the way in. Nobody could park there at any time, not even the ambulances that had their own bay to get patients inside.

He stood up straight, leaning on his mop as the doors of the vehicles opened, and men in bright yellow spacesuits jumped out and began sealing the doors shut.

The doctors, nurses and security men were stretched to the limit inside the cubicles of the A&E. Too overwhelmed to stop two women blundering into the place. They searched the faces and heads of all the people hurrying about. Three or four of the patients they noticed had the same red-raw marks on their, faces, arms and hands, as Mr. Chambers had. Brita was getting very uneasy. She was out of the concern loop, unlike Ellie. She could pick up things the distraught daughter could not. It looked like an epidemic of some kind, not just Ellie's dad, but loads of people had the same wounds. Like their skin had melted right off their arms, leaving exposed all the blood and muscles underneath. The more Brita looked round, the more cases she spotted. The hospital was struggling to cope with the influx.

"There's Mum." Ellie grabbed Brita's arm and led her through the throng of worried people where Mrs. Chambers was standing head bowed next to a hospital trolley; just left against a corridor wall. Brita noticed it first and tried to stop and hold Ellie back. She failed as Ellie yanked her hand free, as Brita watched her join her mother by the empty white sheet covered trolley.

Mrs. Chambers had her head bowed.

"Mum," Ellie said and then tried to say the word again. Her mouth opened, but the word died somewhere in the back of her throat.

Mrs. Chambers was crying; her eyeliner had run like two clown-like dark lines down her puffy red cheeks. She looked ten years older than this morning.

"Where's Dad?" Ellie croaked, her heart sinking lower and lower; it felt like in her chest cavity.

Mrs. Chambers patted the end of the empty trolley beside her, twice. "He died in the ambulance, darling, before we were even halfway here."

Brita closed her eyes. Grief and sorrow seemed to follow her around like a constant shadow.

Selena froze. The man froze, a crescent moon shaped crisp half-way to his mouth.

Two seconds, no more passed, but it seemed like an eternity to the woman and man staring at each other across the flooded kitchen. They moved in the same instant. Selena running for her set of sharp, expensive kitchen knives. While the bearded man dropped his stolen crisps and ran/waded as best he could through the high water to the half-open back door.

Selena had the knife and was wailing like some ancient Iceni queen, charging after the fleeing intruder. Looking back in fear, the man tripped and fell. The left-hand side of his head smashing against one of the granite worktops. He turned, his eyes flickering up into his sockets, then he sunk unconscious under the dirty water that had invaded Selena's home.

Selena, who had already killed one person this week, was not going to let another die in her very kitchen. She dropped the knife to hurry over to him, water splashing up the inside thighs of her jeans. She grabbed the man by the collar and heaved his submerged head out of the water that stunk like pond scum in high summer. The water though helped her at least. Normally she would have trouble dragging such a man more than a yard. At least with the high water she could pull him through to the lounge, using his collar to keep his head afloat. She managed to get him on the damp sofa, which on bricks was just above the water level. His back and legs might still be sodden, but his head on the arm was out of the dirty water.

Selena checked him over, as best anyone without medical training could. He had a nasty gash on the left-hand side of his head under his sparse looking black bedraggled hair. He was still breathing, *always a bonus*, Selena thought. She left him there and hurried off to find her green emergency medical box. David had bought it when they moved in; along with a fire extinguisher and a blanket to put over frying pan fires. Selena had thought it had been overkill and had mocked him for it. Who was laughing now, the joke was on her the lonely single woman, whose only company was a wet crisps thief. She wondered whether to tie him up before he woke. She tried her mobile, but she had no signal bars on it. Not even the emergency calls only sign was showing. She was on her own with him. Maybe after the rain stopped and the floods died down she could buy seven or eight cats and never visit the hair salon in Surbiton again. She thought about retrieving the knife, from where she'd let it drop under the water in the kitchen, but what was the point? He would either be too groggy to escape or maybe strangle her to death. A violent death was no more than she deserved.

When she came back with the green plastic medical box,

the man had his eyes open. She wasn't sure if he was fully com-pos-mentis, but he didn't try to get up. His bloodshot eyes fixed on Selena. "I'm wet," he simply said in a thin stretched voice, sounding like he smoked forty a day.

"I'm Selena, and this is my house. I'm wet also," she said opening the medical box on the headrest of one of the other armchairs. Keeping a little distance between them. Her eyes on him at all times.

"I hit my head," he wheezed out again trying to sit up but failing.

Selena wondered if he was some White-Spirit quaffing simpleton tramp, with his statements rather than questions or conversation.

"Yes, trying to flee after pilfering my crisps," she replied pulling a wipe in a tinfoil packet and a bandage out for his head wound.

"I'm wet," he repeated again, looking down his nose at his body.

"Yes, I think we've established that fact," Selena said with one of her scowl-grins David used to hate. She moved closer to stand over the dishevelled man. "Now can you tell me your name?"

"Selena," he said as his eyes darted around the ceiling like he was trying to spot an annoying buzzing wasp during high summer.

"Yes I'm Selena, and you are?"

"Wet," he said again.

Selena couldn't help but hold in her laughter. If burst from her mouth like a volcano erupting, and she could do nothing to stop it. She laughed until tears ran down her face. She laughed until her tears turned to sobs. Then she cried over the prone man until her tears dripped between her fingers onto his neck.

"Wet," the man on her ruined £3000 couch said again.

Selena took the damp bandage away from her face to look down at the crisp thief. "Yes wet," she replied with a nod. She dried her eyes as best she could on her sleeve and bent down without fear to dress his wound.

Ann had no more tears to give to the cruel plastic sheeted world she inhabited. Her daughter's other half had just died two minutes ago. Ninety percent of his skin had been eaten away by the infection that had taken Maddy from them. His body giving in to the pain, which caused his weakened heart to stop beating. Had Maddy not died, would he have survived longer? Maybe he just wanted to be with her again, in death. Her husband had raged and fought to escape their isolation, finally having to be restrained and sedated again for his own safety. Ann Gable just stared at her hands. Turning them over and back. Over and back. Waiting for the red spots to start to appear on her skin and start spreading throughout her body. She reckoned due to her body-mass-index it would take her much longer than some skinny bird to die. One advantage to being an overweight tub of lard, she supposed.

Ann examined her arms, then her legs. Still no red marks. She turned her hands over and back once again twice.

Across the way through quadruple plastic, she faintly registered that her daughter was calling for her. In the grief and fog, that was her brain, she was pretty sure that the IV drip going into her arm had added calming meds inside. The doctors and nurses were crowded around her little girl, in their hazmat suits. Plastic people, in a plastic world. She could hardly see anything of her daughter Stacey. Then a hand thrust up in the air, echoed with a howl of pain. The hand was red and dripping blood.

From somewhere deep inside Ann Gable found some more tears to cry.

Ayesha and Charlie had been led away to a family room nearby. Deposited there to get them out of the way. The windows' all metal frames clouded with condensation were covered up with sheets of plastic held in position with reams of new yellow and black tape. The Doctors and nurses had been arguing with the men in hazmat suits, as Siobhan showed them into their claustrophobic room of despair. It was just a small place, with two brown sofas and an odd assortment of different shaped and coloured plastic chairs. There was a yucca in one corner, a plastic looking fern in another. The other spare corner had a small table filled with dog-eared magazines and an assortment of broken and incomplete toys.

The two women shared the sofa nearest the door. They held each other, so tight it hurt. But then, everything in their bodies hurt. Their hearts, minds, stomachs, throats were all awash with the pain of the woman they had lost. Mother and wife. Charlie was sobbing quietly, making Ayesha's neck uncomfortably wet. She had been almost hysterical when they had sat down, but emotional fatigue had taken its toll.

Ayesha had not cried yet. She felt cold from the inside out and numb to the point of nothingness. The family room was a vague astral box to her. She knew she was there, in Charlie's embrace, but also somewhere else too. Like she had travelled out of her body and had shrunk to a tiny size. Sitting on top of her own head. Nestling in the follicles, so she had only the faintest connection to her own body. Her stomach was sick and empty. Her throat felt like someone was forcing a cricket ball up into it. She tried to swallow. It was painful but it eased the ball of emotion down again for a few more minutes.

"What are we going to do?" Charlie croaked in a raw voice. She moved for the first time in forty-eight minutes out of Ayesha's embrace.

Ayesha looked at her second mother, letting her arms trail down into her lap. The groin area of her jeans felt very warm for some reason, but at least, not damp. She stared at Charlie. Into her bloodshot eyes, but saw no answers, only pain reflected back. *What was she on about?* Ayesha thought.

"Your mum, my beautiful Pamela is gone," Charlie said reaching out to hold and caress Ayesha's dry cheeks. Ayesha knew Charlie's hands were there; she could look down her nose and see them, all blurry and close. But she hardly felt the touch or the warmth and love in them. Her lips were dry, and her lipstick felt like it had bonded, gluing her lips together.

"How are you feeling darling?"

Ayesha's lips parted with a pained sensation, but she could not speak. The cricket ball of emotion was wedged, it seemed, deep into her vocal cords cutting off her air supply.

She swallowed painfully once more, but the lump in her throat would not budge this time. She had to breathe, get out of this tiny enclosing room. Find her mum. Yes, she needed her mum more than anything.

Ayesha turned and almost lunged for the door of the family waiting room. She faintly heard Charlie crying out her name as she grabbed the doorknob and turned it. The round metal knob twisted in her hand, causing a slight Chinese burn. Then she pulled the door inwards. Only to reveal a wall of plastic, with a hermetically sealed zip running up one side across the top and down the other.

"What's that for?" Charlie said behind her, getting to her feet.

Ayesha wasn't listening to her. She reached down for the lower zip and pulled it up to the top. She did not undo it all, just pushed her way through the thick plastic. She was in a corridor around the corner from the reception area. A man was fitting the same sort of containment seal to the door two along. He was kneeling down but turned to look at her through his plastic visor. "Can you stay inside please, for your own safety," he shouted in a muffled voice.

Charlie appeared at the doorway but did not step through it. She dragged Ayesha's nearest forearm, covering the tiny butterfly tattoo she had there. Ayesha violently shook Charlie's hand off. The man in the hazmat suit was getting to his feet and coming towards her. Ayesha ran down the corridor away from Hazmat Man and the cries of Charlie for her to come back. She ran; the heels of her trainers squealing on the shiny floors as she rounded a corner and ran into two more hazmat clothed figures. An older man and a younger woman went to grab her.

"Who is she?" The man shouted at his female companion.

"Relative of one of the deceased nurses," the woman said back.

Ayesha put her head down and butted an opening between them both. With their plastic gloves on it was hard to keep hold of her hands. Ayesha ran on in search of her mother with three suited people in pursuit of her. She headed off down a well-lit interior corridor with doors on either side. A door banged open four yards further on, and a hazmat-suited person of indeterminable sex pulled a trolley out into the corridor through a plastic opening. The trolley squeaked as it was pulled through the doorway. It also yanked back the white plastic sheet covering the body of a dead person underneath.

Yet there was no face on the female corpse. Just hair and a gory mess where her skin and nose used to be. Ayesha screamed at the top of her lungs, fainting dead away just before her pursuers could catch her.

CHAPTER TEN

THE RED DEATH

"I'm pregnant," Hannah said out loud. It was the fifth time she had said it. Her words drowned out by the beating rain on the hood of her coat. She was wading back towards her home. The waters seemed even higher than when she had left.

"I'm pregnant," she said to the rain.

"I'm pregnant," she said to the red post box, half submerged in the overflow from the River Mole into her street.

She walked on closer to her house. Nearly tripping on the curb, up onto the pavement, which was lost beneath the rising flood waters.

"I'm with child," she said to the flood waters. Maybe putting it a different way would help it all sink in a little more. Yet it didn't. It seemed like a weird dream or a film she was watching. How could another little life be growing inside her, right now? How could all her dreams and future be shot down by her silly affair with her teacher? It was pathetic, sad, like from some tabloids Agony Aunt's page. She was better than this, while he was dropping lower and lower in her affections.

She exhaled as she got within sight of her home. Her grandfather and her sister Hayley were working on some basic flood defences near the step up to the front door. Her grandmother was hanging out of the open doorway, looking out for her.

"Where have you been?" Her grandmother shouted down the drive to her. "We've been worried sick."

"I got the bags you wanted," she simply replied lifting the

carrier bag up high like a quest prize in some computer game. *And a great-grandchild too.*

"Give it here then girl," her grandfather said in a gruff voice, taking off his rubber builders gloves to reach for the bag.

Hannah gave it over.

"Hey, what's that on your hand granddad?" Hayley pointed to the old man's right hand, as he grabbed the bags off Hannah.

"What's what?"

"That red spot there." Hannah pointed, seeing what her sister had spotted.

"How should I know," their grandfather replied rubbing at the five pence sized red spot on his hand. The red skin on it wrinkled and fell off into the water at his feet. The mark looked red raw and was oozing bright blood.

"Better get a plaster on that love before it gets infected," Hannah's grandmother called from her shelter on the dry front porch area.

"Probably a blood blister or something," Hannah's grandfather cursed and headed for the doorway.

"You girls better come in and get warm before you catch your death-of-cold," their grandmother urged. Both Hayley and Hannah didn't need to be asked twice. They stripped off their wet gear in the hall and headed for the kitchen, always the warmest part of the house.

Her grandmother put the kettle on for a cuppa and Hannah, and her sister devoured half a packet of digestive biscuits, by the time the tea was made, brewed and poured. She wasn't feeling sick anymore. In fact, quite the opposite, she was starving. Her mobile chimed in her jeans pocket twice. She pulled it out and just turned it off, she knew who the messages would be from.

"Who's that, your boyfriend?" Hayley sneered with practiced younger-sister glee.

"Fuck off," Hannah shot back so vehemently it shocked even her. *Mood swings.*

"Hannah Louise Britton, I didn't bring you up to hear you speak such language to your sister. Apologise right away," her grandmother croned, setting down her mug of tea loudly on the kitchen worktop next to her.

"Sorry Gran," Hannah said standing up and grabbing her *Time-Team* mug of tea by the handle. "I'll go to my room before you send me there."

"Hmmm," her grandmother tutted, hands on her thin hips.

Hannah left her sneering younger sister behind and thundered up the stairs, spilling some of her tea on the worn red carpet on the way up. She had to pass the open doorway of the bathroom to get to her room. Her grandfather was inside, shirt off, showing off his white vest underneath. He was washing his right hand under the cold tap. The usual floorboard outside the bathroom creaked, and her grandfather turned round in shock. Seeing Hannah there he hurriedly kicked the bathroom door shut. Not before Hannah spotted a second red bloody mark on his hand two centimetres from the first one. Her grandfather must have scraped his hand on the hard driveway or something. Both the red sore blisters looked pretty painful to her. Hannah leant on the bedroom side of her door, shutting her inside, and the outside world out. She put down the tea on a clear bit of her untidy desk and went and lay on her bed.

She turned on her mobile phone and went to delete the four messages of her needy teacher lover without looking at them. Then changed her mind and looked at them. The first was a pleading bile rising text saying that they needed to talk more about the baby and their futures. The second was a bitch of a bitchy *bunny-boiler* rant, she easily deleted with a smirk. The third was an apology and an offer to marry her and bring up the baby together. Accompanied by a love heart, a tiny baby picture, and a smiley face emoticon.

Hannah raised her eyebrows at the near marriage proposal.

"Desperate," she muttered deleting it like the others without replying.

The last was totally different. Saying he was sorry but he had to get to the hospital because his friend's father had just died.

Hannah stared long at this text, wondering if it was a plan to try and gain sympathy from her. She thought many things of him at the moment, but he wouldn't stoop that low. She pondered and rewrote her reply three times before her finger hovered over the send button.

Soz to hear your friend's bad news, hope you will be of comfort to him. We'll chat laters, she typed and sent. Then ignoring all the news, Facebook, Twitter, and the entire attention seeking world, she turned off her mobile and drank her tea in silence.

Only the constant drumming of the rain on her window made any noise.

"Where's my dad?" Ellie screamed at the poor junior doctor she managed to grab by either end of his stethoscope and drag from his chat with another patient. The doctor was shocked and beyond his depth in this crisis. "What's going on, where is my father's body?"

Brita managed to grab one of her girlfriend's very unnaturally strong hands and using both of hers forced her fists open, so the doctor could free the ear parts of the stethoscope, and the poor young man could drag himself back from Ellie. Yet he was not entirely free. A crowd of patients, nurses and friends and relatives had encircled him baying for answers. Panicked the junior A&E doctor jumped onto a nearby table next to a row of occupied chairs.

He looked like a scared rabbit caught in the headlights of an oncoming truck.

"Please, please let me tell you what I know. If you all keep calm, I'll explain as best I can on what is happening here." He pleaded with lowering open hands. "Certain protocols have come into immediate effect, and there is no cause for alarm."

The word *calm* and the phrase *no cause for alarm*, of course, raised the braying for an explanation from the crowd surrounding him.

"What fucking protocols?" a beefy skin-head of man in his forties with a biker jacket and long beard shouted up to him. The man's arm was bandaged from hand to up to his pulled-up sleeve Brita noted. Blood was seeping through in different places.

"Due to the nature of the epidemic running through this hospital, the authorities have had to quarantine this building for your own safety." If the doctor thought the truth would ease the people's worries, he was sadly mistaken.

"What do you bleedin' mean we've been quarantined for our own safety?" biker man yelled, the designated voice of the mob.

"Where is my dead father?" Ellie yelled like a crazy woman Brita hardly recognised. She looked around for Mrs. Chambers. She was lying down on an empty gurney. Her eyes staring blankly at the ceiling, her arms crossed like an Egyptian Queen after mummification.

"I need to get home to feed my kids!" A not so young looking woman, with a tattoo saying Brandon on her neck, yelled.

"What are these bloody sores, everyone is getting?" cried out a green-uniformed parking attendant, rubbing at a bloody mess that was her left wrist.

"When do we get out, when do we get treatment for this?" a man in a charcoal grey suit and purple tie yelled up at the beleaguered doctor.

"The hospital is in lockdown at the moment. I need you all to keep calm, and you will be seen as soon as-we can get to you... the staff are very much overstretched at the moment." People weren't even listening; they were scared for their very lives.

Then there came a scream from the other side of the room. Brita could not see why at first until people began to part like the red sea. Out of a cubicle staggered an Asian woman in a once white smock. It was soaked through with blood, but worse was her appearance. Forgotten and unchecked for over two hours, she staggered towards the doctor wailing like a banshee. Her hands, arms, legs and face were ninety-percent devoid of skin. She looked like someone who had been flayed alive in some Eastern European torture-porn film.

"Helb-me," she muttered through her half-eaten away lips. She grabbed at the biker, but he reacted like most people would and shoved her away from him hard. She fell easily; hitting her head on the table the doctor was standing on. She did not get up, as far as Brita could see.

"Come on, let's grab your mother and get clear of this shit," Brita took Ellie's arm and led her back away from the terrible scene. They made it over to the trolley, just as all forms of civility and control left the frightened crowd.

"Let's get the fuck out of here," the biker yelled and hurried off down the corridor that led to where the ambulance bay was. Half the A&E mob followed him. The junior doctor's yells for calm were lost in the maelstrom of noise. Fifteen people ran past Brita, Ellie, and Mrs. Chambers. Brita was knocked hard on the left shoulder but grabbed the trolley to save her from going down where she would have been trampled underfoot. She used her body to flatten Ellie against the wall. Protecting her as the mob ran past. They were soon gone, wailing and screaming. All English stiff-upper-lip gone. They did not get far, all the shutters were down in the ambulance bays, and the outside door was locked tight.

"We need to get your mother somewhere safe," Brita said to Ellie letting go of her body.

Ellie just nodded silently in agreement. There was a disabled toilet not far down the wall behind them. "This way," Brita urged as they pulled Ellie's mother off the trolley. Mrs. Chambers seemed in some catatonic state of shock, but her legs still moved under her. They got into the toilet just as a red fire extinguisher was thrown at the junior doctor. Brita heard the cry and crunch of the impact as she closed the door behind them. She locked it tight and then helped Ellie sit her dumbstruck mother onto the seat of the toilet.

Ellie heard the sound of cries and something hit the wall outside loudly. She began to weep with a mixture of grief and fear. Brita took her trembling body in her arms and held her close. She kissed Ellie's wet cheek and buried her head into her long hair. All the while looking around the confines of the disabled toilet for anything she could use as a weapon if the mob tried to gain access. Unless she pulled one of the hand rails from the wall, there was nothing to use. She held Ellie tight and just hoped the door would hold against the blind panic and desperate destruction happening on the other side of it.

"So, *Wet*, how are you feeling now?" Selena asked her new uninvited house guest as he sat up in the bed of one of her spare upstairs rooms. Getting the groggy and not very lucid man upstairs had taken a herculean effort on her part. She had stripped the man and bed-bathed all but his underpants. They looked like they hadn't seen a wash in a month-of-Sundays.

Wet as she nicknamed him, as she could not get his proper name from the man, was very passive during the washing of his body. Like he recalled better days when maybe his mother or carer did the same. She was pretty sure that this was how he was normally and not the result of the blow to his head. She had dealt with quite a few people like him in the past as a judge. She was a tough nut, but she always dealt kindly with the disadvantaged in society. She thought that Wet must be one of those poor souls, abandoned by the system when their mother or carer dies and with a child's mind in an adult's body, find their way onto the streets. Sadly, most, never get rescued from that hell or are given the help and medication they so dearly need to lead a happy, productive life.

"So my new friend, are you still hungry?" She sat on the side of the spare bed, drying off her damp hands. A purple plastic bowl with a dirty sponge floated in a sea of filthy water at her feet.

"Not wet now, hungry," he nodded pointing at his open mouth and then his tummy area.

Selena chuckled at this. "What would you like to eat? Soup,, baked beans?" She was trying to think of food that she had in tins up in high cupboards.

"Crips," he just replied.

"Crisps?"

"Yep crips." He nodded several times.

"Anything else apart from crisps, a can of coke or something?"

"Terry likes coke," he said.

"Oh are you called Terry then," Selena asked, sitting up on the bed straight, excited that she had discovered his name by accident.

"No, Terry was my friend."

"What is your name then?" Selena pressed.

"Terry got the Red Death," Wet said in a strange almost adult tone, she hadn't heard him speak in before.

"What's the Red Death?" Selena said laying the long fingers

of her left hand on his bare, hairy forearm.

"Crips please Mummy Selena," Wet said going back to his childish tones again.

"Okay," she said clapping her hands and rising from the bed. "Crips it is then."

Selena went onto the first-floor landing and grabbed her waders off the balcony rail. She wondered what her house guest was on about and what she would do with him when he was fit to travel. Company and someone to care for had made her forget her own thoughts or cutting herself or suicide. She waded down through the kitchen again only to find two dead water rats floating upside down in the ever rising flood waters. She took a shopping-bag-for-life and stuffed as much dry food and tins and drinks into it from the cupboard above the waterline. She and Wet looked like they weren't going anywhere fast, except possibly by boat.

Ann woke from a sleep she did not intend to take. Her head and vision was fuzzy to begin with but cleared a minute after she pushed herself up into her plump pillows. She looked around the plastic lined isolation ward, but could see no signs of activity at all. No movement in the others' beds and no sounds but the pinging of medical monitors. She sat up from her pillows. Her cold hands pushed into the mattress to stop her falling back. No dizziness attacked her, so she swung her legs round and out of the bed. She was relieved to see she had no red blotches on her hands, arms or legs. Well, none that weren't there before.

She sniffed and looked over at the IV drip leading down a clear tube into her arm. It looked empty and in need of changing. She licked her parched lips, she must have been snoring lying on her back. There was a bottle of water with a curved straw on a cabinet beside her bed so she took a long slug of that. She used the water on her tongue to wet her dry lips. Ann looked around the ward again, and something occurred to her. There were no doctors or nurses present. She looked behind her bed and saw a call button and pressed it. The light next to it turned orange. She sat, her bare legs dangling over the side of the bed, waiting for someone to come. Ann reached up her smock and confirmed what she feared, the bush was running free.

Five minutes passed, and no one came. She could hear the soft breathing of her husband nearby. It annoyed the hell out of her back in their marital bed, but at this time, she found it oddly comforting. Patience was not one of her strong points, so she hopped off the bed. The floor felt icy cold to the soles of her bare feet. Ann reached down to open the bedside cupboard to see if any of her clothes were in there when the IV line reminded her it was still attached to her arm in a painful taut manner.

She hated needles. A look down at her left arm, glad that there was surgical tape covering most of the metal of the needle in her vein. Ann reached over to gingerly touch the blue plastic that was attached to the needle and fed up to the clear tube. She hissed at the scratching pain in her arm. Luckily the IV bag was hung on a metal stand with casters. So she grabbed that instead and brought it along for the ride. It also gave her something to lean on, as her head felt like it was floating just above the tips of her hair.

Exhaling hard, and fighting a wave of nausea that rippled from her large overhanging belly up to her throat, she pressed on. Reaching the edge of her plastic bubble-world, was an effort she found solace in to carry on. The zipped-up cubicle took some opening. She had to draw the IV stand closer and lean down with her right hand to grab the inside/outside double zip. Her short, flabby arms and large belly only hindered the situation. Just when Ann thought she might throw up, she managed to tug the zip upwards and let some air into her plastic confinement.

Yet, it was not fresh air. It was tainted with a sickly smell of rotting vegetables. It mingled with the smell of sick, defecation and death. It was a smell she knew all too well, having nursed her cancer-ridden mother at her home every day. Two years had passed since that dark time in Ann's life. But the funk of the isolation ward brought it all back. The darkened bedroom, with the nicotine stained old curtains drawn to keep the light off her mum's jaundiced face. The oxygen mask on her face, the sunken look of despair in her mother's eyes knowing she had woken to another day of pain and suffering and not passed in the night.

Ann's mother had hardly eaten anything at those late stages of her terminal cancer, so Ann had done enough eating for both of them.

The ward stunk like her mother's deathbed. Ann felt suddenly scared for her family. She headed over, and with more strength from somewhere unzipped the cubicle her daughter had been in. The bed inside was empty. The covers stripped off it, but there were stains of brown and yellow down the core of the mattress.

"Stacey," she muttered, her fingertips just resting on the corner edge of the mattress.

Her granddaughter was dead, and her daughter might be the same. She backed out of the cubicle, a motherly resolve forming in the marrow of her bones. Moved up the centre of the ward, ignoring the blurred form of her husband snoring away on his back. She knew he was still alive. She headed over to the bed opposite, which had someone lying still under the covers. Yet something was wrong. Even through the distorting plastic she could see red, where there should only be flesh. She opened up the zip, took a gulp and pushed her head inside.

The man inside was dead. His face a mask of red, looking like someone had been at it with a filleting knife and then finished him off with acid. The ears, nose, lips were gone and all the flesh that made up his features. Only his wide staring dead eyes, locked on the ceiling tiles and his hair remained to give him any human resemblance at all. It reminded Ann of a poster on her old biology class wall back in the eighties showing the layers that built up a human face.

He could be anyone. You could not tell what colour or creed he was. Only the fullness of his jaw and the style of his hair showed he was a man at all. Ann reached down and picked up the clipboard in the holder at the end of his bed. The sight of him and the bleachy smell of the hospital, made her swallow down some sick as she looked at the notes.

Then she saw his name. It was Steve, her daughter's partner.

Then vomit came again up her throat and this time, she could not stop it.

Ayesha pushed herself from her dream like a baby born free from her mother. Ghosts and nightmares tried to drag her back to her unconscious state, but her mind willed her on.

Where's my mother!

Ayesha could feel herself on the fringes of sleep. She could feel the inside of her eyelids like they were led weighted curtains that did not want to be pulled to reveal a new day. Her subconscious mind battled with her will to wake and find her mum. Parts of her brain that knew her mother was dead tried to keep her safe in the fuzzy world of unconsciousness, but her determination to see her mother again won through.

Ayesha's eyes flicked open.

Instantly she regretted it as she looked around her new surroundings, wanting the dreamworld to take her back with soft lullabies. All she got was the screams of the dying.

CHAPTER ELEVEN

HOSPITAL HORRORS

"Hannah get up, we need to take your grandfather to the hospital," her grandmother screamed from the landing.

Hannah blinked away the nap she had taken and sat up to see her bedroom door was open. Her grandfather was lying on his side on the landing, with her worried looking grandmother and sister above him. He was breathing in ragged breaths, but Hannah held hers and did not let it out until her burning lungs forced her to. Her grandfather's hands and arms up to where they met his white shirt were red and oozing with blood. The arms of his shirt were stained with red and a yellow ichor.

"I'll call an ambulance," Hannah said back with concern, picking up her mobile to turn on and dial 999.

"I've tried that. All I get is a busy tone. Nine-nine-nine is never busy and a message saying that due to the large numbers of emergencies my call is in a queuing system. We need to get him in the car and drive there now," her grandmother yelled, tears welling in her eyes.

"But what about the flood water?"

"Your granddad parked the car on the slip road two days ago, it should be good to go. Come on get your shoes on, I need your help to get him to the car."

Dressed up in coats, hats, and gloves; their short journey was a nightmare. Her grandfather was in a delirious state, his large brow covered with sweat. They half-dragged, half-pulled him downstairs and pulled a coat over his arms. His fingers looked almost skeletal to Hannah. The flesh on his forearms seemed to skew away and slip off leading a yellow pus mingled with blood.

Hannah opened the front door and was shocked to see the water from the nearby river was lapping over their meagre flood defences. The first step of the house was underwater. "We'll never bloody get him to the car this way," she yelled back at her gran.

"Don't swear," was her grandmother's automatic reply. Like her swearing would make this terrible day get any worse? Hannah's grandmother stood where her husband was propped up against the bottom banister of the stairs and peered into the flood waters. The sky was laden with dark clouds, and the rain was still coming down. A smell of ponds and rotted vegetation wafted through the open front door on the wind. "Oh gawd," her gran simply said.

"I've got an idea," Hayley piped up and suddenly rushed off to the cupboard under the stairs. She disappeared inside the mess that was old shoes; granddad's fishing gear and the electricity meter.

"What ya doing?" Hannah called after her, as chilly rain carried on a gust of strong wind blew against the left side of her face.

"Got it," Hayley cried out in triumph and came hurrying back with a black, red and clear lilo they had got on holiday in Worthing two years ago. She began to unfold it as she pulled the stopper and began to blow it up. Both Hannah and her gran went to speak to tell her to stop, but it suddenly dawned on them both that instead of carrying granddad they could use the flood water to just float him out.

Once inflated Hayley took it outside and kicked down the overrun flood defences. The wind nearly took the lilo twice, but she pushed it out of her face and held it in the water. Hannah took her granddad's legs, while her gran took his shoulders and between them they carried him the short distance to the lilo and heaved him on it. He cried out from his fever as the cold water soaked his back and legs and the lilo gave a little under his weight. But it did not sink. Gran pulled the lilo from the front, with Hayley on the right-hand side and Hannah at the back. They floated him down the drive and onto the pavement lost under the waters that went over Hannah's bellybutton. She felt a quiver deep inside her, like her baby, had shivered too, but she dismissed it as idle fancy. The baby as it was, was no bigger than a peanut at the moment.

The three females pushed and pulled the stricken body on the lilo around the end of the road and up onto the higher slip road towards the family car. Its wheels were half underwater, but Hannah thought it should still go. They dragged and bundled her grandfather onto the back seat, the lilo cartwheeling off behind Hayley into the grey distance. Hayley got in with him and placed his wet legs over hers. While Hannah and their gran got in the front.

Hannah actually prayed as her gran started the car. It whined and spluttered, but soon revved into life. They were soon on their way down around the roundabout and down the bypass heading towards the hospital.

Brita grunted. Her full set of teeth exposed. Her lips drawn back. As she pulled the handrail free from where it had been bolted to the wall. It had taken twenty minutes of kicks first; then pulling, kicking again, before it had come loose.

Ellie's mother had sat on the closed toilet seat, weeping to herself. While her daughter had paced the six foot by seven foot disabled toilet, like a prowling predator. They had heard shrieks, crying and raging howls of anger from the other side of the door. It seemed humanity had lost its way in a manner of hours, beyond the heavy wooden door.

They had been inside for forty minutes. The screaming from outside shredding their already raw nerves. Brita flexed her right hand which ached from freeing the handrail. She looked at Ellie, her Ellie. She was leaving a mark on the floor with her turning in circles. Her hands running through her hair as her grief, agitation and claustrophobia mingled into a Molotov cocktail in her mind. "We got to get out of here," she repeated over and over.

Brita, who had held her back several times from opening the toilet door agreed with her. Brita lent the handrail against the door and took her lover in her arms, stopping her perpetual motion. Her eyes were red and puffy. Ellie stared right through Brita.

"Hey," Brita said, taking Ellie's hands from her hair and pulling them around her. "We are going to get out of here okay. Things have gone to shit, for sure, but if we stick together, we'll be okay."

Ellie saw her but said nothing.

Brita placed her open palms on Ellie's neck under her small delicate ears. Brita recalled how they had burnt on their Greek adventure. How she had applied aftersun to them every night and kissed them better. This had always tickled Ellie and made her giggle. It seemed another lifetime ago. "I love you, we are leaving, okay, you hear me?"

Ellie nodded. Her eyes returning to the present danger they faced.

"Good," Brita smiled warmly. "Now I want you to lead your mother and follow me. I won't let anything hurt you, baby."

"I know, it's just…" Ellie let the words hang.

"I know, and you will have time to grieve later. So now we have to get out of this place. Now go and fetch your mother."

Ellie left her arms and went over to coax her mother to her feet. "Are we going home?" Mrs. Chambers asked.

"Yes," Brita said picking up the metal handrail. She moved to the door and listened. Things seemed to have calmed down in the last five minutes. Brita turned back to the Chambers women. "Okay, we're going now, fast as we can. Stay together."

Ellie and her mother nodded back. Brita turned to the door and exhaled a long breath. Her hand rested on the lock. She turned the knob and heard the bolt unlock. She gripped the handrail as a weapon and pulled open the disabled toilet door. What horrors she had expected to see had not prepared her for the grisly scenes that awaited them in the A&E. The usual green and blue hues had been turned bloody red.

Selena spent most of the day ferrying stuff from her kitchen up to the first floor of her house. Wet, stayed upstairs eating crisps and would not venture anywhere near the landing, as the sight of the rising flood waters seemed to terrify the man-child.

He watched her for a while. He was dressed in one of David's old brown dressing gowns that she had hated when they were married. Yet she had never thrown it out. On dark, lonely nights she would sniff it just to get the smell of him, but those days were dark period days and laced with gin and tonic.

Wet had taken himself back to bed after a couple of hours. He was constantly scratching at his left lumber area, and she wondered if he had flees or scabies, from living rough. It was lunchtime before she had finished moving all she could save, or wanted to save. Food and drink suddenly became more important than family photo albums and expensive art that hung on her walls. The water downstairs was waist high and covered the first five steps of her stairs. She had limited choices, stay upstairs for the time being, or trying to wade to safety. Having an uninvited guest in her spare bedroom, made the leaving option a little more difficult. Putting a box of tins into her second bedroom, now her storeroom, caused a sharp pain to run up her right kidney area. She let the box slide onto the bed and grimaced at the muscle pain.

"I must be getting old," she muttered rubbing the dull ache as she left the second bedroom. "That's enough Bear Grylls survival stuff for one day."

Selena managed to take off her waders and boots on the newspapers on the landing carpet. Her own little isolation zone for her water foraging clothes. The seat of her jeans and the tails of her blouse were wet, so she went to her own bedroom to find something else to wear. Even with her extensive wardrobe, she would run out of clean clothes soon, the washing machine being totally underwater in the utility room.

"I'll be down to the ball gowns and dominatrix gear," she said, as she went through her walk-in wardrobe for something comfortable to wear. She found a pair of black leggings with the price tag still attached in the dark confines of her wardrobe and put them on with a check shirt she'd worn for some fancy-dress charity gig last June. Feeling like a modern day Doris Day, she headed for the spare room to check on her patient.

It had been an hour and forty minutes since she had looked

in on him. All had been quiet, and she assumed he had been sleeping. The hot sweaty sheen on his brow had her worried as she approached the guest bed. He was in some sort of sleep, but turning his head from side-to-side like he was having a feverish nightmare. The curtains were open as it was dull outside from the never-ending rainclouds. She sat on the bed and called his nickname, to no avail. Licking her lips, she touched his forehead with the back of her hand. He felt clammy and burning hot. His forehead was living up to his nickname. She went to move her hand back, but his eyes flicked open, and he grabbed her wrist tightly.

"Everyone is death," he said with more gravitas than a Shakespearean thespian. It was not like him at all, well not the Wet tramp she knew.

"Are you okay? Do you feel ill?"

He stared at her for four seconds, but it seemed like a minute to her. Then his eyes fluttered closed, and his hand slipped away from her wrist onto the covers.

"Feverish." She grabbed the electric thermometer from the bedside cabinet and put it into his nearest dirty ear cavity. "Not good." Wet's temperature was a hundred and one.

She stood up and patted her leggings, they had no pockets. Her mobile phone must be in her bedroom somewhere.

She found it on her dresser. It had no signal. She dialed the emergency services anyway but got a constant engaged tone. She tried her landline, but that just *burred* in her ear, maybe the water had killed the main socket in the downstairs hall. She could not lug him out of the house. She would need steroids and a boat for that. She had no choice but to try and look after him herself. She went to the bathroom, filled up a plastic jug she used to dye her hair with cold water and grabbed a flannel from the bathroom cabinet. She let the flannel sink into the cool water as she entered the guest bedroom.

A foul flatulent smell assaulted her nostrils as she re-entered the guest bedroom. She hoped he had just passed wind and not soiled the bed. Breathing through her mouth, she put the jug on the bedside table and rung out the flannel. Then she pressed it to his sweaty forehead and left it there. The smell still hadn't dissipated, so holding her breath she lifted up the covers to have a check.

She was glad to see no brown stains under his bottom area, but something else caught her eye. The pyjamas she had dressed him in had been a little too short for him and showed off his belly and lower side. There were livid red sores, like some infectious psoriasis running from his back up his side and were forming in his hairy belly area. Yet they were not dry and white at the edges, but wet with blood. Selena let the covers fall again. She wondered what type of illness this could be. He had been wandering around in dirty flood water, he could have picked up any number of diseases or infections.

Selena went to rub her nose and then stopped herself in time. Instead, she went to the main bathroom and washed her hands thoroughly. She sat down on the closed toilet seat as she dried her hands and wondered what to do for the best. She could see if he gets any better or try to wade out to find help?

A scream from her spare bedroom ended any thoughts she had of leaving her house for the time being.

Gibbering with spittle and sick, she could not take any more. Ann made for her husband's cubicle and nearly tore it down trying to get through the zipped plastic opening to see him. She wiped her wet chin on her shoulder and moved next to his bed. The IV stand had been left behind with Steve's dead body. It had been pulled from her arm, as she'd doubled up on the floor vomiting. She hardly noticed the dribble of blood running down her arm. It was just another fluid that was spattered over her body. She pulled back the covers and ripped at the flimsy paper gown Tony was wearing.

She searched all over his body, well the bits she could see. Even parted his legs and lifted up his balls and large but flaccid cock. As she touched him, it stirred into life like it was Sunday morning special time.

"'Ear, there's a time and a place love."

She stood up to see her husband's confused face. His eyes were suspicious of where her bowed head and hands had just been. He licked his dry lips, his eyes only half-open.

"Are you okay Tone?" Ann moved up to his hairy chest, her hand on his heart.

"Why, shouldn't I be?" he asked groggily.

"You need to get up and help me find Stacey," She urged, as his eyes closed. Ann grabbed his meaty arms and shook him as best she could.

"Whatsup?" he muttered, turning his head towards her.

"Do you remember where you are and what's happened?"

Tony looked back at her like she was a stranger. Then a set of tiny bulbs clicked alight in his brain, and the side of his face slackened. "Maddy," he murmured.

Ann nodded, fighting back her own tears. "I think we are in trouble Tony; I need you to get up now okay?"

"If you say so luv," he muttered, sat up and swung his thick legs over the side of the bed. Ann knew her husband's high tolerance for beer and medicating drugs. It took three attempts to knock him out to have his wisdom teeth out four years ago. The dentist joked that he would need the elephant tranquilizers next. Lucky for the dentist Tony went under before he could lamp the man for his cheek.

Tony stood up and pulled at the flimsy gown covering his broad hairy frame. "I think they fucking drugged me," he murmured as his legs gave way under him and he crashed to the floor.

Ann tried to help him up, but her bad back and bingo wing arms could not budge his bulk from the floor. She passed him a bottle of water with a fixed plastic straw on the end and let him suck that down. Half a minute later, using the bed for support, he rose again on more steady footing. Ann ducked under his left arm to give him a little support, even though her back protested. They walked awkwardly to the torn plastic opening.

Tony looked up from his feet; his eyes coming to rest on the bloody mess that was Steve across the ward. "What the fuck happened to that bloke?"

"Tony, that's Stacey's Steve, luv." She let her words sink in for a moment. "Looks like the thing that killed our Maddy is spreading."

"That's Steve," Tony's deep, loud voice was barely a whisper. "And he's dead?"

"Yes," Ann sniffed. She turned her husband away from the red-faced corpse towards more plastic tombs ahead. "We need to find Mike, Stacey, and our Jayden."

"Jesus wept," Tony muttered as Ann helped him walk.

The bed to their left seemed sterile, clean and thankfully empty. The same could not be said for the last bed on the right. It looked like an explosion in a red paint factory. Blood was streaked over many parts of the plastic cubicle. It wasn't until they reached the end of the ward, that they saw a ragged hole had been ripped in the side of the plastic. A dead, but uninfected nurse in blue scrubs lay on her side, halfway out of the cubicle. Her blue eyes staring up towards Ann and Tony, unblinking and still. Her throat had been savagely ripped open. Her head lay in a halo of blood. The married couple inched forwards to peer inside. A doctor lay face down on the bed, his face towards them. His hazmat mask lay on the pillow beside him. His eyes were dark red holes like someone had pushed them back into his skull. He, like the nurse, seemed free from the red skin eating infection.

"Let's find our clothes and get the fuck out of here, Ann," Tony said pulling himself up to his normal towering height. He took his arm off his wife's shoulder and kicked open the door to the ward with the bare sole of his right foot. The door swung open with ease and wedged that way. Ann noticed a set of small bloody footprints leading out of the ward and down the corridor.

"We have to find the kids and Jayden first," she reminded him.

"We will, but not dressed like this."

Ayesha woke once again from the dream of men in spacesuits hovering close over her face. She tried to get up, but something held her down at the neck, waist and legs. She raised her neck off the pillowless as far as she could and looked down at her body. She was strapped down in those three places in some sort of emergency ward.

She was in an area by a door. There seemed to be a corridor of plastic running down the length of the long ward. On either side were sectioned off plastic covered beds. Each was occupied, and several hazmat-suited medical staff attended to the victims of the plague that had killed Ayesha's mother.

"Get me the fuck off this fucking trolley," she screamed, causing a nearby nurse to drop a tray of needles. She felt no grief, only pure molten rage. Two hazmat figures hurried over to her. One was a man with spectacles behind his clear facemask and the other a younger woman, with a lazy left eye.

"Is she the one, do you think doctor?" the woman said over her to the man.

"She could be, too early to tell at the moment, we know so little about this epidemic, nothing is concrete." The doctor spoke to the nurse, ignoring Ayesha struggling to free herself from her bonds.

"Hey fuckers, get these things offame." Ayesha struggled hard against her bonds, but all she got was hot and agitated.

"And all the others?" The nurse still ignored her pleas.

"Every single one has the infection in one stage or the other. Except her," the doctor at least nodded down at her.

"I'm going to bloody kill you when I get free," Ayesha hissed at him, the veins in her strained neck standing out.

"Strip her and check her every ten minutes for signs of the infection. I want blood and urine samples too, but don't unstrap her. If she becomes too noisesome, gag and sedate her." The doctor walked off with barely a cursory glance at her.

"Hey, don't you go walking away from me! Where is my mother and Charlie, the woman I came here with?"

"Try and stay calm. And quiet if you can. People are dying in droves in here, and the last thing they want to hear is some silly girl cursing to high heaven." The nurse's voice was calm and sedate like she was giving a weather report on a sunny day.

"Are you friggin' kidding me, girlfriend? Calm, my mum is dead, and I can't see my other mother here either, now tell me what the hell is going on?" Ayesha strained her head left and right, trying to get a better view of the patients in the plastic cells. A hand shot up from the nearest bed, grabbing the plastic sheeting confining the bed. It twisted the plastic and then fell limp, leaving a smudged bloody handprint behind.

What Ayesha did not see was the needle until it pricked her bare forearm and sent her back to her world of scary dreams.

CHAPTER TWELVE

HOSPITAL HELL

The hospital car park was a gridlocked nightmare. Hannah's Gran had sworn under her breath after fifteen minutes queuing behind lines of other cars, vans and ambulances. She indicated and drove into the empty exit lane of the hospital round until she was stopped by a crowd of onlookers holding, carrying, and dragging sick people.

Hannah glanced left in panic at what she saw. In the other lane, a girl her age with red sores all over her once pretty, pale face puked blood over the car window she was looking out. Hannah closed her eyes, the familiar sickness flowing up like a cold wind from her stomach area. She had taken off her seatbelt five minutes ago. She managed to scramble out of the car before she vomited on the box bushes separating the two lanes. Through her tears, she was glad to see carrots and not blood.

"Hannah, are you alright?" her gran called in a worried voice from inside the car.

Hannah waved her back, as she spat onto the muddy soil under the low hedging.

"Bloody hell, are you okay Han?"

Hannah stood up at the new, familiar voice coming from three yards away. "Oh no," she whispered, as Matt left the rear of the crowd and hurried over to her.

"Gran, Gran," Hayley screamed from inside the car.

Hannah looked from the father of her unborn child to the rear window of the car, not sure which situation was worse.

All her life's ills were crashing together, and all she wanted to do was have it away on her toes.

"You okay?" her Geography teacher and secret lover asked getting closer.

She couldn't reply. She couldn't move or speak; she was trapped between two hells. Instead, she doubled up again and puked yellow soup on Matt's shoes.

It meant she didn't see her grandfather sit up, his head a red mass of blood and press his skinless thumbs into his youngest granddaughter's wide eyes.

Brita gripped the handrail/weapon so hard it hurt her fingers. The A&E looked like an invading Viking army of berserkers had crashed through it. The junior doctor lay slumped over the low table he'd stood on to speak to the people inside. His skull had been crushed flat it seemed by the blood covered fire extinguisher dropped by his left hand. Other corpses littered the beds and floor. Other bodies looked like they had been flayed by some medieval torture instrument.

"Oh my God," Ellie cried behind her.

Then a man staggered from behind a cubicle. His face and hands looked like they had been attacked with a sander. His eyes were the only thing not affected by the flesh-eating bacteria that had claimed his features. He grunted deep from within his ravaged throat and made a B-line for the three women.

"That way," Brita pointed, letting the two Chambers women go through the double doors they had come through earlier, which led to the main waiting room reception area of the A&E. Brita kept her eyes on the bloody fleshless man as she backed to the doors. His eyes were on her, so did not see the corpse at his feet. He tumbled over and was lost from view. Brita took the time to turn and follow Ellie and her mum through the double doors. They raced for the sliding doors they had entered through, but they were closed, locked and covered outside with opaque plastic sheeting.

Ellie rattled the doors, but they would not budge.

"STEP AWAY FROM THE DOORS! THIS HOSPITAL IS UNDER STRICT QUARANTINE CONDITIONS. PLEASE

STAY INSIDE, SIT DOWN AND WAIT FOR FURTHER INSTRUCTIONS, TRY NOT TO PANIC." A megaphone aided voice ordered from outside.

Ellie flinched back from the doors and put her arm around her bemused mother for comfort.

"What do we do?" Ellie looked Brita dead in the eyes. Brita could see panic setting in. She knew a little about control, and some of her army training kicked in.

"We can't stay here. It's not safe, we need to get to a higher clear window to assess the situation." Brita looked around the reception area. A pair of legs in jeans and wearing Converse Allstars stuck out from under the seating area. There had been many people here before, including the staff and cleaner. Where had they gone? Had they been evacuated before the door had been sealed, or had they fled somewhere?

A raging noise, scream and the sounding of many feet approaching spurred Brita into action. "Come on behind here." Brita dragged Ellie, who in turn was hanging on to her mother towards the glass fronted reception area. Blood was splattered up in an arc across two of the windows. There seemed to be no way in from the reception area, so Brita urged them around a corner to a left-hand side corridor. The corridor stretched on with doors and signs everywhere. Three bodies were along the green and blue painted floor. A sheet covered patient lay on a trolley; blood from its face seeping through its white shroud. A nurse was lying against the side of the corridor as if asleep. Yet a fire extinguisher, lying next to her bloody caved in head, told another violent story. At the far end, was a portly man in every-day clothes slumped against the wall, half of his face a mass of red living sores. The first heavy right-hand door must lead to the closed off reception desks. She tried the door, but it was locked. An electronic swipe pad sat next to the stumpy round metal handle.

The rumbling swelling of people approaching the main reception waiting area was getting louder and more worrying. Brita ran down to where the poor nurse lay, obviously dead. She tried not to look at her caved in temple and the odd angle her left eye was looking in its crushed socket. But it was like trying not to rubber-neck as you passed a bad accident on the other side of a motorway.

"Brita," Ellie hissed in panic, which spurred her into action. She grabbed the security badge off the dead nurse and ran back to Ellie and her mother. She swiped the door, as a raging primal shout came from the reception area around the corner. The door access pad beeped way too loudly for her liking, but the light turned from red to green. She pushed the door inwards, as smashing sounds were heard nearby. As they entered the office part of the back reception area, they could see why through the windows. Biker rage man and his mob of angry followers were trying to smash through the locked glass doors of the A&E. Their numbers looked less than before.

A scared short looking woman in her late-forties with short blonde hair, a little too much weight around the middle was hiding under the long reception desk. She hurriedly waved them down. They followed her instructions, even Mrs. Chambers, without being asked. They ducked down and hid before the mob noticed them.

"You're not infected are you," she whispered to Brita, who was crouching nearest to her. Some of her words were drowned out by the smashing sounds the mob was making, so she had to lip-read and guess what she was asking.

Brita just shook her head vigorously from side-to-side in reply.

"STEP AWAY FROM THE DOORS, THIS IS YOUR ONLY WARNING OR YOU WILL BE MET WITH LETHAL FORCE. THE HOSPITAL IS A QUARANTINED ZONE. PLEASE KEEP CALM AND WAIT FOR FURTHER INSTRUCTIONS," the voice outside boomed again.

"What does lethal force mean?" Ellie whispered, her breath warm and fast in Brita's right ear. Normally it would have been a turn-on, but not in these circumstances.

"I think they might shoot them?" Brita said.

"They won't do that, this is England," the stubby nosed blonde receptionist hissed. "This is a hospital, not an American action film."

"Fuck you!" Shouted one of the mob and the sounds of

something heavy hitting shatter-proof glass continued.

"Let us out of here you bastards," called a female voice. "I have kids."

"There are infected people in here that have gone mad and are trying to kill people, please let us out," said an older man.

The four women hiding in the reception office exchanged worried looks.

The sound of glass shattering and raining onto a hard surface could be heard. "This way, one of the male mob voices called. More sounds of breaking glass, being hit or kicked away could be heard.

"DO NOT LEAVE THE BUILDING. THIS IS YOUR FINAL WARNING. WE WILL SHOOT!" The loud megaphone voice shouted losing some of the calm in his voice.

"They are bluffing," the male voice said before ten rapid rounds were fired from outside. Screaming came from outside, inside and behind the reception counter. The sounding of dispersing running feet could be heard as the mob ran in panic from the firing.

"They can't have, they can't have," the receptionist repeated over and over again to herself while Brita pulled a sobbing and shaking Ellie close and held her tight.

"Wha-what will we do?" Ellie asked through her sobs and sniffles.

"For the moment, stay in here." Brita could not think of anything they could do at the present time. She would like to get to a higher window on the building and find out what was going on outside. But the risk of leaving the semi-secure office was too high at the moment. They had swapped the disabled toilet for another prison. All they could do was wait it out some more and hope some sort of organised, non-lethal help arrived from outside.

Selena sat on her bony behind, legs up, her arms resting on her raised kneecaps. She wore a builder's mask she had found on her last mission to the *cupboard of crap*, under the stairs. Luckily it was on a high shelf next to a duster and some WD40.

She sat on the floor of her guest bedroom, looking like an extra from some Japanese inspired horror movie. *Wet* lay in her guest bed, soaked once again in his own urine, sweat covering his face. His breath had become more rapid in the last twenty minutes, and she could not wake him. The mask that smelt faintly of paint still did not keep out the foul odours of illness emanating from the bed. The red sores had spread, like an infectious version of join the dots. His belly, groin, and upper thighs were red. Yet not red, it was like the upper layers of his skin were being eaten away as he slept. Her last attempt to wash his wounds with bottled water, had left a chunk of his morbid skin in her left rubber marigold glove.

It took all her willpower not to throw up on him. By some miracle, she kept her meagre lunch down. It had left her, where she was. Where she had sat for the past fifteen minutes. She could not contact the outside world. The flood water had cut her house and road off from vehicles anyway. She could not get him out of bed, even if she built a raft to take his weight.

They were stuck with each other.

And she was scared. Scared that she would catch the red skin eating bug from him and die alone and unfound for weeks in her own bed. With a stranger's corpse for company nearby. What would the papers and the people at work make of that?

"It's what I deserve," she said into her mask. She resolved not to suffer like Wet, though. A bottle of pills with a gin chaser should do the trick. Go to sleep and never wake up. Maybe the flood water would rise so high they would take her and float her off to Hell.

Wet coughed, nearly choking. Selena jumped to her feet and hurried over to the bed.

"It's okay, it's okay, I'm here." She put a rubber-gloved hand on his burning forehead, not sure what comfort it might bring. He opened his eyes. They fluttered like tiny butterflies trying to escape a spider's web but did not open. She pulled up the covers and let out a gasp of shock. The flesh below, just a red raw mass of sinew and muscles with no healthy skin in sight. Even Selena, with no medical training at all, could see that he was not going to recover from this. She swallowed down her own bile and laid the covers back over him.

She knew he would be dead sooner than later.

Ann and Tony stared at the dead man. The dead man's wide open brown eyes stared back at them. Caught in a painful, fearful, moment of death. He sat at a foldout table in front of the sterile ward they had exited.

His hazmat hood had been torn off his head and used to strangle him in the swivel chair he sat. Red finger marks were over the suit, his cheeks, and chin.

"What the hell is going on in this hospital," Tony said in a whispered voice that was not his usual bellow.

"I dunno Tone, but we got to find Mike, Stacey and Jayden and get as far away from here as possible."

"We still need clothes," he said absently.

"What about those." Ann pointed across the corridor to a metal gurney with piles of new blue scrubs were, still in their plastic wrappings.

"Yeah, they'll do," Tony said glad to look away from the dead man and his unnerving eyes. They changed in an empty private room. The scrubs were better than the paper thin nightgowns, but Ann had no bra to disguise her droopy large boobs that rested on the top of her big belly. Tony moaned as they put on the croc-like holey shoes. Tony never went anywhere, not even the beach without a pair of socks on. They left the private room and walked down the corridor to where three ways met. There was a nurse's station there. A man in a security uniform was slumped headfirst onto a computer keyboard, spelling out pages and pages of the letter *J*. His face seemed eaten away so he had no nose or features at all. They moved on as quickly as the pair could manage.

The small red footprints had faded away to nothing, but they continued onwards. They had little choice. There was a crash up ahead, then a stifled scream. As they hurried to the end of the corridor, there were a set of double doors. A red handprint of a child was on the right-hand side one. Tony, who was much taller than Ann, peered through the wire lattice glass. He saw a man in a hazmat suit fall to the floor, the metal pole of part of an IV stand protruding out the back of his head. His body gave off spasmodic twitches as his brain sent confusing signals to his extremities.

A figure bent down to examine the dead twitching man. It was Jayden.

"Jayden," Tony cried out pushing open the door, as Ann bustled through after him.

The boy turned around. He had no face.

Ayesha woke from a slurred dream of being chased through a railway tunnel cut through the side of some mountain. She tried to lift her head, but her neck felt like it was made of jelly. All she could do was turn her head and try and blink out the muck that was blurring up her crusted eyes. Things in the isolation ward she was in had taken a dramatic change since she had been forced into unconsciousness. A strip light in the ceiling was swinging hypnotically back and forwards between her trolley and the transparent plastic cubicles. She blinked tears from her eyes, remembering once again that her mother was dead. She watched the light swing on thick white wires pulled from the ceiling panels above. She closed her eyes and pressed her dry lips together. Blue and yellow neon flashes continued to swing behind the blackness of her tightly closed eyelids.

Ayesha opened them again, taking in more of the ward. The nearest clear plastic cubicle was splattered with blood. The one opposite ripped to shreds like a wild tiger had escaped from it. She could see nobody at all from her gurney. She tried to move. Her head did a woozy spin, and she had to lay it back down again. She let a second or two pass and then raised it again only to see that she was still strapped to the trolley in three places. She wasn't going anywhere fast without aid.

Ayesha frowned deep furrows in her usually smooth forehead. She puffed out her cheeks and raised her head to look down at her body again. "And I'm naked."

A grunting noise rose up from the far side of the ward, a moment after she spoke aloud. It stopped her cold. Something primeval deep inside her DNA made her go into a wary quiet mode. The grunting continued like a base rhythmical beast, which sounded very much to Ayesha that someone was hard shagging somebody. The grunts were followed by cracking sounds and then after a while a wet slapping noise.

Ayesha tried to swallow, but her mouth was too dry with fear. She could not see what was making the thrusting grunting noises, and that made things even worse. She was trapped on the trolley. She tried to move her hands to release her bonds, but they were wrapped round twice and strapped down hard next to her bare hips. All she could do was move her head and dart her eyes this way and that. The slowing swing of the strip light did little to aid her view.

Why wasn't there anybody with the patients?

If there are any patients left alive?

Ayesha shook her head a little. All she needed now was the nagging little voices in her head making a bad situation even worse. *Where were the arsehole nurse and doctor from earlier?*

Dead, and their corpses being dry humped in a bloody pool on the floor.

Her imagination and thoughts were going haywire. She had to try to get out of her bonds, off the trolley, get out of the ward and find her clothes pronto. Her wrists and ankles were tightly bound, but maybe she could wriggle down under her chest strap and at least sit up and see what was going on. She was very bendy. Many of her male fuck-buddies had commented on that in the past. The strap was just under her boobs, but they weren't the biggest when she was lying flat. So she started to wiggle her hips and push herself under the tight chest strap. She grimaced, as the straps rolled up her small chest and caught on her erect nipples. Cold and frightened they pointed upwards, making the slow limbo under the strap even more painful than it needed to be. She wanted to cry out and hiss with the hurt but knew in her present unsure situation, that would be a bad idea. She pushed her body as far to the left as she could manage, the strap leaving her tender nipples and she made fast progress. The belt was looser at her neck as she turned her head and ducked down under the strap, with sharp pains coming from her neck and spine areas.

"Yesss," she hissed and knew immediately that was a bad idea.

The humping sounds suddenly stopped. It was followed by a wet hissing sound from the far end of the ward. Ayesha went rigid with fear and had to fight her aching bladder to keep from pissing herself. She heard something being dropped heavily to the floor with a squelching wet noise. Then wet slopping foot-steps approaching from end of the ward.

Ayesha sat up, and she could see it, and it could see her.

A man with a red, raw massive erection was moving down the centre of the ward towards her. He had no skin on his entire body, no hair, just a blood seeping mess of a disease ravaged man. Only the whites of his blue eyes showing any other colour than blood red. The once-man ambled slowly towards her, look-ing like it was in great pain. Its skin-shredded cock fixed and hard for her.

Ayesha struggled with her bonds and screamed for her mother, as the red man advanced on her.

CHAPTER THIRTEEN

THE END OF ALL FLESH

There was a wall of screaming surrounding Hannah in every direction.

Then she realised that she was screaming herself.

Her grandfather dropped Hayley's lifeless head and lunged forwards around the driver's headrest to snap his wife of thirty-eight years' neck. Hannah's grandmother slumped forwards against the constraining tug of her seatbelt. Bloody fingerprints covered her cheeks and neck, as her head lolled downwards and she collapsed in on herself, like a jack-in-the-box forced back into its square abode.

Hannah felt someone grab her and tried weakly to fight him off. It was her teacher and lover and father of the child inside her. He pulled her to her feet as her grandfather tried to get out of the car, his face a red mask of hatred. Another victim of the red death shattered the crowd in all directions. Shots were fired; screams punctured the air, as Hannah's legs gave way under her. Then she felt Mr. Davies pick her up in his strong arms, and they were running away through the lines of parked and idling cars to the exit of the hospital. Hannah's bobbing head looked back as an armed person in a grey hazmat suit shot her deranged grandfather five times in the head. Blood begat blood.

Hannah saw no more as her lover carried her across the road and behind a slow moving bus through the still driving rain. The hospital was on a hill, so the floods had not had the devastating effect as on the lower ground. They were both soaked through as he ran up a side road and ran on past some bins and down a side alley and away from the hospital. Hannah didn't know what was going on; her already small family was all gone, leaving only her and her unborn baby. Hayley and her grandparents had joined her parents in the deathplace she kept vaulted in the back of her mind. She felt the rain and Mr. Davies strong arms holding her, but nothing else.

Brita, Ellie, her mother and the receptionist called Pauline had waited in the reception office for twenty-five minutes since the shooting. Brita needed to pee. It was ironic that their last hiding place was a toilet, and she desperately wished they were back there. She had moved to the locked door to listen, when screaming, shouts and running feet outside were followed by lots of automatic weapons firing.

The receptionist looked appalled as the firing and chaotic noises outside continued. "They can't shoot people, this is England," she said, not for the first time.

"We need to get out of here." Ellie anxiously pawed at Brita's passing left leg.

"I know," Brita replied, with a curt nod.

The noise outside made it hard for her to hear anything clearly. The coast sounded clear enough. She stood slowly from her crouching position, expecting her back to twinge in protest, but it didn't. She scanned the reception area through the windows. Apart from three dead people who had been trying to smash through the quarantine, the place seemed empty. She put her hand on the doorframe and unlocked the office door and opened it a crack. Nothing attacked the door, so she opened it wider and risked popping her head outside. No living people were in the corridor, only the dead from before.

Brita closed the door and looked over at Pauline. "Where is the nearest stairs upwards?"

"Erm...down the end of the corridor, through the doors there are lifts and a staircase that goes up and down." Pauline was pulling absently at her fake long blonde hair extensions, some of it coming away in her tiny nervous hands.

"Down? Down where?" Brita pressed.

"Erm... to the basements, they run under all of the

buildings, for the porters and maintenance men to move about quickly, Boilers and Incinerators down there too. It's like a fucking maze down there." The woman was rubbing at her caked on makeup, which covered spots that even concealer could not hide. Brita had thought the woman pretty for her age when they had entered the office, not so now. The closer you looked at even beautiful women, the more flaws you eventually saw.

"Could we use them to get out somehow?" Brita crouched down again, for safety's sake.

"Erm…they lead over to the boiler room right on the far side of the site, near the staff car parks, right near the back road. Yes, we could." The short, frightened woman nodded.

"Then that is what we shall do," Brita said pulling Ellie to her feet with her. "Are we all agreed?"

Ellie and her mother nodded quickly.

Pauline stood up, she was even shorter than Brita had expected. She was shocked when the woman picked up her handbag and pulled out her lipstick and started applying it.

"Are you coming too?" Ellie said to the dolled-up receptionist who was trying desperately to cling onto her fading looks.

"Yes, just needed a bit of lippy to brave the outside world," Pauline said, dropping the lipstick back into her bag.

Brita thought she looked much better without the greasy covering on her lips. Brita rarely wore makeup and lipstick just made her thin lips look even thinner. "Come, we go."

She opened the door slowly and peered out into the corridor again. Nobody alive was there. So she waved them out, holding onto the toilet rail before her.

They hurried down to the double doors. Ellie leading her mother, Pauline close behind with her designer handbag held to her ample chest, like the price of it would ward off an attack. The lift area beyond the double doors was free of people and bodies. There were two small lifts and a larger freight and trolley one. A green sign pointed to a door with a glass panel. Brita peered through and saw steps leading down and up. She pulled it open quickly and waved the other three women inside.

The women ran into the stairwell, and Brita used her hands to keep the spring-loaded door from banging as it closed. She turned to see the three other women congregating around the centre handrail that curved up and downwards. They looked like lost sheep. Her strong feminist hackles rose for a moment, then she remembered what Ellie and her mother recently lost and chided herself for that. They looked to her to be strong, for guidance and to be a leader.

She walked towards them, trying to force a smile from her thin lips. She just hoped it wasn't the one that came out as a grimace in photographs of her. Caught unaware, she thought she was fine, but posing like a super-thin photoshopped model: she could not manage a proper natural smile.

A sudden cry of panic from below brought them back to the scary reality of the situation. Fleeing boots on the steps below brought the cleaner they had asked directions from come running and panting up the stairs from below ground. He was wide-eyed and ran past them and out of the stairwell door without a second glance at them. Throaty cries and sounds of many feet in pursuit came from below.

"Up," she quickly herded the three other women. As she pushed them up, she gave the closing door a meaty kick to send it flying open again. Then she followed after the fleeing women up the stairs. When she got them to the first-floor exit, she grabbed them to get their attention and pressed her forefinger to her lips to silence them. Then she crept to the railing and hung onto them as she peered down below, the way they had come. Luckily for her, the two men and one girl that ran through the still slowly closing door did not look up. They took the bait that Brita had laid.

She stepped back from the railings, slightly aghast at what she had seen. She could only tell the sex of the figures below by their hairstyles. What flesh that showed seemed to be gone, showing the bloody layers below the epidermis layers of skin that were missing. They looked like some cartoon villain from a comic, one of her fellow soldiers used to read in the bunk next to her, during her National Service. Brita hated all that super-hero shit; she preferred stories of real people doing extraordinary brave things.

Something was happening here that she could not

comprehend. Some disease or infection, whatever the correct term was eating the skin off people in rapid time. Most people like Mr. Chambers died, while a few turned mad by the pain, she assumed; went after every living thing. Ellie ducked aside from the window in the door to the first floor. She pointed, and then took a sneaky peak.

"Someone just ran past," she whispered.

Brita pointed upwards again. She wanted to both take point and be at the rear also. In the end they went up like the animals into the ark; two-by-two. Pauline next to her; Ellie and her mother, one step behind. They moved up to the next floor. But that's where the stairwell ended. They were just approaching the exit, when two men, one a doctor in a white coat and a nurse rushing through the door jumped at the sight of the four women.

"What the hell is wrong with this hospital?" Mrs. Chambers piped up, a sudden raw rage in her hoarse throat.

Then she saw. They all saw: a woman with no flesh on her face ran through the door after the fleeing men.

Selena couldn't take the sound of Wet's laboured breathing anymore. She sat on the soft carpeted floor of her guest bedroom. Her back and head leant back against an old freestanding wardrobe. Her legs were parted, and a half bottle of vodka lay pressed tightly against her crotch. Of the missing vodka, half she had used as an antiseptic on her guest and half she had drunk to keep her light breakfast down.

Wet was breathing erratically. He had gone through a feverish panting stage, then had thrashed about and called for someone named Deirdre. His breathing was painfully slow, with pregnant pauses, during which times Selena held her breath also until his next breath came. The gaps in his catching breath were getting longer. Two seconds had passed since his last intake, then a third, before he lightly exhaled.

Selena could not look at him anymore. She stared down at the bottle, wondering if her pelvic floor muscles could break the glass of the vodka bottle. His neck and his cheek facing her were gone. Eaten away by the flesh-eating bug that was slowly consuming his skin, inch-by-morbid-inch. Selena tapped at the top of the bottle lid with her nails, wondering whether to take another slug of alcohol.

One more breath in and out and I will, she promised herself.

Wet breathed in, and she held her breath also. Her thumb and fingers were resting on the screw cap; ready to twist it open. It wasn't until she felt the burning pain in her lungs, did she realised Wet had not exhaled. She had to. She stood up, the bottle tipping sideways onto the carpet; the liquid inside sloshing back and forth like a clear tide.

She was tall anyway but stood where she was on tip-toe to look at the stranger in her guest bed. Wet's lips had been nearly eaten away, showing his rotten and missing teeth underneath. His mouth was slightly parted; his tongue poking out of his mouth; He was no longer breathing.

Selena once again checked her hands and arms for any red marks. Thankfully there were none. She had no real idea what had killed this nameless man, or if she would catch it also. She had a dead body in her guest bed, and she did not know what to do. Wet didn't look peaceful in death, he looked demonic and unsettling. Selena pulled the blood-stained sheet over his eternally grinning death mask and then doused her hands in vodka afterwards. She had some idea from a pirate film she had seen to sow him up in his sheets, but then what? Drag him down into the waters below and give him a burial at sea?

In the end, she left him and the vodka in the guest bedroom and reverently closed the door behind her, with the barest click of the lock. She wondered how long it would take for him to start to smell. Or smell worse than he already did.

"Disease, death and decomposing," she began, "a poem by Selena Wright-Fenshaw aged forty-six." She wandered along the landing and peered down at the silent rising water. It was still raining outside. She could hear it against the window directly behind her. Something from her Catholic nun taught education suddenly sprung to mind. "Then God said to Noah, the end of all flesh has come before Me; for the Earth is filled with violence because of them; and behold, I am about to destroy them with the Earth."

"Balls, give me Thor and Odin any day of the week," she said turning to peer out the rain rivulets on the window panes. "Give me thunder and lightning and floods and wash away my *fucking* tears."

The vodka on a nearly empty stomach had more of an effect she noticed since she stood up. No thunder or lightening came, only more rain. She wandered into her bedroom, lay down and fell quickly into a deep sleep.

Ann fell backwards on her considerable backside. As what remained of her grandson's snarling face tried to bite at her nose. Her hands slipped on the gore and puss, as the remains of the skin on his neck slewed off as she tried desperately to fend him off.

Tony lay half through the open doors, groaning and clutching at his head where Jayden had whacked it with the IV pole. He was not in a fit state to save her from the lipless snarling faceless thing her grandson had become. Her left hand slipped in the dermis of his neck, and she had to turn her head sharply to stop his teeth latching onto her nose. She could feel her grip slipping off his blood-soaked neck, the pain in her wrists rising under the strain of holding him back.

She felt a rush of air in front of her and a clonking sound. Jayden's weight and red deranged face were no longer pressing painfully on her large bosom. He lay in a wretched heap beside her. More a red skeleton than the boy she loved. She looked up. Standing over her was a woman holding a large red fire extinguisher.

"Are you bitten, are you infected?" The woman asked, breathing hard.

"No." Ann shook her head.

The tall, elegant woman, with dark auburn hair, reached down a hand to help her up. Ann took it but used most of her own strength to stand up. No way was this athletic shaped woman was going to pull her bulk from the floor.

"Charlie," the woman said, then pointed at Ann.

"Ann Gable and this is my husband Tony and..." she let her words falter. What was the skinless thing that attacked them, surely not her grandson anymore? All the flesh that made him what he was, was gone. Ann hurried over to help Tony get to his feet. There was blood on his hands and head from the wound he had received.

"What the fuck is going on around here?"

"I wish I knew," Charlie replied. She started walking through the double doors.

"Where are you going?" Ann asked looking from the back of her retreating saviour to Jayden's unconscious, blood-covered body on the sterile hospital floor.

"To find my daughter," Charlie simply replied, not waiting for them.

Tony pulled the dazed Ann towards the doors, his large arm resting heavily on her shoulder.

"What about Jayden?" she asked as they left what remained of their grandson behind.

"I don't think that is Jayden anymore. Do you want to be here when he wakes up? I don't. So let's get out of here." Tony said, letting the doors bang behind him.

Ann said nothing in response. She did not want to leave her grandson, but what was left of him, no features of the sweet boy he had been. Just a crazed skinless beast. What could they do for him anyway, they could not replace his face or skin, Ann felt hopeless as they followed after Charlie, down a left-hand corridor.

Ayesha could not free her hands. She managed to kick open one shackle on her right leg as the walking red erection moved ever closer. His lipless mouth was wide open, and his tongue that looked like raw liver slivered in his mouth and over his teeth. He had to step around a monitor to get to her. It meant he came at her from her bottom end. Ayesha was naked, strapped to a trolley with a skinless man after her. Would he rape her, kill her or do both in whatever order he pleased?

She pulled up her right leg, ready to kick out at him when the doors to the closed ward burst open.

"Get away from my daughter you bastard," Charlie screamed running at the erect red man. Ayesha saw something red and heavy connect with the remains of the man's face. She heard the bones in his face break as Charlie slammed the end of the fire extinguisher into the right side of his cheek. With extra maternal strength from somewhere deep in her core, she knocked the man to the floor. But seeing his red raging phallus did not stop there. She smashed the end of the fire extinguisher into his skull, with increasing grunts like a tennis pro in a long rally. Sure his face was caved in, she stamped on his withering cock, just for good measure. That used the last of her adrenaline, she turned and staggered away from the dead thing, towards Ayesha on the trolley.

"Better not piss her off eh, Ann," a deep bass voice said from the doorway.

Ayesha wanted to cover herself but was unable to. She wanted to see who was with her second mum, but Charlie fell upon her kissing her forehead and pulling her tight.

"I thought I'd lost you too," Charlie cried with relief into Ayesha's neck.

"You saved my bare arse." Ayesha wanted to hug her back, but she was naked and still strapped to the trolley.

"We'll try and find some clothes," a woman's voice came from the open doorway. "Come on Tone, stop staring."

"Eh-what...no," he mumbled apologetically, as the door swung shut behind them.

"Who are they?" Ayesha wanted to know as Charlie worked on her bonds to free her at last.

"Dunno, I met them in the corridor, helped them out. This hospital has gone mad. Half the people are dead, and some people are infected like the man after you. All flesh and features gone, only eyes left, and they want to kill everyone. There!" At last, Charlie had got the straps off Ayesha.

She sat up and hugged Charlie properly. "Thanks, mum," she said into her neck, closing her eyes from the sight of the red man with the bashed in head and brains all over the clean floor. She hopped off the table and looked around. Nobody else seemed to have survived the red man's attack in the isolation ward: staff and patients alike. She spotted a clear plastic bag on the floor near a medical waste bin. It had some familiar looking clothes inside. She rushed over, tore it open from the side with her long nails and hurried into her things.

A plump middle-aged woman came through the door carrying some green scrub gowns. "Oh, I see you found something better," she said spotting Ayesha pulling on her left trainer.

"Look at us," the huge bulky man said hobbling after her, tugging at his tight medical clothes with ire. "Look like fucking casualty extras, me and the missus do."

"This is Ann?" Charlie said waiting for the plump middle-aged woman to give a nod that she remembered her name right. "And her husband, Tony."

"Alright?" Tony waved a huge hand at her.

"Is this your daughter?" Ann asked moving hesitantly into the ward filled with dead people.

Charlie looked at Ayesha with pride. "Yes, she is."

Ayesha smiled back for a second, glad to have Charlie around, but it hit her again that her birth mother was dead. She had died of the same disease as the red man on the floor. Ayesha began to weep, imagining the suffering her mother must have endured as she died without her family around her. How frightened she must have been. Had she called out for Charlie and her; had she hated them for not coming sooner and being with her at the end?

Charlie pulled her head into her belly. Ayesha with one trainer still not fully on hugged her around the middle, finding comfort in Charlie's hands in her hair.

"Look, I know I might sound terrible, but you've found your daughter. We need to try and find ours." Ann moved a step closer to the hugging women.

"Then we better check all the beds here first," Charlie said turning around to face her. An intensely strong, but grim look on her face.

Ayesha wiped her eyes on the edges of the cuffs of her top. Sniffed up her tears and stood up. "We really got to do this, can't we just get the fuck out of here, tell the police?"

"We'll look," Charlie said rubbing Ayesha's back. It reminded her of the time she had a terrible chest infection. Mum had been at work and Charlie had stayed up all night with her feeding her Calpol. "You stand at the door and keep a look out, Ayesha."

Ayesha nodded. Charlie, who was taller and willowy, kissed through her hair onto the top of her head. Ayesha moved slowly over to the door of the isolation ward and peered outside. The place seemed empty enough. There was only a dark bundle at the far end of the corridor behind and under a set of connected plastic waiting chairs outside a day clinic. Ayesha tried to imagine it was just a pile of clothes dumped there, but she knew better. She peeked behind her, jumping at every little noise she heard. Charlie, Ann, and Tony were moving down the centre aisle of the plastic sheeted beds. Talking in hushed voices, probably not to scare her even more. But she was frightened to death. All the bravado had left her. She was a frightened teenager, feeling more like a scared kid, than a woman.

The sounds of a wail, followed by the unmistakable sounds of someone puking their guts out followed. It grabbed her attention, nearly as much as the chemical and shit smell coming from inside the ward. She breathed out. She felt hungry, and the smell of sick wafted her way, making her struggle to keep from throwing up. She turned and moved out into the clearer air of the corridor. Past the open door.

A boy with no face was standing only three yards away from her.

CHAPTER FOURTEEN

THE RISING RED TIDE

Hannah felt Matt's strength give out before he did. She swung her legs down as he struggled over some rubbish strewn across a walled path between two rows of houses. He graciously fought to keep her upright as he fell and she only went down a little way banging her right knee in the process.

The path was like a mini-river coming down from a slight rise. It chilled her exposed hands as she pushed up, wincing at her banged kneecap. At least she had not fallen on her side or belly. Matt was breathing hard. He looked up at her, his face awash with the constant rain coming down from the heavens. He seemed like a beaten tired old mutt on its last legs. "Are you okay?"

Hannah noticed that instead of her boobs his eyes immediately went to her belly area. She nodded; she was so less than okay. "You?"

"I'll live," he said, using the wall to push himself up. "We need to get out of here, find some shelter from this bloody rain… time to think." He was breathing hard, harder than in the sex sessions they had in the back of his car.

An army helicopter, followed immediately after by another flew low overhead. "Chinooks," he said as they had passed.

Like she really cared what type they were. The sounds of the helicopters were replaced by the sounds of many sirens from all directions converging on the hospital.

"We better get moving again, Hannah." He offered his hand to her.

She took it to keep him happy rather than any other reason. There was no warmth in either of their palms or fingers, the constant cold rain had been to that. Matt rubbed his other hand through his short damp hair. It looked to Hannah like it was going thin on top already. She wondered if she had a boy, would it have its daddy's hair?

They moved off through the rain, at last, finding shelter in a bicycle shed near a set of tennis courts. The courts looked like slick mini swimming pools at the moment. She was glad to be out of the driving rain. Though it had washed away her tears.

Matt bent and took her in a wet embrace. It was nice to feel the tiniest body heat between them. She felt numb, letting him pull her close. All hope and reason and thoughts of the future were gone for her at present. She was an orphan and pregnant. The rain, near-silent outside, battered the corrugated roof with unending drum-solos of despair. Thoughts went to her immediate predicament. She could not live in her drowning grandparent's house alone. Social workers and care jumped into her mind. Of people taking the baby from her, foster care and gymslip mum, all rushed into her mind like a bad soap opera script. Maybe she could lie about her age, all of her past life taken by the flood. Take Matt up on his offer if he avoided jail. A baby needed a father. A mother needed a roof over her head. Not a bicycle shed.

Then she felt his hands slip down to her backside to rub and squeeze her.

Her future died a little more.

She stayed in his arms, letting the whole sorry tale play out. He lifted her chin and kissed her numb lips.

She let him.

Only when his hands brushed her belly to grab her breasts through her coat did she respond. Hannah stepped back and shoved him with both hands. He stumbled backwards, tripped over a metal bike rack and fell on his cute arse into a crater of a puddle.

"What did you do that for? I was only trying to make you feel better," he said, splashing his hands in the puddle before pushing himself to the side to rise from an awkward kneeling position.

"What you trying for, twins?" she spat back. "My family are all dead, and you thought a quick fumble in a bicycle shed would make me feel better? Did you! Are you that much of an inconsiderate cunt?"

"Okay, I'm sorry." He moved towards her wet palms out-stretched. Hannah took a step back. "Things have just gone mental that's all...I wasn't thinking straight. Let's find a way into town and get a taxi back to my place. Get you warm and dry and some food inside you." He saw her look. "Nothing more I swear. Then we can figure out what to do, together."

"Let's fucking go then," she stormed off back into the rain leaving him trailing in her wake. Anger was a better substitute for grief any day.

The fleeing men knocked Brita to the floor as they tried to escape the woman. In the end, they did her a favour. It saved her life.

The blood soaked snarling woman's next target was the unfortunate Pauline. She fell upon the short blonde, who screamed in shock and then pain as the red woman tore out her hair extensions, exposing her double-chinned neck. Brita was pulled up under her armpits by a worried looking Ellie as the red woman bit down into Pauline's neck. Her screams turned to gurgles at the second, third and then fourth ferocious attacks on the soft skin of her neck. The three other women just watched on in shock as the red woman savaged Pauline like a wasp stung Rottweiler.

Brita, even with her quick army training could do nothing to save her.

The doctor reappeared, swinging his stethoscope over the red woman's head and down around her neck. He put a black expensive Italian leather shoe onto the back of her neck and pulled hard. The crazed skinless woman tried hard to claw behind her at the doctor while trying to whip her body round to attack him, but he just pushed his shoe down harder. Brita could see the veins in his young neck sticking out like cords, his face turning from pink to flushed red. The shocked Asian nurse reappeared, looking even more aghast when he saw what his colleague was doing. Brita wanted to turn away from the woman's death struggle but couldn't. Ellie turned into her neck, though, when the sole of the doctor's shoe slipped sideward, taking off most of the woman's matted black hair. It slid off like she had been scalped, but her struggles were over, her breath and movement done. She was dead.

The doctor with rubber gloves on his hands already pulled the red woman off Pauline. He knelt down, his hands going to her blood pumping neck. Her eyes were wide in shock, her mouth opening and closing like a caught guppy on a river bank.

"Paul," she croaked before letting out her last breath on Earth. Brita did not know if this was the name of her other half, son, brother, or that she was trying to say her own name before dying. She would never know.

"She's gone," the doctor exhaled, then staggered backwards from the two corpses on bent knees until he fell backwards on his behind. He had been so brave and strong moments ago trying to save Pauline, but he began to weep and breathe heavily. The nurse moved up and patted him on the shoulder.

"There was nothing you could have done," the male nurse offered in Pakistani accented English.

The young doctor scratched at his head, then realised he had blood on his gloves. He ripped them off and flung them down the stairwell. "I'm supposed to save lives, not take them," he muttered in a cut upper-middle-class Home Counties accent.

Brita let go of Ellie and moved closer to the sitting doctor and nurse. "We need to get the hell out of here, is there a way?" She really wanted to get Ellie and her mother someplace else than next to the two dead women.

"What about those zombie-things?" the nurse pointed at the red woman.

"I told you, Wasim, they are not dead, or reanimated corpses, they are very much alive and in pain. Pain so bad it drives them mad. Also, the ACTV-7 virus they have eats away at the brain, causing a dumbing-down of cognitive function. It suddenly decreases visual processing and motor speeds, turning the patient into some base subhuman throwback to before the Stone Age. Adding to that it is airborne, virulent, and not touched by antibiotics, surgery, or hyperbaric oxygen therapy, means we had little defence against it but containment. If this escapes this hospital, thousands, if not millions of people could die." Brita did not understand half of what the scared doctor motored off. Even if she had been a native of these shores, she probably would have still not caught half of what he said. She reached down to the terrified doctor. "We need to get out of here and fast."

"But the hospital is on lockdown, they won't let anyone escape in case the virus spreads. The military and police have been given licence to use lethal force to keep everyone inside. We are trapped in here with the buggers, with no means of escape."

"Then what do you intend to do, give up, sit down and wait for the virus or one of those skinless people to eat your face off?" Brita extended her hand again. "You showed bravery to kill her and try and save Pauline. Show it again by getting up and helping us escape this hellhole."

The doctor looked around from Wasim to the corpses and then up to Brita again. He took her hand, and she helped him to his feet. "I don't want to die here today," he said. He tried to look brave, but his flushed boyish cheeks didn't help him.

"What do we do now?" Wasim gesticulated his worried words with both hands.

"We need to see what is going on, right?" Brita nodded at the doctor.

"The roof!" he said clicking his fingers.

"Good a place as any to start for sure," Brita said. She pointed up the stairwell. "This way?"

"Yes. I'm Doctor Kieran Noble, by the way," he said, offering her his hand. Frowning slightly Brita took it and shook it vigorously.

"Wasim," the nurse said raising his left hand.

"Let's go up," she said, turning to guide Ellie and her mother up past the two female corpses. They pressed on up another single flight of steps to the roof exit.

"So what is causing this virus, outbreak thing?" Ellie asked as they moved cautiously up the next flight of steps.

"We are not totally sure. The flood waters might have

brought something new to the surface. We had a little girl brought in that had been playing in the flood waters next to a pond that had burst its banks. Something stung or bit her, we could not tell as the bite area had necrotized and was gone by the time she was brought in. She seems to be the first reported victim we know of, but since then the virus has mutated out of control. It kills ninety-five percent of its victims. The survivors if you want to call them that lose all their layers of epidermis... erm skin and it kills the humane part of their brain. Sends them bat-shit crazy and homicidal." Doctor Noble reached the red door marked *trained personnel beyond this point only*. He rattled the door, but it was locked. "No escape this way."

He turned as the others reached the small concrete landing he was on.

"We shall see," Brita walked past him with a grim smile on her face. She stepped back and kicked at the lock next to the handle. The old weathered doorframe outside gave way, and the door juddered a foot outwards before stopping on the bituminous covered flat roof. It was still raining hard, and the water soon moved under her trainers to pool under everyone's feet.

"Lead the way," the doctor said in impressed tones. Brita paved the way, followed by the doctor, Ellie and her mother and Wasim bringing up the rear. They had to round some large air conditioning units to get to the edge of the roof to look down and see what was going on outside. That's if the driving rain allowed them to see much.

Brita rounded the tall oblong structure and saw movement ahead. Immediately, her words of warning were drowned out by a mouthful of rain. Harsh lights blazed suddenly in the faces of the survivors, followed by the dreaded shouted order of, "Fire!"

Selena woke in darkness and immediately thought she had slept through the night. She checked the watch with the broken catch she kept on the bedside table to tell the time, but it was too gloomy to see the hands however much she squinted. She leant over and reached out to turn on her bedside lamp. The thumbed white button clicked, but it brought no illumination to the darkened room. Frowning, she wiped some drool from her left cheek and went to the window.

"Still raining," she said. She could see it was not night, but still daytime. The sky through her net curtains was leaden grey, with smudges of charcoal. The rain was coming down unabated. The back garden looked like a scene from Venice rather than her Walton-on-Thames garden on the private road on which she lived. Lived? That was a joke, she barely existed. She hadn't been into work in days, no one had bothered to come and check on her. She had no real friends, only colleagues, and the occasional bedfellow. Plus, a dead nameless tramp in her guest bedroom, she remembered.

She angled the watch face towards what light shone through the window. It was only a quarter past three in the afternoon. She padded barefoot across the bedroom carpet, sure she had left the light on before she had fallen asleep. The switch was down, she flicked it up and down again. Nothing. Then again three times more.

"Brilliant," she muttered exiting her bedroom. She accepted it and let it into her brain. She tried the landing light, nothing. Either the fuse box downstairs was underwater, or the National Grid was playing up. Either way, it would be a gloomy place to stay. She went back to her bedroom and through into the en-suite bathroom. She knelt down to open the cupboard under the sink and pulled a pack of T-lights with ten left in the opened package. Selena was still holding the watch so she put that up on the sink so she could grab the long metal lighter she had too. She went to close the cupboard and then opened it again to dig out four stands of the metal encased fragrant candles. She carried her booty back to the bedroom and dumped them on the end of the bed.

Soon the room was lit by four twinkling candles. It was nice to smell something other than her sweat and the funk of death. Her bedroom lit, her thoughts went back to what she would do next. Her stomach rumbled, so she dug out a packet of digestives from her limited supplies in her spare bedroom. She was halfway through the packet before she realised she had formulated no plans on whether to stay or risk leaving the house.

She thought of David, living on the most sensible thing a boathouse, during these floods. Hoping he and his new little family were safe and sound. Selena twisted the biscuit packet shut and put it next to her on the bed. Standing up she brushed crumbs off her chest and wandered to the spare room again. It had a view of the front drive and the two houses closest to her on the waterlogged street.

If the back garden was a lake, then the front was a river of water. The low brick wall, with tall black iron spikes, had been washed away by the fast-moving water in places. The power of nature could be shockingly beautiful sometimes. She could see no lights from her neighbours on either side. It could mean they had evacuated to their London residences or country retreats in South Wales. Not that the valleys would be any safer bet than here. But it probably meant the whole street was devoid of electricity. She could not see that being mended while it was still raining. Electricity and water: a lethal combination.

Selena pressed her forehead against the cold glass.

No one loved her.

No one cared enough to check on her or save her.

She was alone in a dark house, with a corpse for company.

Ann wanted to hold her son and daughter in death, but Tony held her back. She wailed, beating at his arms and her own large chest in the process. But he was strong. She blinked out her tears, gaining some vision again. Visions of her daughter slumped against the back wall of the isolation ward. Her legs and arms pointing one way while her head lay at an almost obtuse broken angle side down to the skirting board. She was dead. Beyond dead even to Ann, because half her face was missing. Eaten away by the infection that had claimed half her family already. One eye closed the other staring right at her. It's blue tinge dulled by death, the eyelid and skin around the socket ravaged by the disease that had decimated her family in such a short period of time. Her son Mike lay on his deathbed nearby choked in blood and staring up at the ceiling tiles.

Finally, Tony's arms were too strong for her, and he dragged her backwards along the floor of the ward. Her loose fitting bottoms pulled off her behind and halfway down her thighs. It would have been funny in any other circumstance. Now, it was undignified, but so was death. She pulled her thin hospital trousers up as Tony lifted her under the armpits into a standing position. He did not let go, just in case she collapsed again and maybe because he had lost so much too and wanted to hold onto what he had left.

"I'm so sorry," the woman...*Charlie?* said to them from behind her and her husband.

"We need to get out of this fucking place and find out some bloody answers, find someone in charge and throttle the truth out of them." That was Tony's response, Ann thought. On time. Running as clockwork as Mussolini's trains, a phrase her granddad used to say. Hate, anger, fist and shouting, got him where he was today, she hoped he liked the view.

"Your husband is right," Charlie said, coming into view from behind her, through the blur of her tears. "We need to get out of here, this charnel house and find some answers."

Ann tried to speak, but her voice box was empty. So she nodded instead. Tony guided her in his big arms around, just to see the young mixed-race girl run back into the ward and close the door. She was very pretty, like her daughter had been, her late daughter. Lying dead on the floor behind her. She wanted to run back and kiss her one more time, but she knew it might be a kiss of death to her. Did that matter anymore, wouldn't she rather be dead than live without her kids and grandkids.

Charlie's daughter screamed as the door she was holding was banged open an inch and she had to push with all her might to keep it shut.

"Help me!" Ayesha screamed at Charlie and the large couple beside her. Even though she was distracted by the faceless boy trying to get in, she could see that the couple had found their children, and it wasn't a happy ending. Charlie ran to help her followed by the lumbering hulk of a man. The boy hit the door with such force it surprised Ayesha, knocking her back two strides. Only Charlie crashing into the door beside her stopped the snarling boy from getting in.

"What's out there?" the hulk of a man asked using his hands above their heads to secure the doors. His blue scrubs barely did the job of covering his rotund hairy beer belly and his pits stank to high heaven. Ayesha realised he had said *what*, instead of *who*? He was right, the faceless red thing had once been a boy, but the disease that had taken his skin seemed to have scrambled his brain too.

"A boy with no face or skin, he's gone nuts," Ayesha replied.

"Fuck me old boots, no," the large man moaned as he looked through the round portal window in the door to see what remained of his grandson snarling with lipless teeth up at him.

"What are we going to do Tony?" the large man's wife asked moving closer to them at the door.

"We need to get rid of him and get out of this fucking horror nuthouse," Ayesha suggested in a loud almost squeaky voice for her.

"That's my fucking grandson out there," Tony snarled at her.

"Well I didn't fucking know, did I," Ayesha said in a sulky but sarcastic voice.

"I don't think there is anything of your grandson left out there," Charlie said in a low voice, trying to calm the situation. It was one of her life skills, Ayesha wished she had learnt off her.

"Tony, what are we gonna do?" the wife pleaded with her husband.

"Fuck this for a game of soldiers," Tony said looking around. "Hold the fucking doors." He grunted at Charlie and Ayesha then moved to the nearest bed and began ripping down the blood stained plastic curtain around the bed.

Ayesha yelped as the door banged against her shoulder, but pushed as hard as she could manage to keep the sick feral boy out.

"Ann make yourself useful, gal and dig out some surgical tape from somewhere," Tony barked at his wife, not caring what suffering she must be going through.

Ayesha watched as Ann's head dipped and she moved over to a sink with some cupboards above and below it and searched for what her oaf of a husband was after. The door whacked into her shoulder painfully again. *That's going to leave a bruise,* she thought.

"Got some," Ann said, hurrying back to her husband carrying the tape she had found in a drawer.

Tony stood to his full height of over six foot four and held the plastic out between his outstretched hands. "When I shout now, open the door, and I'll grab him in this and wrap it round him. Ann get ready with the tape to wind round him to keep him and us all safe, right?"

"You sure about this?" Ayesha said, thinking it might not be such a hot idea, but at least her shoulder would get some peace. The boy must be taking a battering himself, running and jumping at the door to get them.

"Got a better idea luv?"

Ayesha shook her head. "Get on with it then."

"One, two, three...now!" Tony shouted. Charlie backpcdalled to the right as Ayesha pulled the ward door open. By a sheer fluke she had timed it right. The faceless boy was on a charge and ran right into the plastic held by his grandfather. Tony wrapped the confused Jayden in the plastic. Before Ann rushed around and around with the wide surgical tape securing the poor struggling boy, as Tony knelt to grapple his legs as she did it. Then when the tape ran out, Tony lifted the plastic wrapped boy and slammed him down on the trolley. He held the struggling red form down. "Somebody strap him down."

Charlie and Ayesha both rushed forwards to strap the faceless boy down on the table as best they could. Ann was clinging to the wall near the doors, emotionally and physically spent.

"Come on let's get the bloody hell out of here," Ayesha cried when the boy was held firm by the straps. She grabbed Charlie's hand and dragged her across to the doors.

Tony looked grim-faced at the thing that had once been his grandson, struggling to bite through the plastic to get to him. He shook his large head and moved around the table and joined Charlie and Ayesha at the open doors. Ayesha peered out into the corridor and was glad to find it was devoid of life.

Tony turned to Ann, "Come on we got to go luv."

His voice sounded almost tender to Ayesha, or Tony's version of tender anyway.

"What about Jayden we can't just leave him here like that," Ann said, not moving.

"Well we can't take him with us like that can we, we need to get out of this hospital and get help for him, medical people and all that. Now, come on." His last three words were barked with malice and laced with threat to Ayesha's ears.

"Left or right Charlie?" she said, squeezing her other mother's hand.

"Right," Charlie said, and they headed off towards some double doors at the end of the corridor.

"Where you two going?" Tony said, too-loudly for safety's sake behind them.

"Find a bloody way out, that okay with you?" Ayesha called back to him as they reached the double doors and slowly pushed them open.

"Suppose," he replied gruffly, obviously used to getting the last word at home. But he wasn't at home with his submissive wife; Ayesha was in-the-house.

"Catch up then bigboy," she said cheekily, as she and Charlie moved through the doors to find a set of lifts or a door to a stairwell.

"Better take the stairs to be safe hun," Charlie suggested as Ayesha pressed the down button in the centre of two lifts. "Don't want to be stuck in a lift now."

"Not with lardy boy eh?"

"What'd you say?" Tony said half dragging his sobbing wife through the double doors to join them.

"No time for a lift party boys and girls, let's take the stairs." Ayesha did not wait for approval. She headed into the stairwell and peered down. It seemed empty and silent enough. She and Charlie began to gingerly head down the steps. Tony paused with Ann behind them, apparently not used to a woman taking the lead.

So when the bashing open of a door above and the mad raging sounds of pursuit hit them, they at least had somewhere to run. Down and around. Fear making them all move faster than they had done in years. Ayesha hadn't run properly since her last school sports day. She had been a fine long-distance runner until she discovered boys and booze. She was flying down the steps like an Olympic sprinter, dragging Charlie behind her. The Gables moving as swiftly as their combined bulk allowed. The thing or things behind them would soon catch them up, Ayesha knew that for a fact. She was just glad she and Charlie were nearly three-quarters of a set of steps ahead of the married couple. She would gladly sacrifice them both if she and Charlie got away scot-free.

CHAPTER FIFTEEN

FIGHT OR FLEE

Hannah couldn't remember ever walking so far in her life. Her feet and calves were burning, and she was soaked through in places, where rain should never reach. Matt hadn't spoken to her for at least fifteen minutes, which was a bonus at least. They were in Surbiton, the iconic suburb of all London commuter belt suburbs.

People were hurrying along under brollies, hats and copies of Metro newspapers over their heads, but not in a panic. Everything seemed normal, day-to-day. News of the happenings at the hospital had not reached here yet. Sure, the roads were like mini rivers, but people were just getting on with their lives. Matt looked at her, the confusion on his face told her he was feeling the same way.

"Let's get a train home then?" he said, wanting to get out of the cold rain and home again.

"Okay," Hannah replied, not sure what else to do instead. She thought there would have been roadblocks, police, army and the sky awash with helicopters, but there was nothing but real life. They hurried into the station, glad to be out of the rain. Matt went to get the tickets from a machine while she stood shivering nearby. A rail worker was trying to mop up the puddles of water on the floors from the leaky roof with little success.

"Got them," Matt said handing over her single to Hersham. She took it with numb fingers and headed up the steps that led up and then down onto the platform they wanted. The rains had caused many problems over the whole of the rail network, but most of the suburban to London lines were high up on embankments and luckily away from the water. Parts of the rail network in Hedge End, Eastleigh, and Southampton in Hampshire had been washed away by mudslides. Their train was delayed by five minutes, but that wasn't too bad considering the atrocious conditions. The carriage floor was slick with water: drippings from coats, shoes, and umbrellas. It was warm, dry and the windows misty inside and rain-washed outside.

They were back at Hersham before they knew it. They hurried down the long steps out of the tiny station and back to dodging the rain again.

"Do you want to go back to your place to pick up some stuff?"

"What?" Hannah replied from under her hood again. The driving rain on the man-made material made it hard to hear what he was saying.

"Do you want to pop back to your house and gather up some dry clothes and stuff, before heading back to my flat?" he repeated, stopping in the rain to turn her towards him.

She hadn't really thought what would happen next. Her grandparents and annoying younger sister were dead like her parents. *Annoying, no more.* The words echoed around her brain. She had nothing but a probably half sunken house by now, full of memories of the dead. She just wanted to lie down on the slick pavement and join them. A large lorry thundered by, spraying them both with even more water. It woke her a little from her grief.

Matt was waving his fist and swearing at the monster of a lorry which was already fading into the grey distance. Then she laughed at the stupidity of his actions. Swearing because a truck had splashed them while they were already soaked down to their skin. And under her skin, a new life was growing; her only remaining blood relative in the world.

"What's so fucking funny?" He passed his anger onto her, giving his sternness teacher voice.

"You are, now let's get back to your place. I don't have a home to go back to anymore."

Bemused he led her to his flat. It was near to the station,

and they could both get dry and take stock of the situation. The clouds above were turning from grey to black. So much so she wasn't sure if it was day or night anymore.

Brita woke suddenly. Her world was bright white light and spinning blue stars. She turned over the edge of the military bunk she was on and vomited up ochre liquid onto a canvas flooring.

"That will be the tranquilizer darts exiting your system the best way it knows how," an unfamiliar female voice said from nearby. Brita couldn't turn around to face the voice, her throwing up had her entire attention for the moment. A metal kidney dish appeared above the pool of sick, a thick gloved hand was holding it. Brita snatched it into her own hands as she heaved up again, glad to have something to throw up in. The result of her heaves soon dried to dry ones and spittle hung from her lips to the metal bowl. She placed the metal dish on the uneven ground and rolled onto her back on the cot. Usings her bare arm to wipe the spittle from her thin lips. Eyes closed against the cramps in her stomach and the harsh lights in her eyes.

She put her left arm over her eyes to shield them and exhaled. "Where the hell am I?"

"You are in a British Army mobile field hospital set up on a rec in Surbiton Surrey, are you a foreign national?" The female voice was slightly muffled.

Brita peeked from under her warm arm to see a woman in a full hazmat suit was kneeling beside the military cot she was lying upon. There seemed to be heavy plastic curtains around her isolated cot. "My name is Brita Mikkelson I'm from Denmark. I was with my girlfriend Eloise Chambers, her mother and a doctor and a nurse from the hospital, where are they?" Brita tried to sit up and look around, but a wave of nausea made her lie down again quickly before she threw up again.

"Yes, the helicopter that brought you in had two women and two medical staff also. I must apologise on behalf of Her Majesties Armed Forces, for the darts used to knock you all out. The men on the ground were faced with a difficult and hostile situation. You should be thankful you weren't shot with live rounds. I will check on your friends though for you." Brita helplessly lay on the bed as the woman unzipped the inside of her plastic isolation chamber.

"Can I ask your name, as you have mine now?" Brita said in a tired voice.

"Corporal Jan Jones, I'm a nurse with the Army Medical Corps. Be assured you are in good hands now and show no symptoms of the virus that infected the hospital." The nurse said in a slightly kinder tone than before.

"I was a corporal in the Royal Danish Army once," Brita murmured before the remaining drugs in her system and exhaustion led her to nod off again.

Selena ate cold meats and other perishable foods for dinner as darkness sank over her two-million-pound home in Walton-on-Thames. She ate by candle light, relishing the simplicity of her life. She had separated her food and drinks into separate piles of what she would take and what she would leave behind. She had plenty of canned food, but realised nearly straight away, that would be the heaviest to carry. So she had a mixture; glad of her addiction to cheese n' onion crisps as they were on the light side to take. She had all her remaining candles, a carving knife, a penknife, matches, waterproofs, and bars of chocolate.

She wasn't sure what she would find outside her gated house, so she prepared for the worst. It was like a biblical flood outside anyway. She would leave a note for the emergency services about the dead tramp in her upstairs guest bedroom. No point being tried for two murders instead of one. She felt sorry for poor Wet, having to leave him all alone in the house in the morning. It wasn't like she could bury him in the garden as it was three feet underwater still. She tried on her backpack, a deep cupboard remnant of a walking holiday she and David once took. It had been fun for the most part, for a soggy English summer. They made a pact to do it again, get near to nature. But her career always seemed to get in the way and the often promised walking holiday never happened again.

The cans she had taken were too near her back and kidney area for comfort, so she had to repack it again. She wrapped her clothes and perishables in plastic bags, for when the rain made it through the backpack lining. She tried it on again, but still she had to delve deep inside to move something pokey from the wrong area. On the third try, she was satisfied by the comfort of the thing. She leant it up against the wall and thought about the water. She had her wellington boots, but the water was thigh high in places she guessed. Bin liners taped around her jeans was the best idea she could work out. Maybe a bin liner with arm and head holes to cover her waterproofs too maybe?

She grabbed two ski poles she had got for a holiday in the Alps with one of her lusty young lawyers. Not that they had done that much skiing at all. Her young buck had wanted sex and champagne day-noon-and-night. She left the holiday sorer than if she had taken a tumble on the piste. She thought they might help keep her balance in the water and check the way ahead underwater. She tried to think of anything else, but nothing new came to mind in the survival stakes. She lay on the bed, watching the constant drumming on the windows of the relentless deluge of rain from the heavens.

She tried to read a bit of Jane Austin but found the candlelight made her eyes water after six pages. She wondered how people coped working or reading by candlelight, it wasn't as romantic an idea as she hoped. She put her book down and took off her reading glasses, rubbing the bridge of her nose. Selena lay back in her soft pillows, wondering where her first port of call should be tomorrow. Probably the nearest police station.

She was asleep before she knew it.

The first thing Ann knew about the attack from behind, was when Tony shoved her staggering down the last two steps of the landing bend of the stairwell. She thought she might go base-over-apex for half a second, but reached out and crashed into the wall to keep herself upright. Her shoulder flared with pain, but it was soon forgotten, and she turned her head in panic to see what was happening behind her.

What remained of a man was trying to claw and bite at her. Her attacker was dressed in a suit, belying the grotesque skull like features of his head and its bloody red hands. Lucky for her she had her husband between her and the raving creature. Tony grunted, pushed the suited man back, but he would not give in. Baring too much-exposed teeth, he launched himself off three steps high at Tony. Tony bent at the knees and caught the man about his groin and collars area. With an angry bellow of effort, he hoisted the suited attacker above his head and slammed him down back first on the interior railing of the stairwell. She heard the suited man's back break as Tony let him roll off and fall to the floor. The Infected suited man flopped down like a caught fish on dry land. His head moved side-to-side like a snapping spaniel, but the impact seemed to have paralysed his arms and legs.

"Fuck me," Tony said staggering down the steps to join Ann. He wiped his blood-stained hands down his scrubs. "What the fucking hell is going on?"

"I don't know, Tone," Ann said. She stopped by a hand wash dispenser on the wall and tugged her husband's arm towards it. "'Ere Tone, use this to sanctify your hands."

"Yeah, good plan, Batman," he mumbled cleansing his hands in the clear gel. His eyes not leaving the broken Infected man lying near them.

"What's going...what-the-fuck," Ayesha exclaimed seeing the broken Infected man lying alive but unmoving on the stairwell landing as she ran back up.

"He attacked us," Ann said, pointing at the teeth chomping man in a smart suit.

"So I took the cunt down!" Tony added.

"Well, no use hanging about, let's get moving. Charlie and I have found a way into a basement area. There are loads of long corridors with pipes running under the hospital, could lead to a way out of here."

"Come on then," Tony said with a determined snarl of his top lip.

Tony reminded her of a Rottweiler one of her fuck-buddy boyfriends once owned. The thing scared the crap out of her but had still been cuter than her short-lived fling with its meathead owner. She skipped back down the stairs while the Gables made more heavy weather of it behind her. Both were huffing and puffing like asthma sufferers forced to do a cross-country run. The basement area was larger than she expected, well-lit with wide corridors big enough to get beds and trolleys along. A lift with a wide set of double doors stood open and empty, next to the stairwell.

Charlie was waiting nervously, holding open the stairwell doors for Ayesha and the Gables. They moved off down the long corridor, glad to be on the move and have a clear line of sight, just in case one of the Infected wanted to attack them again.

"Where the hell are we going?" Tony grumbled when they had made it two-thirds of the way down the long corridor.

"How the hell should I know," Ayesha shot back. "But anywhere far away from those bloody isolation wards is good for this girl." Ayesha could feel Tony building up for some simmering terse reply when there came a wailing sound from the bend twenty feet up ahead. All four of them stopped dead in their tracks. Ayesha could feel goose bumps running up her arms from her hands. A woman with half of the skin of her face missing came running around the bend and slammed into the ochre painted wall with a slight splatting sound. She shook her head, sending bits of her cheeks and nose to join the bloody marks she left on the gloss painted wall. She became aware of the four of them standing watching her with horror. She let out a piercing gurgling scream and pushed off the wall to run at them. She had made it two steps when her right arm, neck, and chest were disintegrated by a hail of defeating machine gun fire. The entire group threw themselves onto the floor, even big scary Tony.

Ayesha lowered her cowering arms to see a man dressed head-to-toe in black with a matching gas mask on, stride around the corner. He was carrying a serious looking machine gun and pointing it at the four of them.

"Who the fuck is next?" The soldier said in a loud distorted, Welsh accent.

Ayesha peed herself for only the second time in the last ten years.

CHAPTER SIXTEEN

ESCAPE PLANS

Hannah counted two ambulances, one fire engine and three police cars streaking past on the busy road from the bedroom window of Matt's flat. She had never been here before, their sex lives ruled by the safety of his car, woods and a local leisure centre changing room once. He would never bring her back here, and now she knew why. She had just had a warming shower—alone thankfully—in his en-suite bathroom. It had two doors connecting to the living area, a spare bedroom, and the kitchen.

She stood naked except for a fluffy (and strangely pink) large bath towel wrapped around her. She was trying to dry her hair with one corner when she spotted the montage of pictures in a cream frame on the wall next to the window. It featured Matt and a very attractive woman in her early twenties. They were on holiday, at a rugby match, at someone else's wedding and then of them at a dinner table, the attractive woman showing off an engagement ring to the camera.

Hannah frowned. *Something you forgot to tell me perhaps Mister Davies?*

Matt was cooking up something hot for dinner. Her sodden clothes lay in a wet pile on the bathroom lino. She wondered if Matt's *fiancée* had any clothes left there to put on. A pair of knickers would be a great start. She wandered over to his wardrobe and slid its mirrored doors open. *Kinky Bastard.*

It was quite tidy inside for a man. Ties on a special pull-out rack, drawers for socks and underwear. She searched through his clothes, but could not find any really suitable for her. She donned one of his white shirts, with a cream collar he had worn on their first date. Date? More like dogging in woods near Hinchley Wood. A quick couple of drinks in a dark pub corner and then fucking in the back of his car; hardly romantic.

She let the towel drop to the floor as she buttoned up the shirt. Her bare arse was getting chilly, she needed something more than this, or he would get the wrong idea. Hannah focused on the clothes problem while other thoughts pressed like a tidal wave to get to the forefront of her mind. She had to keep herself occupied and not think of her grief. If she let that in, she knew she would surely drown in it. She wiped a lone tear from her right eye and then spotted a large red velvet box hidden under a pair of trainers. She moved the trainers and lifted the large box out onto her knees; the other end resting on the inside of the wardrobe. Lifting off the lid to find a pair of handcuffs with fluffy red fur attached to them.

She raised her eyebrows and moved them off. There were clothes underneath, but not normal clothes. She stared at them, realising suddenly what sort of man she had fallen for, what sort of father to her child he would be. She hoped like hell it was a boy. Then a cruel smile crossed her lips, and she lifted the clothes from the box and decided to put them on. If this was what he wanted, maybe she should give it to him. Underneath the clothes were a Polaroid camera and some pictures of Matt's fiancée dressed up and posing in the same clothes in various lewd poses.

Old-school kinky.

She was definitely putting it on, just to see his reaction. *And the knickers are a welcome, dry relief.*

"Do you want some bacon lardons with your breakfast, I think I have some in the fridge somewhere?" Matt Davies asked hearing his bedroom door open. He was bent down under the counter, rooting through his fridge.

"I've been a bad girl Mister Davies and forgotten my home-work, will you discipline me?" Hannah laid on her best approx-imation of a thick sexy voice from the open bedroom doorway.

"Eh? What you on about?" he asked rising to his feet to see

her. Then he realised right away what she was wearing. He felt sick to his stomach, angry, afraid and also had a massive hard-on rising in his pants.

Hannah stood posing at the doorway, one arm up on the frame. She was wearing the secret gear that he sometimes got his fiancée to wear. She had to be a bit drunk to do it, but she saw it as harmless fun in the end. Hannah was dressed in black patent leather flat slip-on shoes, thick tights that went up just over her knees to the near-belt of a black pleated skirt. She wore a white shirt tied at her midriff exposing her belly button and cleavage and had a tiny grey pointless cardi on top. Her hair was in pigtails, just as he liked.

He gulped, his secrets exposed.

"Do you want to fuck me, Mister Davies?" Hannah purred sauntering into the room.

Matt took a gulp of brandy from his nearby glass he was having to warm himsef up and stepped around the counter to meet her in the middle of the living room.

"Yes," he said in a timid voice like all his dreams had suddenly come true at once.

His dreams were shattered by a stinging flat-palm slap to the left side of his face.

"You dirty fucking paedo," Hannah raged at him and stormed off back to his bedroom and slammed the door shut.

Matt rubbed his face and went to follow her, then stopped. His right hand went into his pants to rearrange his erection. It was, even more, iron hard than before. The world was going to shit; her family was all dead. She had no one left, but him, and the pregnancy meant he had a hold over her, an unbreakable connection. He moved over to his front door and locked it up tight, then went back to his cooking. He was feeling ravenous.

Hannah flung herself on the double bed and the floodgates opened. She cried about her situation, then her pregnancy and then her grief. It would be hours before the sobs would subside.

Brita felt a warm hand touch her cheek, which drew her from her bad dream of her childhood and back into the harsh cold, wet world. The tent she was in smelt of mud and damp grass and the electric lights strung about the place were on full and dazzlingly bright. There were grim shadows everywhere, telling her that night had fallen outside.

She sat up to find a smiling Ellie perched on the edge of her cot, smiling at her.

"Glad you are awake and hopefully not feeling pukey?" Ellie her hand still on Brita's face lowered her head and kissed her briefly on the lips. "Could do with a mint, though."

"Thanks," Brita smiled back at her. Glad to see her girlfriend was well and with her again. "Where are we and how is everyone else?"

"I saw the doctor; he is helping the military out with the infection. The nurse has died, though; the infection took him within an hour of arriving. They don't say much, but I think they are all very worried how quickly and deadly this disease spreads." Ellie pressed her lips together, her hands reaching down to grab Brita's.

Her hands were trembling, belying the forced smile on her lips.

"And your mother?"

"Oh god Brita, she has it too now." Brita caught Ellie as she flung herself at her. Tears bursting from her eyes, sobbing into her neck as she clung onto her for grim death. Brita pushed herself into a better sitting posture and wrapped her arms around her girlfriend. Brita felt so sorry for Ellie, knowing the burden grief can lay on oneself, but she had hardly known Mr. & Mrs. Chambers. Her focus was on keeping Ellie safe and well. They were okay for now, and had to stay because of Ellie's mother's condition, but Brita did not feel safe here at all. All the armies and guns in the world could not protect you or the ones you love from death, nothing could. She wanted out of here, as soon as possible. Maybe even take Ellie back to Denmark if that was possible, but she sure the border controls would be very tight now.

"Can we go see your mother?"

Ellie pulled herself back from the embrace. Brita had to resist wiping the side of her damp neck. She dragged the tears from her eyes and cheeks but more came to replace them making it a hopeless task.

"The-they said wer-we are in the non-infected tent and ha-have to stay here." Ellie struggled to say. Brita kissed her tear stained cheeks and then pulled her into a tight hug.

"It will be okay *min elskede*, I will love you and take care of you forever." Brita only hoped that this red infection would let her keep her promises.

Selena woke out of a sudden nightmare gasping for air. She had her fists to her chest, and she fought to control her breathing. The rain was still coming down hard outside, and the candles around her room showed she had been asleep for at least two to three hours.

The terrible dream about Wet coming back to life and appearing red raw and naked in her doorway began to subside. She looked at her bedroom door; it was still closed, as she had left it. Exhaling hard, she swung her legs over the side of the bed and bashed her heel on a hard part of the backpack she had left there.

"Crap," she hissed rubbing the pain away. She let out a deep sigh and stood up anyway. Selena moved across the bedroom floor on tip-toes and rested her hand on the door handle. She unlocked it and pulled it open, just to dispel the silly nightmare she had suffered. The landing outside her master bedroom was empty and full of depressing shadows.

"See, nothing to be scared of," she said aloud to dispel the night.

Selena was about to return to her comfortable bed, when she heard a scuttling noise down the way, near Wet's room. She froze and held her breath. She was rewarded with hearing the sound again, and something like many fingernails scraping on wood somewhere. That was it. Retreating back into her room she grabbed her mobile phone and switched it on. It might not be any good for phone calls, internet or texts, but it had a good torch App on it. After what seemed like ages, it turned on fully so she could put the App on full beam. Satisfied she had enough illumination to investigate, she headed off onto the landing towards her guest bedroom and the source of the noise.

Something slick brushed past her left foot as she moved

towards the doorway of the guest bedroom. She flicked her mobile downwards, catching the darting scurry of movement vanishing into the shadows by the closed door. At first, she thought she must have left the door ajar, but she found it was closed as she approached. Movement caused her to hastily skip back two steps as two giant soggy rats shot past her and through a gnawed hole in the bottom left-hand corner of the door. She put her hand to her mouth and gagged a little. The thought of rats invading her house was abhorrent to her clean living mind. She had no fears or phobias about them, but to have them rushing upstairs and into her sanctuary, just confirmed to her; that her decision to leave in the morning was the correct one.

Three more bedraggled rats hurried up from the ground floor to slip under the ragged gap in the eaten away door. They seemed oblivious to her very presence.

This is my house!

Feeling riled up and mildly disgusted by the presence of vermin in her guest bedroom, she barged into the bedroom and was almost instantly knocked back from the vile, putrid stench coming from the bed. She staggered back to the doorway, as more cold, wet rats hurried over her feet to get to the bed.

Or was it their dining table?

At first, she thought Wet was still alive, and she had misdiagnosed his death. She was wrong in so many ways. The sheet, illuminated in the glare of her mobile phone was half shredded. Poor Wet's face, or what remained of it jerked on loose neck muscles this way and that. Not from any life in his dead body, from the twenty or so rats covering his chest downwards and under the tattered sheet: eating away at the remains of his muscles and internal organs. Wet's body was alive again, with fur, sharp teeth, and long worm-like tails. Selena closed the door and ran to her room. She managed to close and lock her door and then dragged a chest of drawers in front of it, before rushing off to the bathroom to throw up.

Selena spent the rest of the night cross-legged on the middle of her bed, watching her own doorway. She lit all the candles she could find. Her ears straining, sure she could hear the rats chewing down on poor Wet in her guest bedroom, but that was probably her overworked imagination.

She didn't sleep a wink until dawn.

Ann could not believe what she was seeing. A black clad soldier who had just killed one of the deadly red Infected walked up and pointed his automatic rifle at the face of the pretty mixed race girl.

She was sure he was going to shoot her and then probably kill them all for trying to escape the quarantined hospital. Her white mother flung herself over the girl in a desperate attempt to shield her from the weapon's deadly rounds. Ann had fallen on her ample arse and was trying to back pedal, but the worn heels of her white hospital crocs were gaining little traction on the polished basement floor.

"Corporal Young, stand down," a loud posh-voice, echoed down the corridor with an authoritative edge. The black clad soldier dithered for a second and then retreated from the frightened girl and her mother. Three more black-clad soldiers hurried up to join the trigger happy Corporal.

"Are any of you hurt, bitten infected or suffering any effects of the ACTV-7 virus?" The plummy voiced officer-type said to the four of them.

"No," Tony managed to bark back, but the three women just shook their heads.

"Good," the officer nodded. "Now I need you all to lie face down with your hands on your heads while our medics give you the once over. This is merely a precautionary measure. Some of the rather badly infected have tended to get a tad over-aggressive. Hope you understand."

Ann nodded and did what the masked soldier told her to do. It was only then she caught a whiff of urine from the young girl. Poor thing must have wet herself with fear. Ann felt sorry for the her, she was barely holding onto her tight bladder as it was.

Only her Tony did not turn over.

"Look, mate, I was in the fucking army too, what the fuck is going on here?"

Ann closed her eyes and wished he would shut up; he was only making a tense situation worse.

"Then you know how to fucking take orders," another of the black-clad soldiers said, pointing his weapon at her hubby's head. "Now turn over mate, or do I have to make you?"

Tony eyed the deadly automatic rifle so close to his face.

Ann closed her eyes, wishing him to comply.

He turned over and put his big hands on his head. "Like to see you frigging try mate," he muttered as he did so.

"Say something?" interrogated the trigger happy corporal, pointing his weapon at Tony's head also.

One-two-three-four, Ann counted. He did not reply; she was glad her Tony finally had the sense to shut his big fat gob.

"Jennings, check them over," the officer-type ordered, and then he spoke to them all. "Jennings here is our medic and will give you a quick once over. Once you get a preliminary all-clear, we will escort you all single file outside to a waiting helicopter that will take you to a local evac medical station. There you will be thoroughly examined, taken care of by top military medical personnel. Once you are all tested and cleared, you will be set free again. They will have warm, dry clothes and hot meals on the go. So best you follow orders and do as we say when we say it, and we will all get along fine. Understood?"

Ann nodded and managed to say a feeble, "Yes." More than anyone else managed. They were tired, scared and in shock.

"Good, now follow Sergeant Reynolds's lead, and we will all get out of here alive and away onto the chopper to safety. Let's move out please."

The officer and the gung-ho Corporal guarded the way that Ann and the others had come while the medic and Reynolds ushered them single file past the infected dead person, and around the corridor. Ann walked on, her mind blank, just following the orders she was given, like some sort of automaton. A brief burst of weapons fire made them all, even Tony jump. It was not repeated, and the other two soldiers soon caught up to them. They made two lefts and one right, before walking up a short flight of concrete steps. She trudged through some angled doors and into the driving rain and cool night air. They were in some dark car park on the far end of the hospital. A helicopter sat up a slick grass bank, near a low wall seemingly waiting for Ann and the other survivors of the terrors inside Kingston Hospital. Other soldiers in green camouflage took over, escorting them to the waiting helicopter. Ann had always wanted to fly in one, nagging Tony every birthday and Christmas but never getting anywhere. Now she could not think of a worse thing to be walking through the rain towards. She turned to look backwards to see the four black silhouettes of the men who had found them hurry back down into the bowels of the hospital to continue their sweep.

"Hurry up," one of the green masked soldiers grunted. Ann held her over-large bosoms with one arm, as one of the helicopter crew pulled her into the waiting chopper. They were strapped in and up and away in seconds. Leaving the dark remains of the hospital behind and most of her immediate family also. She cried all the way to their destination, missing her trip of a lifetime, as the world zipped past below.

Ayesha had been glad of the rain that soaked them the fifty yards from the exit of the hospital to the waiting chopper. It had at least made the rest of her clothes join in with her soaking wet thighs and crotch area. One of her dreams was to take a helicopter ride. In her imagination, it would have been over the Grand Canyon or Niagara Falls, not a soggy South-West London. It was only when sitting in her wet knickers, under her damp clothes on the fast chopper journey that she wished for her home in Surbiton. And for a while, she thought, that was their destination.

She could see the hill and the nearby church. The helicopter started to descend, raising her vague hopes of a warm bath and her own dry pyjamas, but it was not to be. The helicopter swiftly passed over the brightly lit train station and the rest of the shops on Victoria Road. They flew swiftly over her place of work, towards the dark rows of rain swept houses. Then the helicopter began to descend even lower, and Ayesha was disorientated in the darkness on her exact location. They should be over Victoria Recreation Ground. Yet, instead of dark playing fields, she saw a shanty town of tents and lights everywhere. It wasn't until they landed with a bump on a yellow lit landing zone, and seeing the railway embankment nearby, did she realise that this was the rec.

Then all her thoughts were washed away as the door to the chopper was pulled open by soldiers and rain splattered her only just dry face. She glanced back at Charlie, only to nearly fall from the helicopter doorway as hazmat-suited people, with eye-dazzling lights on their helmets manhandled her from the aircraft.

She went to swear back at them, but a gush of heavy rain choked down her words. She knew they would be drowned out by the rotor blades and helicopter engine anyway. She was cold, damp and urine soaked. Grieving for her lost mother and defeated. The normal Ayesha would have stamped her stilettos and swore until the air turned blue from her profanity. But there was little of that girl left at the moment. She, with Charlie behind her and the little and large couple from the hospital, were escorted—two hazmat soldiers to either arm—through the rain and into the outer tunnel like tent.

The tent was damp underfoot and cold as armed soldiers in different colour hazmat suits ordered them to take off their shoes and socks. The tent was so bright in contrast to the darkness outside, Ayesha's eyes leaked at each corner at the harshness. Nurses in white hazmat suits handed each of the four of them facemasks via tongs, from sterilised boxes and told them to put them on. Not even the large angry Tony, refused, even his thick skull could see the wisdom of protecting himself from the deadly flesh-eating bug. They were suddenly each unceremoniously sprayed down with a fine watery looking, but not smelling, liquid from bottles strapped to two of the hazmat medical team's backs.

Then before they could protest were herded into two separate zip sealed tunnels ahead of them. The fat woman tried to go with her husband to the right-hand tunnel but was ordered to go with Ayesha and Charlie. She screamed about her *human rights*, but automatic weapons pointed at her and her husband's heads, soon ruled them defunct. Armed hazmat wearing soldiers ushered them into the separate male and female tunnels, where two women in hazmat suits awaited their arrival. What also awaited them was what looked to Ayesha like a sunken blue kiddie's paddling pool, covered with something from a carwash. Clear plastic boxes were situated on the near side and other boxes on the other end of the pool, and another armed guard.

"Please strip off all clothing and jewellery and put them in the boxes provided. You have one each. They will be decontaminated and returned to you when safe to do so." The nearest nurse in a white suit said through a speaker system attached to the side of her suit's helmet.

The three women looked at each other warily, united in fear and grief.

"Strip please, or we will do it for you." the nurse said. There was much more of a warning to her words.

The three women looked at each other again. Their recent losses; the cold and dampness of their clothes had taken all the fight from them temporarily. Ayesha started first; thinking dry, non-urine soaked clothes might not be such a bad thing. Charlie followed and then the other woman: Ann? She had little to strip off out of her hospital scrubs, but the most to hide. She was a real beached white whale of a woman. Ayesha would offer her a free tan at the salon after this was all over. She had never seen a white woman with such a big arse and drooping belly before. Her breasts were like sacks of flesh which she tried to cover, without much success they were so big. Only good thing was her big fat belly hid her ladybush from sight. Her tattooed upper arms, wrist and ankles doing her body image no favours.

Ayesha stripped off quickly, not afraid to be naked. She knew she had a banging toned body, with near perfect skin. She would always seek out any nudist beaches on her frequent holidays in the sun. Ayesha had trouble peeling her jeans and underwear off, leaving marks on the inside of her thighs.

Charlie was the most indignant and last to undress. Her skin nearly as pale as Ann's to her ginger hair, Ayesha had no idea she shaved her haven, though. With rings, earrings and bracelets following their clothes into the boxes.

"Step into the decontamination area, please. This is for your own safety and the safety of others in the camps to help fight the contagion." The nearest white suited nurse said

As they were all three buck naked, nothing could really get any worse so together they stepped into the ankle deep hospital smelling liquid. Ayesha winced at the cold, goose bumps mounting the ones she already had.

"Please close your mouthes and eyes and breathe normally as you can through your nose. Extend your arms outwards horizontally like this and stand with your legs a foot apart." The nurse on the other side with a Cornish accent ordered and demonstrated the stance she wanted them to assume.

Exposing breasts and lady parts for all to see was hard, even for Ayesha. Then the icy cold spray hit her from above and the side, taking all the breath from her lungs. All three of them yelped with the cold, as it hit them. It was worse than any cold beach shower Ayesha had ever used.

"Turn around please," the Cornish nurse said.

Ayesha did as she asked. Lips and eyes closed tightly shut. The sterilising liquid hitting her skin smelt like something you'd put down the sink to unblock it. It would ruin her moistening regime, she idly thought. The temperature changed, feeling a little less cold as water was jetting onto her body at a higher velocity.

"Please move forwards out of the decontamination area. Use the towels provided to dry yourselves before dressing. All towels must be placed in the red bins after use."

Ayesha hurried from the pool. Glad to be drying herself off. She felt like she had just been caught skinny-dipping after breaking into the YMCA swimming pool late at night. Their new clothes were papery plastic stretch pants, a white sports type bra and blue shirts and trousers and matching crocs. Ayesha was glad to be out of the rain, glad to be out of the pool, and happy to be in dry clothes; but the crocs would haunt her fashion sense for a long time to come. They were given new masks to put on and led through another airlock into a huge well-lit and humid, damp smelling place. Tony re-joined them, Ann glad to see her husband safe after their recent losses.

What waited for them were examination tables like the ones she had been strapped down to in the hospital. Medical staff in white hazmat suits, two to each bed awaiting them. Before Ayesha could even think of turning and running, something metal and solid was prodded into her spine. Two soldiers in green hazmat suits had passed behind them as they entered the vast hospital tent. Ayesha didn't need to look to know what it was, as the soldiers ushered the four of them to the waiting examination tables.

CHAPTER SEVENTEEN

FLESH AND BLOOD

Hannah silently cursed her rumbling tummy.

It had forced her out of his bedroom, still dressed in the fantasy schoolgirl gear he had his fiancée wear. She wondered if she liked it, or just did it to keep him happy. Thinking it was harmless fun and he wasn't really grooming and banging schoolgirls in real life. She pulled his oversized dressing gown over the schoolgirl fantasy clothes, as she could find little else in his wardrobe that would fit her.

He had apologised until her hunger pains nearly made her throw up for real. But she was eating for two now, and the little kidney bean inside her needed energy. She wolfed down the dinner he had reheated in the microwave for her. She said nothing, trying to drown out his endless *sorrys* with the sound of her mastication. Hannah drank his coke and ate his food and carried his baby, she just didn't want to listen to his mock-adult shit anymore. She had little choice at the moment but to share his flat and food, she had nowhere else to go at the moment. Even if she inherited her grandparents' house after this, what watery state would it be in? Surely she would be taken into care and not left alone to bring up her baby in that empty house. She wasn't even sure she could go back in there, knowing that her grandparents and sister were dead. All their things, smells, and memories would be there. She never felt more alone since her father died. Dropping her fork onto the near empty plate she began to sob for her lost loved ones. Hannah heard him move and felt him kneel down and wrap his arms around her. She resisted for a second and then gave in. He was alive and better than being utterly alone with the emptiness she felt in her heart. She let him pick her up and take her to bed. And in the dark naked hours, she let him make love to her again. Just to feel life again and not wallow in death and despair.

It's not like I can get double-pregnant, she thought as he finished inside her.

The nurse with the armed guard would not let them past a certain point in what Ellie dubbed *'the clean tent.'* She and the guard held them at bay so they could only glimpse the outside world. It was still raining, but not that heavily. Brita could see the whole encampment was built on wooden cargo pallets. They were under the tents, raising them off the saturated grass below, with boards over them. More pallets ran like paths through the muddy and submerged grass. It looked like a war zone out here rather than a recreational area for kiddies to run around care-free and for adults to play football and cricket, depending on the time of year.

They could see soldiers in and out of hazmat clothes, hurrying this way and that. The hospital shanty town took up most of the rec. The pavilion was in the middle of two grassy playing fields, doubling as the company HQ. She could hear the barking of orders and the incoming roar of helicopters nearby. It brought back her time in the army. Mostly fond memories, where she had learnt to control and channel her anger into positive ways.

Ellie was in a terrible state, demanding to see her ill mother. Brita could understand this, but she also understood why the nurse and soldier stopped them. This deadly red virus or infection had to be contained somehow. The hospital quarantine had been an unmitigated disaster. Brita was sure the British Government and famed NHS had certain contingencies in place for such an outbreak, just not for the patients to refuse to die and start killing the living. Brita tried to console her as much as her own stunted emotions would allow. She had no family and no ties, only Ellie and she was suffering her father's loss and the impending loss of her mother too. Brita had yet to see anyone infected with the red death recover. They mainly died, or if not became some savage skinless creature hell-bent on infecting and killing others.

She hugged Ellie, said soothing words she thought Ellie would like to hear, not really believing in them herself. She told her lover that her mother was strong and would be okay, but in reality thought she was a corpse waiting to happen. She felt no emotion about Mrs. Chamber dying or her husband for that fact. They were nothing to her; only because of Ellie did their deaths matter.

The mobile hospital was filling up fast. Helicopters were buzzing overhead and others landing unseen behind their tent. The whole place outside lit up like a fairyland ride at some Disney resort. Generator fueled lights were strung up on either side of the pallet roads to give the poor squaddies, doctors and nurses light to work as they hurried through the mud and rain.

It was after seven in the dark morning when a surgeon-major came to tell Ellie that her mother should be clinically dead, just could not technically acknowledge this fact by lying down and dying.

Selena, with an aching back, gingerly got out of bed. Some sort of grey dawn had come at last outside. The rain had eased to a pitter-patter on the windows. She never felt less like leaving her bed, since she had the flu last winter.

She knew she had to go. Her once beloved show-home had been compromised badly. How long would it be before the water born rats finished feasting on Wet and turn on living flesh? The thought of it brought her stumbling on pins-and-needles stricken legs to the en-suite to throw up. She wearily cleaned her teeth and used her mouthwash to take the taste of sick from her mouth, then popped both in her survival back-pack. Selena drank a can of coke, that she was leaving behind, but couldn't stomach anything to eat. She put on her wellies and then bin liners over them and taped them around her legs with black tape. She put two bin liners over her backpack and found a large floppy cricket hat she had worn to Lords. She had been a guest in a corporate box, she could no longer recall the name of the person or company who had invited her. She got the hat to keep the sun off her face. Armed with her ski poles, she headed onto the landing. Pulling on her gloves, she felt more like an astronaut than a judge ready to leave her sinking home to the rats and the water. The daylight showed no signs of her rodent invaders. Breathing through her mouth only, she descended the stairs into the cold, murky water waiting for her.

This was no descending into a sun warmed pool on a sunny holiday, nor even getting into a cold river for a moonlight swim. The water was muddy brown and stank like rotted boiled cabbage. Debris of her privileged life floated on the surface, with the dead rats, green foamy scum, and flotsam from the rear garden. She shivered as her body lost warmth as she went step-by-step deeper into the water that had invaded her home.

"Ugh," she said, with disgust as another dead rat with bloated guts bobbed into her. Then she slipped on the carpet below her less than steady wellies. She managed to grab onto the banister for dear-life and stop herself going fully under. The thought of swallowing the tainted water scared her more than her little trip. She steadied herself and using the banister, descended into the icy water that hovered around her midriff.

Using the ski poles in both hands, she made it across the hall to her front door. Then she felt it, all her protection, wellies, and bin liners had failed. Cold waters seeped into her socks and underwear; chilling her core temperature even more. She could do nothing, but struggle on. Putting both ski poles in her left hand, she reached out to unlock the door. Then tried to pull the door inwards. It would not budge. Gallons of dirty flood water stood on either side, preventing her from pulling it inwards, even a millimetre.

"Let me fucking out," she hissed at the door.

Selena turned to look down the hallway, pondering her options. She could go out through the open back door, round the side gate. Or the easier option might be to clamber out one of the downstairs bay windows. Selena chose the window option. The dining room one was nearest. Its side windows were large enough for her to scramble through with her pack. She trudged on through the water that soaked her from the belly button downwards and made for the window. The bay was just an inch above the water level, so she unlocked and flung the side window out as far as it could go on its hinges. Getting onto the bay and her legs through was easy enough. The passage through the rose beds was muddy and painful. Her pack caught on every jutting out piece of window, latch and catch before snagging in a pink rose bush. Eventually, she was through, out of the mud and onto her curved drive. It was easier going, heading for her gate. The world outside seemed even more silent than the dead house that she had just left. It was, or had been before the non-stop rain, a quiet, prosperous suburban private road. Now, there were no sounds, no signs of life.

Glad to have left her house behind, though feeling a little unnerved by the lack of life around her; Selena pressed on through her open gate and into the real world again. The rain on her hood and the lake of water that once was the private road, made her stop in her tracks. It didn't seem like the same road that she had driven into only a few days ago, with the blood of an innocent cyclist on the bumper.

She guessed where the road would be, from the position of two large elms that had stood there for three hundred years apiece, and pressed on through the floodwaters, in search of life.

Ann felt like a pin-cushion after the doctors and medics were finished with her. She hissed as she rolled down her sleeve over the pulling plaster that covered the crook of her inner elbow joint. It was the same on the other side too. Tony nor the mother and daughter brought in had faired any better. Tony had shouted and threatened a bit, but grief and fatigue had sapped his strength.

After an anxious hour's wait, where they were kept apart, all four of them had been given the all clear. Only then could she and Tony hug and console each other. Her tired, aching eyes seemed to have run dry of tears for the time-being. Tony and Charlie had tried to get answers from the military medical staff, but apart from the all-clear and that they were taking them to a tent for the non-infected, they got little out of them, but vague, evasive answers.

The light of morning outside was a shock. It was still dull grey, but the rain seemed to have lightened. The pallet paths underfoot seemed to be half-floating in watery mud as they were led across the mobile military hospital's temporary base on the rec. The cricket pavilion in the centre had been taken over as a headquarters, and the concrete tennis courts turned into helicopter pads. There were hundreds of displaced, and military personnel everywhere. Helicopters buzzed the base and were landing with more refugees of the flood and red death virus.

They were shown through into a tent with a double entrance. They had to walk through a half inch trough of disinfectant before they could enter the inner part of the large green tent. Beds had been set up in two rows four feet apart, running down each side of the oblong tent. If this was the uninfected tent, it did not fill Ann with any confidence. It was nearly empty. Out of the twenty available military cots, only three were occupied. A couple of pretty girls in their twenties were holding onto each other lying on one cot. One was sobbing silently and the other trying to soothe whatever loss she had suffered. At the far end of the tent lay a man with one of those trendy bushy beards. He had his arms crossed over his face and seemed asleep.

"Are we allocated a certain bunk?" Charlie asked behind her.

"Take anyone you like," said their soldier escort in a tired voice, before she zipped them inside and left them to it.

Ann looked through the clear plastic that separated them from the military hospital personnel and then down the line of basic looking bunks. *Hope they can take my weight,* was her only thought as she picked the nearest one to the ante-chamber entrance. She sat on the bed; it sunk very low but did not give. Tony took the cot next to her and sat down. His elbows went to his knees, as his big hands pushed through his hair and then stayed there. Ann had never seen her husband so quiet and defeated looking in all their turbulent years together. He just stared at the ground, unmoving.

Ann wanted to comfort him but had no energy left at all. So she lay down on the cot and curled up into a ball, and tried to find out if sleep could take her from her living nightmare of loss.

Ayesha moved down the large tent, one cot away from the huddled up entwined girls, who seemed only a couple of years older than her. They both looked very attractive in each different ways. One was pale white of skin, with natural blonde hair and athletic of build. The other had more feminine curves and softer features. With regular everyday clothes and makeup, they could nearly be a match for her looks. But no one in this tent was winning beauty pageants today. Not with the blue and green scrubs, croc shoes and zero make-up. She could kill for a nail file and cuticle stick.

She sat on her bunk, which dipped lower than expected. Charlie kissed the top of her frizzy hair and sat down beside her, making the bunk sink even lower. Ayesha was glad she did not have a mirror at the moment. She didn't look too bad without make-up. No man had ever seen her without eyeliner on, though. It was her hair that concerned her most, it must look like she had been tasered. She tried to lick her fingers and damp it down like she was a cat, but it felt stiff like wire and unruly. She pushed, and combed with her fingers, tried to dampen it down but nothing was working.

"Fucking hair," she hissed, trying manically to get her hair under control. If she could do that one thing, just that one thing, she might get some grasp on the situation. She had to control something but was failing badly.

Ayesha felt the cool gentle hands of Charlie grab hers. She took them from her head and pulled them firmly down into her lap. She was shocked to see strands of her own hair caught under her broken and chipped nails. Ayesha felt herself rocking to-and-throw, the state of her nails and hair making her cry. She knew deep down these were just surface problems she was focusing on, so she didn't have to face the greater hurt in her heart.

"Look at my nails," she blubbed, showing them to Charlie.

Charlie just ignored her and pulled her tight into her body. Both of them were sobbing. Rocking each other back and forth in collective grief. They had both lost the best thing in their lives and could do nothing about it.

The man at the far end of the tent suddenly sat up. The top half of his face from forehead to his upper lip was just one mass of fleshless red. His lidless orbs fixed on the others in the tent and he let forth a raging roar of hunger.

CHAPTER EIGHTEEN

NOWHERE IS SAFE

Hannah crept out of Matt's bed and into his bathroom. She peed and flushed, wondering if her life would be easier if her baby went the same way as her urine. The light through the frosted small window showed it was dawn at least. The rain was still coming down, but with less force than yesterday.

She touched her bare belly and wondered how long before her pubes and then feet would disappear from sight. She wanted to look out on the new morning but didn't want to wake Matt up. She had enough dealing with the baby inside her, let alone having an adult man-child to mollycoddle. She took the second door out into the main living/kitchen area of the flat and went across the room to quietly twist the blinds so she could see outside. Whereas the bedroom window looked over the road by the station, the living room one looked inwards into the gated communal parking area for the people that owned the flats. The rain wasn't too heavy, but it was still a dull grey wet world outside.

Would that ever change? she thought to herself. She could see a few lights on in some of the other flats, but no signs of life. A shiver ran through her and looking down at the goose bumps on her body, she knew she needed to get dressed. She turned away when movement caught her peripheral vision. She turned back, thinking she had seen someone moving down there in the rain. Something red hurried from behind a small parked van to behind a pink mini. Hannah crossed her chest with one arm, before opening the gap wider in the blinds with her other to get a better look.

A bald man with a scary odd looking red face and hands under his dark, sodden clothes jumped onto the bonnet of the Mini and looked directly up at her. His primal cry of rage scared her back to the side of the window, with a squeak of shock. She pressed her bare back against the wall and fumbled the blinds shut. Then hurried over to where her clothes were on a white plastic airer next to a radiator. Her knickers, socks, and bra, were dry, so she pulled them on quickly. The trousers and top were a little damp feeling at the extremities, but she tugged them on anyway. It was either that or Matt's paedo schoolgirl outfit again.

She went to the kitchen, grabbed a wine glass from last night and filled it with tap water and drank it all down in four gulps. Her shoes had been on top of the radiator and were warm inside as she put them on sitting on the sofa. She needed more clothes, she needed to get away from Matt and the crazy situation she had found herself in. Grabbing her coat, Hannah unlocked the front door quietly and tiptoed outside. It was only when she closed the door behind her did she realise that she was not alone.

Down two flights of steps in the communal hallway, the bald red face infected man was looking up at her with ravenous bulging eyes. The red-faced man began to ascend the steps slowly after her, like a lion stalking its prey. Hannah shrieked and began banging and kicking the door to Matt's flat with all her terrified might.

Brita looked up as the infected man got up from his cot and rolled off her bunk with Ellie still in her arms. They grunted as they hit the floor, with Brita rolling on top to protect her lover. "Stay down," she ordered Ellie.

"Guard," the large, tall new man of the tent cried out as he got up and balled his fists.

The two other women cried out in fright and ran down the centre aisle to try and get out of the tent. Brita grabbed the next vacant bunk along and picked it up at one end. It was bulky, but not heavy and she rested it on her hip as the infected half-faced man charged at her. She had one shot at this. She charged at him to gain some momentum. The end of the bunk hit the half-faced man in the stomach winding him, and Brita pressed her advantage pushing him a couple of steps backwards. Then raging at her, with the flesh peeling from his face in strips he gained his footing and pushed back. Brita staggered and felt she was going down before the man mountain from the other cot grabbed the bunk from her and pushed the infected man back to the side of the tent. The half-faced man toppled backwards, and Brita got to her feet where the bulky man had brushed her aside.

The infected man was up again, as the big man used his great strength to wield the bunk like a club and hit his opponent on the side of the cheek sending more disease ravaged flesh from his face. The infected man sprang at the big man again, knocking the bunk aside. Brita was quicker and kicked at the infected man's nearest knee sending him tumbling sideways. She and the large man retreated, as the half-face man rose once again.

A shot rang out, making Brita cringe down into her body. The infected man's red face exploded, and he fell to the floor with the top of his skull missing. Brita and the large man turned to thank the soldier. He was incredibly young looking under his combat gear. Pink of cheeks, too red lips quivering nervously. This had been the first time he had fired his rifle in action. Brita bet he never thought it would be on home soil, killing a fellow countryman.

Brita rushed over to help Ellie to her feet.

Outside the tent, screams of pain and fear suddenly erupted in the drizzle filled world.

Selena almost slipped on some unseen underwater obstacle. Lucky for her the closed white gates that showed the poor riff-raff that this was a rich person's road and not to be entered, was close enough to grab. Selena hung onto the white gate and laughed inwardly. It may have kept the odd hawker or gypsy trying to sell you a new driveway from coming in, but it couldn't stop the biblical flood.

The main road ahead that led between Hersham and Walton-on-Thames town centre was underwater, but the water was not as high as her own road. With every step, she rose out of the muddy, watery mire until it was only knee deep on where she recalled the pavement was. She looked around, suddenly wondering what the hell she was going to do. The place seemed devoid of people, cars and the normal sounds of life in the suburbs. It was still raining, but less than before.

She looked left and right down each long road, wondering which way to go.

"Train station," her cold, wet lips muttered. She needed to get out of Surrey. Go somewhere higher, or abroad maybe. So she turned right heading for Walton train station. The water was freezing, and her calves and thighs were aching, after only a couple hundred yards of wading. She was only just around the corner of the *Halfway* crossroads, heading up the road to the station when she heard the screaming. A teenage girl came running, falling and splashing across the small park area, where the Halfway pub had once stood but had been demolished years ago. She had on jeans, a bra and the ragged remains of a once white top on. Selena wondered what the cause of her screaming and flight was, and then she saw. The poor girl was being chased.

A figure with all its flesh stripped away was chasing her through the flooded park. It had no hair; lips, nose or eyelids, and the red gore beneath gave it a look of a Japanese Demon Selena had once seen at an art gallery in Tokyo. The girl saw her standing there and with pleading eyes turned her flight towards Selena.

Selena panicked. Wondering what she had in her rucksack to defend herself and the girl. Then the poor teen tripped and went under the dirty flood water. She came up coughing and retching, her long brown hair a bedraggled mess.

"Look out!" Selena went to cry, but no words came out of her mouth.

The creature, which Selena guessed as a female, fell upon the screaming girl and dragged her under the water again. Selena watched the thrashing of the water and then nothing, but blood rising to the surface to form a watery grave for the girl.

Selena ran as fast as her legs and the water allowed. She

didn't stop until she reached the trains station. It was closed. She beat upon the sign laminated and pinned to the doors:

South West Trains would like to apologise for the closure of this train station at this current time due to the unusual amount of rain, causing parts of the track to become flooded overnight and unsafe for train journeys. Please check our website or call the number listed below for further details and updates.

Selena checked the taxi shed and other shops nearby, but they were all dark, closed, and empty inside. Then she heard the sound of voices coming from the strange round shaped church across the flooded road. Voices were singing inside. She waded across the road, keeping an eye out for the red murderous creature. She saw her/it or something like her, halfway between where the girl was attacked and the station. She hurried through a double metal archway to the glass doors of the church, which were half covered in protective sandbags. The water seemed only ankle height here. She hammered on the glass and wood hoping someone might hear her over the singing and before the red creature reached her.

"Fuck," Ann said, gulping down some air quickly to stop her throwing up.

"Right, we ain't fucking stopping in here, we are going fucking home," Tony bellowed. He took Ann's arm and frogmarched her past the stunned soldier. Behind Ann, the other women followed after them.

A terrified woman's scream halted them in their tracks in the anti-chamber at the front of the hospital tent. The group stopped behind Tony's large frame. Ann peeked back at the soldier. He was sitting on a bunk, sobbing to himself inside his yellow suit. He was *no use to man nor beast*. Tony reached forward to unzip the tent, as he did an officer in an RAF uniform fell inside holding his neck. Blood was pouring from a gaping wound there.

Ann knelt and gathered his head to her lap.

"The site has been compromised, save yourself," he said coughing up dark looking blood.

"Where do we go?" Ann pleaded with the RAF man, but

his breathing had stopped, and his blue eyes stared up at her blankly.

"We are going home, that's where we are going," Tony said grabbing her arm and pulling her up. The dead RAF officer's head slid to the floor, as her husband pulled her from the tent. The other four women followed after. Nowhere was safe it seemed, from the red death. The military hospital site was in chaos. Patients and military staff were running in all directions. Tony led Ann through the rain across the planks heading for a path on the far side of the rec.

Their attention was taken by a helicopter lifting up from the tennis court pads. But something was very wrong with it. They saw a movement of red inside, the whole thing yawed over to the left, its rotors hitting some poles of a nearby tent. The deadly blades hit the path and a drinks fountain nearby sending a blade slicing through two soldiers wrestling with a red-faced man. All three vanished in a spray of red and were gone. The helicopter crashed through two more tents before exploding against the side of the cricket pavilion, sending flames, bodies, and metal into the air.

"Peg it!" Ann yelled and this time dragged her shocked husband towards the path. They ran between two tents to reach it. The other women following after Ann and Tony, thinking they had some sort of escape path and not just a primal urged to run away as fast as they could.

Ann let go of Tony so they could fit through the gap. It was not lost on her, that two slim people could have walked through the gap easily. She and her Tony were not slim people.

A soldier with a red face under his helmet appeared before Ann. In an effort to stop, her feet went from under her and fell on her arse in the muddy grass.

"Fuck off," Tony yelled, punching the soldier on the chin strap. The infected soldier bit off the tip of its own tongue as the punch shattered its jaw in three places and sent it down on the floor in an unconscious heap. Tony charged ahead, leaving the mother and daughter from the hospital to help Ann to her feet. They hurried after Tony, five women in a scared group in the chaos of the emergency hospital site.

They reached the path that led around the far side of the rec by a chain linked fence that backed onto a railway embankment. The fire was spreading from the pavilion area back through the tents to the tennis court, fueled by the crashed helicopter and in spite of the drizzle. Down the other side of the paths, three soldiers were just shooting anything that seemed to move: the infected, the uninfected and fellow military personnel alike.

They looked around for any means of escape, but it looked bleak.

"This friggin way, come on Charlie," Ayesha said above the mayhem, and gently led her second mum by the hand towards the chain linked fence.

"We can't get up there," Tony shouted, pointing up the steep, wet and slippery railway embankment.

"Watch and learn mate," she said and scrambled up and over the fence with youthful ease.

"Where the hell are you going?" Tony shouted at her over the din.

"The Gates of Hell," she replied with a smirk. "Come on Charlie."

Charlie, knowing what her step-daughter was on about clambered a little less agilely over the fence after her. Tony and Ann exchanged worried glances, screams of pain and death brought them closer to the fence, but they both weren't built for climbing. A soldier shedding his hazmat suit ran up to them shouting, "We've got to get the hell out of here!"

He threw his rifle over the fence, kicked off the last of his suit and joined Charlie and Ayesha on the other side.

"I ain't getting over there," Ann said to her husband.

"Yes, you fucking are." He picked her up in his arms, bringing her weighty body to his chest, and then lifted her legs up over the top of the chain linked fence. Ayesha, Charlie, and the soldier ran over to woman-handle her over the other side. They all fell in a wet heap into a bush, with no significant injuries.

Ayesha helped everyone up and then rushed to the fence, to usher the rest of them over. Tony, who was huge, was looking for another way over. While the two other women from their tent were staring at a woman not more than ten metres away from them. Ayesha saw one of them scream, as the woman they were so intent on staring at, turned, revealing she had only half a face. The rest was red skinless gore, with a lidless eye that made her look like some superhero film villain.

"Run," Ayesha screamed at them.

"Run where? Where are we going now?" The soldier shouted in her face as he grabbed her and spun her around.

"In there, you dick!" Ayesha pointed through the bushes and trees to a dark railway arch that ran under the embankment above. "The Gates of Hell."

CHAPTER NINETEEN

ESCAPE FROM HELL

Hannah had nowhere to run. So she turned and hammered on Matt's front door with her fists. She glanced back over her shoulder to see the bald skinless man creeping up the stairs towards her. She rang the doorbell while kicking at the bottom of the door. "Matt open the door!"

She looked back again, and her voice turned to a whimper. The infected man was halfway up the second flight of steps. His lipless mouth opened and blood drooled out from over his teeth. Hannah pressed herself back against the door, as he took another step nearer. He roared at her, and she squealed in surprise as the door opened and she fell past the surprised Matt, rolled to the side and help kick the door shut. Matt had seen the infected man too and slammed the door closed, before locking and bolting it.

The infected man crashed into it from the other side making it judder in its frame and scared Matt from pressing it shut. It held, two more attempts of the infected man shoulder barging it before it went silent outside.

"Do something," Hannah urged the father of her unborn child.

"Shit. Right." Matt dressed only in his boxers and socks grabbed his coffee table and put that in front of the door. Hannah had never seen such a pathetic attempt at a barricade in all her life.

"Is that it?" Hannah pushed herself off the floor and retreated from the door.

"Well, you do better," Matt said back to her, in a whiney voice.

What had she ever seen in him? "Get dressed, we need another way out of here."

"There isn't another way out of here, that's the only door," he said, reverting to sarcastic teacher talking to a dumb teen mode.

"Then we'll make a rope out of bedsheets and climb out the bloody window then," Hannah shouted at him. This brought primal screams of rage and more hammering on the other side of the front door. Both of them shut up and ran back into Matt's bedroom. Hannah pulled a dresser across the bedroom door as her older lover got dressed quickly. She looked at the twisted sheets of the bed, deeply regretting letting him fuck her last night. Then grabbed the top and bottom sheets and rushed over to open the bedroom window. The drizzle hit her face as she pushed the window wide open and peered down. It didn't seem that far a drop down and with the sheets, it should be a doddle. The infected man crashing against the flat's front door spurred her into action.

She knotted the top and fitted bottom sheets together and pulled it tight. Opening up the small top fanlight and tied it with two knots onto the centre window frame. She pulled it leaning back, as Matt laced up his trainers. A crash sounded the alarm that the front door had surrendered to the infected man's vicious onslaught.

"Hannah, quickly," Matt whispered, ushering her towards the open window.

At least he was gentleman enough to let the women and children go first, Hannah thought as she climbed onto the windowsill. The drop down into the front garden of the flats suddenly looked daunting. She had no time to *dilly-dally*, as her old Nan used to say. The grass below was covered in water so it would be a soft landing. Shutting out thoughts of deranged men and her dead Nan, she wiggled around and pushed her bum off the window frame, holding onto the makeshift rope. It gave a few heart-stopping centimetres, as the knots tightened but held. She lowered herself down the side of the brick building, using her feet to walk down as much as possible. She slipped the last metre, landing shin deep in muddy water.

Matt wasn't so lucky with his exit. She heard a crash above and then her teacher come jumping out of the sky over her, landing with a roll through the muddy underwater garden.

"You okay?" She hurried over to him and helped him to his feet.

"Yeah," he said in a shaken voice. "Think so."

A roar from the window above saw the infected man bellow down at them.

"Come on, let's get the hell out of here," Hannah urged dragging him up and towards the gate that led to the pavement and road by the station.

Brita had tried to pull Ellie towards the chain linked fence, but she had stopped in her tracks for some reason.

"Mum?"

Brita turned to see Mrs. Chambers standing side onwards to them not more than a few metres away.

"Mum," Ellie shouted again over the smoke, chaos and commotion.

Mrs. Chambers turned towards her daughter then, causing Ellie and Brita to cry out in shock together. The other half of Ellie's mother's face had been eaten away by the disease. Ellie screamed and cried out at once as her mother turned and with a look of evil hunger on her face, rushed towards them. Ellie gave up her stance and bladder at the same time, letting Brita drag her towards the chain linked fence. Brita knew they would reach it first, but had no time to climb it before Mrs. Chambers could reach them. She flung Ellie at the fence and turned to face their pursuer. The remaining good parts of Mrs. Chambers face exploded as the sounds of the shots echoed in Brita's ears. She fell into a puddle by the path Brita was on and sunk under the water.

"Nooo," Ellie cried, hanging onto the fence with her fingers as her legs gave way under her. Behind the fence, the soldier lowered his rifle and nodded at Brita. She nodded back and hurried over to her lover. Ellie collapsed to the sodden ground.

Next to her, the large man was pulling at the fence next to a concrete pole. Brita watched as she crouched by the wet sobbing Ellie, as he pulled it from the post to make a gap for them all to slip under.

"Mum," Ellie sobbed. Brita knew that there was a time and place to grieve, and it was most definitely not now. The large man held up the fence, and Brita pulled and scrambled through with Ellie, mostly on her soaking behind. The scrubs they had been given were useless in keeping out the wet and cold. The large man somehow forced himself under the fence, with his wife coming to his aid to help pull him. Once through, he used a snapped branch to pin the fence down below the water line to make it look like it was still intact. The hospital camp was descending into utter chaos, nearly all military decorum had gone. Most of the personnel were medical staff or Reservists.

Brita, with the help of the large man, pulled Ellie to her feet and helped her towards a dark, overgrown tunnel under the railway embankment, the rest of the group were moving into. Even though it was morning, the dark skies overhead, the constant drizzle, and the overhanging trees and bushes around the tunnel entrance made it look dark and foreboding. The large wife hugged her tall, huge husband and went inside the tunnel. Brita had her arm around Ellie, her other hand over her eyes leading her inside after the others.

The arched brick walls of the tunnel were dark and slimy wet. She could see the shapes of the other people in the group bunched up in a crowd and wondered what was going on. A torch, held by the soldier clicked on to reveal a bricked up wall ahead of them blocking their escape.

"It's a dead end," the soldier snapped at the pretty teenager who had urged them inside. Brita hoped for Ellie and all their sakes that the girl had another plan up her scrubs sleeves.

Selena's hammering on the doors had produced two things. A black man in a suit and a white woman in a garish green floral dress appeared at the glass doorway. The second effect was a red dripping wet creature had emerged from the waterlogged subway under the train station and was heading across the road towards her. It's features were even worse than the creature coming up the road towards her. It looked like a woman made of red wax that had been half melted away.

Selena banged on the frame of the glass door for divine help. But she didn't get it.

The couple inside had spotted the red death infected creature advancing on her and retreated to a set of inner doors. The woman mouthed the word *sorry* before the man pulled her inside and closed the wooden doors behind them.

"Fuck you and your God," she screamed at the glass door. She spun round to see her escape options were limited. The Infected were approaching her from two sides, and it didn't look like they were here just for hugs. There was a large waist-high plant pot next to the sandbags and doorway. She tried to lift it, to maybe break open the glass panel doorway, but it was too heavy. Yet the round porch area was only one storey high. Dropping her ski poles, she stepped onto the sandbags, hands pressed against the rough white wall and then onto the rim of the planter. It gave her enough height to grab the low, flat roof and kick off and pull and then push herself onto the wet puddled roof. The planter tipped over as she scrambled up. Her palms stung as she pulled herself up and rolled through the puddles on top of the flat roof. She was even damper than before but safe from the Infected, she hoped.

A huge crash of breaking glass jumped her into action, and she rolled over through the two inch puddles of water on the roof to see that the fiercely strong Infected had used the planter to smash one of the large side windows of the modern church. It and its fellow Infected hurried inside, bringing screams of panic from whoever was within. Selena didn't know whether to stay or go. In the end, her cold shivering body told her to get up or get pneumonia or hyperthermia or something.

Wails of panic became screams of pain inside the church. Selena slid down the other side of the roof and across the road as fast as she could manage through the standing water. She made for the left-hand gates at the side of the station and clambered over, hurting the inside of both her thighs in the process. She jumped down from the station and onto the track, wondering which way next would be best. Into London or out into the sticks?

Ann looked around the dank tunnel, surely they hadn't been led into a dead end?

"Up here," Ayesha pointed across to a metal ladder riveted to the left-hand end of the blocked tunnel.

Ann moved forwards to get a better look. The rusty ladder led up to an oblong opening at the top of the embankment. Drizzle fell down from the grey clouds above. Smiling, the girl moved past Ann to grab the ladder and proceeded to climb up the ladder like she was just running upstairs. Ann knew it would be hard work for her. Even running upstairs would bring on heaving breaths and a sweat on for her.

She watched as the girl's mother followed her up at a steadier, but fast enough pace.

The soldier slung his rifle over his shoulder and followed next.

Ann did not want to go next. She turned and ushered the two other women from the tent towards the ladder. Lucky for her, her husband was keeping watch on the terrible things happening in the hospital camp. For all his many, many faults, Tony would always let the women go first.

Ann was scared that she might break the ladder with her weight and trap others down in the tunnel, and feared that anyone else other than Tony might see her huge arse from below as she climbed the ladder.

The crying young woman took a lot of coaxing from her friend. Only Ann heard the soft tender loving words she spoke in her friend's ear or the soft kisses on her cheek. Ann raised her eyebrows, *lesbians*, she thought. With slow cajoling the two very friendly women in their twenties reached the top.

"Tony," she hissed back at her husband, who lumbered over to join her at the bottom of the ladder.

"Up you go luv," he urged, his eyes darting back to the tunnel entrance.

"Here goes nothing," she whispered, and started up the ladder. The rungs were icy cold, wet and crusted with flaking rust. The first few rungs were okay, but the further she climbed the slimier they became. The thought of being six feet off the ground did not help her, she hated heights. Ann took one rung at a time, slowly moving one hand, one foot, next hand, and next foot. Always keeping three hands/feet on a rung at all times.

"Fucking hurry up," her husband hissed from below.

That did not quicken her progress at all.

She was halfway up a narrow (for her anyway) chimney. The oblong shape of freedom and grey skies willing her on. The red-haired woman suddenly blocked the grey light above.

"Come on you can do it," Charlie urged in a caring fashion.

Ann forced herself onwards and upwards, even though her feet seemed to be screaming, go back down to safety. Charlie reached down a hand to her. It was two rungs out of reach, but it was a friendly and helpful beacon for Ann. Her fingers were numb and calves cramping up. The sciatic nerve down her right leg was burning like fuse wire heading for a heap of TNT. She gritted her teeth through the pain and fear and reached the last rung. She steadied her shaking body and reached up to grab the woman's outstretched hand. Then she was out of the tight claustrophobic chimney and found herself on a cold, wind-swept embankment with four sets of railway tracks on either side of her. The trees on the embankment edge masked some of the horrors of the camp down below, but not the fires and screams of the people.

It took a bit more effort for Tony to squeeze up the chimney onto the tracks but he made it. He was panting like she was, from the exertion, both of them bent over with their hands on their knees.

"We did it old girl," Tony said in between heavy breaths, reaching out to touch her in a rare moment of comfort.

"Less...less of the old," she replied with a tired wink.

Ann looked around. It seemed much colder, but equally much safer up on the embankment. She stared down each way, both ending in misty drizzle in the distance.

"So which way do we go now?" she asked the rest of the group.

"That way leads to Surbiton where me and Charlie live and then London. This way down to different places Woking, Guildford, Hinchley Wood and the rest of Surrey, depending which track you follow," Ayesha replied to Ann, the woman they had met at Kingston hospital, as she pointed each way down the tracks.

"But Kingston and this place are overrun. I suggest we head away from London and the denser population centres." The foreign sounding blonde woman suggested.

"But our flat is in Surbiton," Charlie stated, pointing up the straight track towards Surbiton station.

"Yes, but this place ain't safe, and Kingston is that way too, I think we should head down the tracks," Tony said, standing up to his imposing full height.

"What does soldier boy here say," Ayesha pointed a cracked nail towards the soldier in his combat fatigues.

"I'm an RAF Regiment Reservist luv, I just want to get home to my family in Woking, so I'm going this way." The RAF man re-slung his rifle and headed off down the tracks.

"We should have a vote on which way to go," Charlie said in a loud, passionate voice. Ayesha smiled across the track at her. She was all for equal rights, racial equality and gender rights, her second mum.

"We sticking together then?" Tony asked, pulling his wet scrubs from the sides of his immense thighs.

"Safety in numbers," Ayesha shot back before anyone could jump in with the same argument. She had been waiting years to say that in open conversation.

"I'm so fucking cold," Ann said wrapping her arms around herself. "Can we hurry up and vote, before we all freeze our nipples off up here."

"Or those Infected come after us," the Scandinavian-sounding blonde said.

"Okay, I suggest we quickly say who we are, where we are from and which way up the track or down the track, we want to go. Up is towards London and down, the Surrey suburbs and beyond." Charlie, who had taken charge of hundreds of council meetings, spoke up.

"I'm Darren Tiller, and I'm heading home to Woking,

whatever you decide," the RAF man said as he trudged off.

"I'm Charlotte Macmillan. I live in Surbiton with my step-daughter Ayesha. But please feel free to call me Charlie," she said, smiling across at Ayesha and rubbing her cold hands together. "Oh, and I vote up the tracks."

"I'm Ayesha Adebebayo, I live up there," she said pointing up the tracks. "So up the tracks for me."

"I'm Tony Gable, and this is my wife, Ann. We vote down the tracks, and can we please hurry this up before those fuckers or the cold kills us all."

Ayesha noticed the wife threw her husband a dirty look, maybe she wanted to introduce herself and vote.

"And we live in Weston Green," Ann managed to get in, with a smug look on her cold red-cheeked round face.

"Like Ann of Green Gables," Charlie chimed in, only delaying the vote in Ayesha's eyes. There was a time and a place for social interaction, this wasn't it.

"My name is Brita Mikkelson I'm from Denmark. I vote down the railway tracks."

"I'm Ellie Chambers, down the tracks," Ellie said in a low voice, too upset to say where she came from.

"Down it is then?" Charlie said, but the rest of the group had already begun to walk that way already, heads down against the wind-driven drizzle.

"Jesus fucking Christ, red skinless zombie people down there and all you bloody women want to do is have a committee meeting. Fuck me." Tony stormed off, with Ann behind him.

"Come on Charlie," Ayesha put an arm around her second mum and urged her after the others. Maybe going away from the danger was the best plan after all. Ayesha wished she knew where they were going to go and if there were warm beds and hot food at the end of it.

"Okay," Charlie said wanting to get away from the sounds of battle and death and pain below to their right.

"Is the electricity on the tracks off do you think," Ayesha suddenly said in a loud worried voice.

Everyone walking down the tracks stopped dead in them.

CHAPTER TWENTY

TRACKS OF MY TEARS

"Fucking run you knob," Hannah screamed back at Matt as they raced up the steps to Hersham Station. There had been a near lake to wade through near the railway bridge by the flats, blocking their escape from the red infected creature following them. Another two Infected were splashing through the water covered road and pavement from the other side of the Molesey Road. So the only real option was to run up the set of steps up the side of the embankment near the bridge and on to the station platform.

Hannah was glad to get her sodden trainers and cold feet out of the icy water and be able to run up the steps unhindered. Matt commented last night in bed that the trains had not been running since about nine o'clock, and they had heard no sound of them again this morning.

She reached the top first and turned to see Matt was only three steps behind her. The Infected were still slow and hindered by the water and whatever ailed them. Hannah was glad of the protection of the platform roof above as she scanned the tracks up and down. There were no trains in sight and up here no flooding to worry about. The small covered station buildings ended only a few metres away, but to the right the roofless platform stretched on for ages. Fearful of the electrified track she ran along the platform. Matt stopped as he reached her and then had to start running again to catch up again.

"Where the hell are we going?" he shouted after her.

"Anywhere they aren't," she shouted back.

The drizzle hit their faces as the roof above ended. They ran on, for their lives. Hannah had been on this station platform hundreds of times but had never ventured this far up. She kept glancing back expecting to see the murderous Infected coming after them, but the station was empty except for them. Only the sound of their footfalls on the wet platform could be heard. Sides burning, they reached the end of the platform at last. It sloped down to trackside level with warning signs not to trespass any further. They ignored them. There was a thin muddy track leading down the embankment, made by railway engineers. They took the track, but Hannah knew she needed to rest before running anymore. She ducked under the stilted railway platform and hid underneath with all the worms and spiders. Breathing heavy, Matt looked down the steep muddy track. Holding his side, he decided to join her.

They huddled in close under the track and waited, fighting to control their rapid breathing.

They heard the rain hitting the platform above their heads.

Two minutes later, they heard three sets of feet also.

"The railway system is suspended, and the tracks turned off," the RAF regiment reserve informed them all.

Brita looked up, getting rain in her eyes as the armed man led the way down the tracks. She was grateful that they were slowly walking away from the fires, death, and chaos in the rec below. Yet, she wished for better clothing for her and Ellie. They were exposed to the cold wind and rain so high up and their scrubs were soaked through and sticking to them, hardly any use at all. They might as well be naked. Usually, the thought of Ellie naked would bring a smile to her thin lips, but not today. So much had happened in such a short space of time, it was hard, even for her as an outsider to comprehend. She just wanted to get Ellie home, warmed up, dressed and then they would grab their passports and try and get back to Denmark. She wasn't sure if the airports would be shut because of the weather or quarantine procedures in place to stop people leaving the British Isles, but she had to try. Maybe the ferries would still be operating. They needed to get to Ellie's parents' house and try and find out what the hell was happening from the television news or the internet.

She had no idea where she was and hoped Ellie would tell them where to leave the railway embankment. As they crossed over a flooded road below, she looked over the side to see several parked cars abandoned and waterlogged. She wished she had her phone with her to see what Denmark and the rest of the world was saying about the outbreak. That was left behind somewhere in some tent or the burning sport's pavilion somewhere. She could do nothing but hug her lover close and trudge down the tracks like everyone else.

Selena had been walking face-on to the drizzle next to the railway tracks for ages it seemed. She had decided to head for London, thinking the Metropolitan Police and Army would be in greater numbers there. She had a few colleagues she knew there, who might put her up for a while until this crisis and flooding ended. The hood of her coat did little to keep the swirling rain from her cold cheeks. The straps of her rucksack were burning into her shoulders, and it was heavy as hell. The tracks were high up on embankments, for the most part, so she saw little of what was going on below on the flooded ground. She had heard cries of pain, screams of terror and wails of grief-stricken people, but she was isolated up on the tracks. Not safe, but safer than most.

She thought about Wet and how the infection, virus whatever you wanted to call it, had eaten away his skin and killed him in the end. Had the rats finished him off or did everyone infected turn into some crazed monster. She remembered having an abscess under one of her back teeth a year ago. It had driven her mad with agony. High doses of painkillers would hardly touch it, and it had driven her up the wall. She couldn't sleep; drink, eat, work or even concentrate to read a book. She remembered vividly banging her head against the headboard of her bed at three in the morning. Her father, a career officer in the Royal Marines, had told her as a girl if you had a pain somewhere, kick or punch something hard, as the new pain would take your mind off it. He had been blown up by the IRA in 1987, and never even saw her become a lawyer. She wasn't sure his advice really worked that well.

Yet, the point her brain was trying to fathom, was these poor infected creatures had had all their skin rotted away by some highly infectious disease. Surely, they were in agony from that, so much it drove them crazy and prone to violence. Selena decided to avoid them if possible, like the proverbial plague.

When she looked up from watching her boots to keep the rain out of her face, she saw she was approaching the next station up the line.

"Hersham," she muttered to herself through her numb lips and trudged on.

Ann was full of pain, misery and loss. Walking through the wind propelled cold rain, was sending waves of burning lava up and down her right sciatic nerve. Her ill-fitting rubber shoes were rubbing her numb feet raw, and there seemed no end in sight to their flight. Add to that the fugue of grief that enveloped her, she wasn't sure how long she could carry on. They had just passed Esher train station, which seemed to brighten Tony up a little as he looked longingly at Sandown racecourse as they passed it. He had spent many a boozy day and night there, losing thousands on his so-called dead certs.

Two steps later she stubbed her toe on the jutting up concrete track sleeper and went down heavy on her left knee, bashing it hard on the railway line. She gave a cry of pain and curled up into a sobbing ball and rubbed at her hurting kneecap.

Tony turned and went back for her. Ellie and Brita stopped walking and waited while Charlie and Ayesha rushed over to bend down to try and help. The RAF reserve stopped to give Ann a look of worthless disdain, then opened up his canteen to drink from it. He did not offer it around to anyone else.

"Up you get luv," Tony said, not too much concern in his voice.

"Are you hurt?" Charlie had a much kinder and gentle bedside manner than her husband Tony.

Ann tried to speak, but the grief of losing her daughter and grandchildren was eating away at her, worse than any infectious disease. She could only sob and point at her knee. Charlie smiled at her and pulled up the baggy scrub trousers. "No cuts or red marks, can you stand hun?"

"Sitting on your arse freezing to death won't help you, Ann," Tony said with his usual marital belligerence. "Get up, we need to keep moving."

"Oi, let her catch her breath mate, she's had a nasty tumble," Ayesha stood up to her intimidating husband: and even jabbed his big bicep with an indignant finger.

"Don't you fucking tell me how to treat my own fucking wife," Tony bellowed back at the young girl, tiny in frame compared to him.

"I'm okay," Ann said, pushing on the frowning Charlie to stand up between Ayesha and her husband. "Let's not make a fuss over a little tumble eh." Ann held onto Tony for support and rubbed the bicep the girl had prodded.

"*Well,*" Tony grunted and put his arm around Ann's shoulder and frog-marched her off down the track. Ann was in a world of pain from her feet to her left knee and the burning pain in her right thigh, but she soldiered on.

"There's no helping some people," Ayesha called after the large retreating couple. She raised her thin plucked eyebrows at the two raised fingers Tony showed her as he escorted his wife away from her and Charlie.

"Leave it." Charlie's cold, warning hand grabbed Ayesha's equally numb one and gave it a comforting squeeze. "They've lost loved ones today like us."

"Don't mean he has to act like some giant dickhead does it," she said in a lower voice so only Charlie could hear.

"Come on let's catch up to the rest," Charlie managed to smile at her somehow.

"Why, doe?" Ayesha put her freezing hands under each armpit and held her ground on the railway track.

"Why what?" Even Charlie sighed at her this time.

"Why do we have to go wid them, doe, we could head off home and leave those people to do what they like. Our home is back that way." She pointed back up the misty track.

"I know you want to get out of the cold rain and somewhere warm and safe, but after what we saw at Kingston Hospital and the rec, do you think that home is a safe place to be?" Charlie stepped forward and rubbed both of her arms.

Charlie always made sense and knew the right thing to say in all situations.

"Suppose not," Ayesha had to give in. "I just miss my mum and the flat."

Charlie cradled the crying Ayesha to her neck and turned her to follow the others down the track. They seemed to have been walking down the rain pelted tracks for hours. Ayesha couldn't see where they were going or why, just that they were escaping those red infected people. She wondered why some people just died from the infection, and others didn't and turned into mental killing zombie monsters. When she looked up, and her tears cleared a little, she could see they were approaching another train station.

CHAPTER TWENTY-ONE

HERSHAM HORRORS

They had been cramped under the dry, but old spider web covered platform for over thirty minutes. They hadn't heard the wet sounding feet for a while. Had the Infected gone, or were they still around the station area lying in wait for them to show themselves?

Hannah eyed the muddy path down into the wooded area below. She was pretty sure she didn't want to go that way. The Infected could be hiding in wait for them. At least on the railway tracks they could see them coming.

"I'm going to have a look."

"Is that wise?" Matt pawed at her arm, holding her back.

Matt continued weakness was an ongoing surprise to her. She thought he had it all going for him; so mature, alive and sexy as hell. Now she only saw him as a whimpering man-child, hiding behind her bravery. *God, I hope the baby is a girl.*

Easily throwing off his hand, she moved her stiff, cold legs out of the supporting frame of the platform. She crept around the sloping end of the platform and peaked her head up like a Meerkat. Platform 2, where they were hiding was devoid of the Infected. Hannah rose up a little to scan Platform 1; it too seemed clear of Infected. Then she saw someone peer around the corner of the station leading down the other set of steps. It was a bedraggled woman in a bright, outdoorsy coat. They stared at each other; probably both eyeing the other up to see if they were infected.

Hannah waved, fearing the woman might duck back around

the wall and run off down the steps, taking her for Infected by mistake. The woman, her features mostly covered by the hood of her coat, waved a slick glove back at her. Then the woman seemed to stiffen and look up the tracks past Hannah's position. She waved, slightly more animatedly this time and pointed on down the tracks before ducking back around the corner of the station wall. Hannah turned to see several people lumbering down the tracks towards her.

"We got company," Darren the RAF reservists said, pointing ahead with his rifle.

Brita rolled her eyes. She had met so many gun loving, action film quoting men in her time in the Danish army. It was untrue. Most of them were *prickspillers* and cowered at the first sign of combat. They were approaching yet another station, and there was a young woman hiding at one end of the left-hand platform. Darren raised his weapon as a man in his twenties came out of hiding near the tree line with his hands raised.

"Stay with the others," Brita said to Ellie, who just nodded in reply.

Brita moved up the line so she was two steps behind Darren. They were within seven metres of the two strangers.

"What you doing there?" Darren asked them at gunpoint. "Are you infected?"

"No," the man said walking forwards. Darren swung his grey toned L5-A2 rifle towards the man, who stumbled to a dead stop, raising his hands higher. The girl, Brita noted did not raise her arms, but covered her middle instead.

Brita moved up beside Darren and forced the end of his rifle down, easier than she thought it would be.

"Hey," he said like a child whose favourite toy had been taken away by its mother.

"Do they look dangerous to you," Brita told him, before letting the rifle go. Darren frowned at her but kept it pointed down towards the tracks. "Are you okay?"

"Yeah, not bad," the girl replied before the man could speak. The girl walked past the man and up to Brita extending a hand to shake. Darren stiffened and then stepped back a step, but his twitchy rifle did not rise. The teen was much younger looking than Brita had first thought. *Still at school perhaps, pretty little thing, though,* she thought.

"I'm Hannah, and this is Mist-erm, Matt. Some weird infected people with their skin rotted off chased us up here."

Brita shook her cold hand. *The English, always so polite even with the world falling around their ears.*

"I'm Brita, and this is Darren." Brita turned to point at the rest of their approaching group in turn. "That's Ann and her husband, Tony. Charlie and Ayesha and Ellie."

"Are you all hospital staff or something?" Hannah asked pointing at the wholly inadequate clothing all of them except Darren were wearing.

"No, we were in a hospital and then a military one, but we got attacked by Infected and ran away," Brita informed her, as the bedraggled group crowded in to say their hellos.

"Eloise," the man suddenly said moving past Brita to her girlfriend.

"Matt," Ellie said looking up from the grief-stricken state she was in and taking in the world again.

"Look out!" A woman's voice shouted across the tracks.

Brita and Hannah spun around to see the woman on platform 1, waving her arms and pointing to the tree-lined track.

The three Infected—who had been after Matt and Hannah, rushed at the group.

Selena ran down platform 1 at Hersham station, waving frantically. She skidded to a stop just before the roof above her ran out and peered across the fine drizzle swept tracks as the Infected attacked.

A man in some sort of military uniform raised his rifle and blew the face off the first attacking red creature. The rifle fire seemed dull to her ears as the Infected creature died with an explosive fan of red misty blood and brains behind it as it fell. Yet the other two Infected dove under his firing arc and crashed him to the wet tracks, biting and clawing at him as he dropped his rifle.

A very blonde woman in hospital scrubs ran forwards

beating a lumbering mountain of a man in the same sort of ill-fitting attire to the fallen weapon. They had a brief exchange that the wind took from Selena's ears before the white-blonde woman coolly picked up the rifle and shot one of the Infected, who was biting at the screaming military man's neck, in the head. The other small red fleshless creature was biting between the poor man's legs. Unable to shoot, for probable fear of hitting the downed man, the blonde kicked the child-like creature in the head very hard. It had rolled off the wounded man before she shot the Infected red creature five times in the chest until it stopped moving.

Selena shrugged off her backpack and placed it before her. Searching through the things she brought, she grabbed a kitchen knife and the medical kit taken from her bathroom. She left the heavy backpack behind and jumped down off the platform without thought for her own safety and ran across the tracks to where the shocked group were crowding around the wounded man.

"Let me through," Selena called to the group of mostly scrub-clad people. A thin woman with auburn hair plastered to her face was trying her best to help the bitten man.

Selena knelt down and handed the knife to her. "Use this to cut off his clothes."

The shocked woman did so and began to cut away at the man's combat trousers. Selena undid her small medical green plastic box and searched through the contents for anything useful.

"They fucking bit me, I'm going to turn into one of them," the military man cried out through the pain of his wounds. He was holding the bite in his neck, but blood was pumping through his closed fingers.

Selena had only one major wound bandage and decided to use that on his neck. "Let me see, let me see," she urged trying to pry his fingers from his neck wound.

"Bitch bit my bollocks," he spat blood at her. Selena whipped the pressure bandage open and pulled his hands away giving her just enough time to see the wound and pushed the bandage onto it. His bloody hands pressed the bandage to his neck, as

Selena tied the ends of the thing around his neck tight as she could. The wound looked savage and deep.

"What do I do, what do I do?" Auburn asked as she exposed his groin wound.

"It bit one off," a short wide woman from the group circle above gasped, not helping the situation.

"The bitch bit off one of my nuts," the pained man shrieked in horror as he writhed around on the track in a very uncomfortable position.

"You've got one left," Selena said into his face and dug around in her medical box. She had nothing else suitable to use on his groin wound at all. Just gauze, plasters, sterile wipes and a pair of crap looking scissors.

She was biting off her gloves and digging into her jean pockets for a hanky when the man began to shake from tip-to-toe and his eyes rolled up in his head.

"Hold on Darren," a mixed-race girl in her early twenties tried to comfort him.

"He's going into shock," Selena said aloud and peered into the man's face. "Stay with us Darren."

"Balls," he croaked once, and his body went rigid and then seemed to collapse into stillness. Selena slapped at his face and then pressed her left ear down to his heart. She couldn't hear a heartbeat. She made a fist and pumped him once where she guessed his heart would be. A black jet of blood shot up from his groin area, hitting the auburn-haired woman on the cheek and over the trousers of a man and another woman in scrubs behind her. Everyone shrieked at once and retreated from Darren's body, dripping blood.

Selena looked down at the groin wound that was slowly pumping ever-decreasing arcs of blood from his torn scrotum area. "Must have hit a major femoral artery," Selena said in an exhausted, defeated voice. The bitten off testicle or the neck bite looked worse but weren't the problem, another small bite to the thigh had been.

"Is he dead?" The overweight lady asked.

"Yes," Selena said rubbing her face, before closing poor Darren's eyes. "Even with proper medical assistance, he probably didn't stand much of a chance."

"You not a nurse then?" the rotund lady asked her.

"Nor a doctor either," Selena replied a little peeved the woman assumed she could only be a nurse. She was neither in the end. "I thought you lot in scrubs might have helped more?"

"We aren't medical professionals, we were patients," Auburn replied, using a nearby puddle to clean Darren's hot blood from the side of her face.

"Who are you all then?"

"Survivors, I suppose," Ann replied sadly.

"Survivors of what?" the posh sounding stranger asked as she packed away her medical kit.

"Where do I start luv," Ann said trying not to think of her children and grandchildren. Her wet warm tears mingled with the cold rain on her cheeks.

"Shall we all get under cover first at least," the plummy-voiced stranger said pulling on her gloves and rising to her feet.

"What about him?" Ayesha pointed at Darren's corpse lying across the tracks.

"We can't leave him there," Charlie said rising to her feet.

"Take him over to the station under the roof part, I guess," Ann said. Loud voices made her turn around. Tony and Brita seemed to be scrabbling over the rifle. She walked over between them. "What's the matter now?"

"She won't give me the bloody gun, woman," Tony barked at her while jabbing a thick finger at Brita.

"Why the fuck should I, I served with the Royal Danish Army, I know how to handle this weapon, strip it down. I killed those fucking Infected, right?"

"Danish army, fuck me, how many wars have you won. I was in the British Army luv, come back when you've won some world-fucking wars ya dyke." Tony jabbed his finger at her again.

"And started many pointless ones, killing millions of inno-cent men, women and children too. You try and grab this weapon, and I'll shoot that fucking finger you keep jabbing at me, for sure." Brita barked back, standing her ground.

"Tony, we need help moving the body over to the station."

Ann hoped that her husband would see the futility of arguing with the Danish woman and give up on the gun. Even as she thought it, she knew he wasn't built that way.

"Give me the fucking gun, you foreign blonde cunt!"

Nope, Tony wasn't backing down, instead building up his usual arrogant head of steam that might get his head blown off this time. She saw Brita raise the gun and aim it carefully at her husband's chest.

"Look prickspiller, you either calm the fuck down, or I'll put you down."

"You ain't got the balls luv, literally."

Ann had to do something quickly.

She stepped in front of Tony and grabbed his balled fists in her wet hands. She turned to look at Brita. "We've lost our daughter, son and our grandchildren to the infection, he's a bit upset hun."

But Brita wasn't looking at her or Tony anymore. She was looking past them at her girlfriend, who was talking in raised voices with the man and girl they had just met. She suddenly leant the rifle against the platform and hurried past the married couple to see what the argument going on behind her was about.

"See, easily *sorted*," was what she was going to say, but Tony pushed past her knocking her to the ground on purpose as he angrily went for the rifle. Ann fell on the track and banged her knee again. She was back in the world of physical pain again. She was well used to it; at least it took her mind off her loss. The others were too busy arguing or trying to carry the body of the RAF reservist out of the rain to notice. *No change there, then.*

Ann did what she always did. Picked herself up, winced through the pain and carried on. Tony had his prize, as he fiddled with the rifle. It looked like a kid's toy in his large hands. For one dark moment, she hoped he would accidently blow his head off with it. Then the thought was gone, she had lost too much already to lose him too, for all his many faults.

Ann limped over to the others and helped carry Darren to the dry part of the station, where they laid him on a metal mesh-like bench.

"So what the fuck are we going to do now?" Ayesha said, glad to be out of the rain for the moment. Yet, the wind and cold were making her shiver in her scrubs. She rubbed her damp forehead, trying not to think what a frizzy mess her hair would look like. She was glad the station had no mirrors in sight.

"I dunno, report it to the authorities. Police or army perhaps," the new woman suggested. "Or at least find shelter. We haven't been formally introduced. I'm Selena, by the way. Selena Fenshaw-Wright, and you are?"

"Ayesha, this is Charlie. That's Ann," Ayesha said pointing to the people on the platform nearby.

"And the angry ape?"

"That's my husband," Ann replied, rubbing at her knee.

"You have my sincere condolences," Selena said tartly making Ayesha giggle. "And the others?"

Ayesha saw the brief flash of anger in Ann's face but was sure it was nothing new to her ears.

"Erm, Brita and Ellie, who seem to know the new guy and girl, think his name is Matt or something and the girl's called Hayley I think? They sure seemed to be getting in a tizz over there about something." *Tizz* was one of the words her mum used to say. Tears rolled down her cheeks again, and she felt Charlie hug her close.

"I'm pleased to have non-infected company at last. What the hell are we to do?" Selena stated.

Selena, the new lady, was right: *what the hell were they going to do now?*

CHAPTER TWENTY-TWO

IT ALL COMES OUT IN THE WASH

"So, this is the poor misguided woman who wears your ring, eh, Matt? Does she know what you are really like, the poor cow?" Hannah stood on the tracks hands on her hips. She felt hungry, wet, but at least drier than Matt's fiancée.

"Who are you?" Ellie scrunched up her face and looked down her nose at Hannah.

"She's one of my students at school, I rescued her from Kingston Hospital, when things went a bit mad," Matt jumped in before Hannah could jump in with the big reveal.

"You were at the hospital?"

"Yes, in the car park, but all hell broke loose, people went mad, got infected and the police shot people, it was pandemonium. Hannah lost her family, I had to leave the car, and we escaped together. Then there were Infected around the flats and they chased us up here, it's been a nightmare. I'm so glad you are safe and well." Matt moved a step forwards, then stopped, realising he was stuck between a rock and a hard place.

"My mum and dad are dead," Ellie said bleakly.

Matt moved towards Ellie with open arms to hug her. Hannah felt a sudden flush of teenage anger and jealousy.

"My mum, dad, sister, and grandparents are dead," Hannah snapped. Not at Ellie really, but towards Matt and the whole messed up world. "And I'm pregnant with Mr. Davies' baby."

That stopped the cheating Mr. Davies dead on the railway tracks.

"What?" Ellie shouted, shaking her head. "What did she just say?"

Just then Brita walked past and stood next to Ellie and put a comforting arm around her back.

"I said I'm up the duff with Matt's baby. We've been fucking in his car for months. See all that dress up schoolgirl play wasn't enough for him, he liked the real thing, and I stupidly gave it up for him, thinking it was love. What a silly bitch I am."

"Shut the fuck up!" Matt turned on her, his hand raised ready to strike. Brita jumped forwards and pulled said arm around his back in a half-Nelson.

"You don't hit women," she said before sticking out a foot and pushing and tripping him to the wet tracks in one fluid motion.

"You okay?"

Hannah nodded her thanks.

Ellie walked up to Brita and put her hands on her wet cheeks to turn her head. Then she kissed her with obvious passion, *and it was not for the first time either,* Hannah thought. *Good for her.*

Matt looked up at her, confused.

"I'm with Brita now, the wedding is off," Ellie said. "You coming?"

"Me, you sure?" Hannah said.

"We both fell for his pervy crap; I'm sorry he's messed up your life. Let's get you under the platform and out of this bloody rain."

Hannah smiled at her, and they went to join the others on platform 1.

"Your birds a lezza, and you've fucked a schoolgirl. Living the dream eh mate," Tony laughed as he walked past him holding the rifle.

"Where we going to go now? My family are all dead, and there seemed to be these skinless zombie things all over the place?"

"I don't know," Ellie said. "But us girls have to stick together eh." She reached out her hand to Hannah, who took her cold fingers in hers as they walked.

"Hey wait for me," Matt called as the group trudged on down the tracks. From the bridge over the road, they had seen red skinless bodies floating in the water. Other Infected were attacking the living so they decided to move on back down the line. "There's something you should know."

Selena had warned them about Walton Station and the Infected attacking the modern church there, but heading back up the line didn't seem any better. The world appeared to have fallen apart overnight. Maybe if they headed on further down the line, they could outrun the infection and find somewhere safe and secure to hole up.

"What is it?" Tony was the only one to ask. He was in a better mood now that he held the rifle and spare ammo. He had Darren's webbing belt over his shoulder like a Mexican bandit, as it was a foot too small to fit around his gut. The woman majority of the group seemed to be snubbing him; news travelled fast.

"There are Infected behind us," Matt called as he caught them up.

Brita turned in Ellie's arms, and they both peered back through the misty effects of the constant drizzle. Many figures were following them at a distance. They didn't seem to be able to walk fast or in a straight line, but she had the terrible feeling the Infected were pursuing them.

"We made the right choice then," Brita said turning back to the way they were going.

"I did," Ellie said and kissed her on her cheek affectionately.

"I'm starving," Ayesha said, rubbing her flat stomach. "And freezing my tits off in this gear."

Brita agreed. They had to get off these tracks to warm up and eat very soon or run out of energy. Then the Infected would easily catch up and pick them off one-by-one.

Selena stopped and shrugged off her pack. "I have a bit of food for now and some spare clothes to share around." She pulled out a woolly jumper and offered it up. Ann took it but gave it to Ayesha to wear.

"We haven't got time for this, we need to keep moving and find shelter and a fire and a change of clothes," Brita urged looking back down the tracks at the distant stumbling figures.

"For once I agree with the Danish bacon," Tony said. "We need to keep moving."

The group nodded and plodded on in silence. Food would have to wait.

Brita hugged Ellie closer to try and get some body friction going. Any heat was good heat at the moment. With the dark clouds and drizzle in the air, it would be dusk sooner than they thought. They needed to be in the warm by then or risk hypothermia, or stumbling into the Infected. Both would mean their deaths in the end.

Selena wasn't sure what to make of the group she had joined. She was glad the overall majority were women but frowned upon the fact Tony had the rifle because he had a penis, above the equally trained Brita. She tried not to think about it and focus on their shared survival in this crisis. The stories they told her while she had been insulated in her own home were horrific to hear. She was glad to have people to talk to, even though they were not her usual friend-set. They hurried past Walton Station, which was nearer to ground level than the last two. They saw no sign of the Infected, so kept on moving as best they could.

Being on the railway tracks was a different type of isolation. Before they were on a high embankment surveying the floods and carnage, now it was the other way. Steep embankments of earth were on either side, excluding them from the outside horrors of infected Surrey. The inclines on either side were lined with trees and overgrown bushes, so they only saw fleeting signs of life beyond the gaps in the trees. They saw the odd side of a house or building, but not much else. They heard cries, sirens; car and home alarms. The waters flowed down the muddy embankments like waterfalls in places. The water on the tracks was only ankle deep; the stones and soil beneath giving good drainage.

Ann jumped as a scream punctuated the near-silence in which they walked. The beating of the rain on the leaves of the trees and tracks soon returned. She moved on with the others when the scream was not repeated. Apart from two helicopters, they heard nothing else fly overhead.

"No planes."

"What?" Tony grunted at her. She hadn't realised she'd even spoken aloud.

"I've not heard any planes fly over today," she said in a small voice, wishing she hadn't said anything.

"So?" Tony shrugged.

"Nor me," Selena the new lady said, turning to look at her and got a smile of solidarity. "Maybe they have stopped all flights in and out of the UK to stop the infection spreading abroad."

"You think its spread beyond Surrey and London then?" Ayesha sounded worried.

"It does seem to have a rapid infection rate. From what you've told me, it has a high mortality rate. You either die or become some rabid Typhoid Mary." Selena said wiping the cold droplets of rain from her face, for what seemed like the hundredth time today.

"Mary who?" Tony, much to Ann's annoyance, loved to share his ignorance loudly.

"A carrier of the disease. This Red Death, virus, call it what you will, seems like the perfect killing infection. Those it doesn't kill, are sent out to either kill or spread the infection to others, and it appears to be spreading and killing faster as it grows," Selena pointed out.

"You make it sound like the living thinking Hitler of all flu bugs," Matt joined in.

"Not thinking as such, but evolving. Like those hospital superbugs you hear about, that cannot be killed off with antibiotics. Like the plague, but for modern times, drug resistant, fast acting, rapid infection rates and crazed living carriers to spread it. The government will need to get a handle on this quickly, or the whole country could be affected."

"The rain and flooding around here don't help," Ann piped up.

"No, it hampers a cohesive plan of action, how can you save people or evacuate an area if you can only reach it with boats or helicopters. You can't move the whole of the South-East of England like that, would be a logistical impossibility," Selena said.

"Why not just the infected places around here, why the whole of the South-East?" Ayesha asked, her south-east coming out as *sarf cast*.

"Because you need to build up a fire break, between infected and non-infected areas and make sure no infected cross that area." They looked round to see Hannah had spoken for the first time. "Or build a bloody big wall, that always helped over the ages."

"So, you are basically saying, that we are fucked," Tony said, with another shrug.

"Look, the next station," Ellie said, ending the conversation.

Ahead through the misty drizzle, they could see a larger station built into the side of the embankment. There were lights on, but they could see nobody moving about.

"Somewhere to get dry and spend the night," Brita said, to nods and murmurs of agreement. Those in scrubs were freezing and needed food and warmth quickly.

"Me and soggybollocks can go scout it out first," Tony said, pointing to Matt.

"Oi," said Matt and Brita together, but for different reasons.

"Okay, you too Danish Bacon, you are so flat chested and could pass for a geezer anyway." Smiling, Tony hefted the rifle and led the way, leaving the female protests in his wake.

"What an arse," Ellie said to the steaming Brita, then whispered in her ear. "You have lovely boobs."

"I'll show him, the prick." Brita hurried after the two leading men.

The other women were appalled at Tony's sexist words but were too tired and cold to join the scouting party or overly object. Selena wanted to give the *Misogynistic Man Mountain* an earful, but her pack had slowed her to an exhausted snail's pace. She let the three of them go ahead, she would take him down a peg or two another time.

Brita moved up to the side of the smiling Tony. Matt was frowning, trying to keep up on the left-hand side of the big man. He may be large, but he was tall and walked fast.

A large brick bridge hid some of the approaching station.

It reminded Brita of those Native American dwellings carved out of the mountainside a little. The station seemed embedded and had buildings dug into the side of the towering embankment behind it. When they reached the dry shadows under the bridge, they all slowed their advance to scope the place out. The buildings on the other side of the bridge seemed abandoned and not used for decades, but the station was fully lit, with waiting rooms, offices and a closed coffee kiosk, plus water and food vending machines; Brita's empty stomach noted. The signs for the toilets, also made her suddenly want to pee.

The place looked invitingly dry and deserted. She exchanged a glance with Ellie's ex-fiancee, and they nodded despite the strange circumstances. Both of them pulled themselves up onto the platform, leaving Tony behind.

"I'll check out the stairs and exits," Matt suggested, pointing to the main exit/entrance from the station platforms. Brita nodded again, she didn't want to be that close to him anyway. She looked back to see the others sheltering under the arched road bridge, that ran above the tracks. She shivered, feeling as miserable and cold as the rest of the group, all of them female she noted.

Tony, who was a giant of a man, over two metres tall she reckoned, put down the rifle and crawled up onto the platform. When she was on the track, the platform reached up to the underside of her chest; with Tony, it just about reached his waist. The platform vibrated under his heavy footsteps: she would not like to guess how much he weighed, slightly less than a small Volvo maybe.

Grinning despite the cold, damp and the situation, she made for the waiting room, rubbing at her bare exposed arms. The cold was an old friend to her, she loved the snow training she did with the Danish Army. She knew that they needed warmth, shelter, water, food and more importantly, to get out of their damp useless scrubs.

The waiting room felt like a baking sauna as she entered, covering her body all over like she had been dipped in a chocolate fountain. Her soaked clothes soon felt icy and like the enemy as she rushed over to an over-painted dusty radiator and hovered her hands two millimetres from its boiling hot top. The place was sparse; it had grey flooring, white walls and three uncomfortable black metal mesh benches to sit on.

At least it was warm, Brita thought, as she forced herself to leave the waiting room and wave the others up.

Matt came down the steps as she moved back onto the platform. "The exits are all shuttered and locked up both ends, no one is getting down that way."

The sudden shattering of glass grabbed hold of their attention. They turned to see Tony further down the platform smashing not one, but four panes of glass in the windows of the station office buildings. They hurried over and found Tony peering through the window of the station office.

The rest of the group had grown tired of waiting and were clambering and pulling themselves up on the far end of the platform, nearest the bridge.

"Oi Danish Dike," Tony boomed, "clamber in 'ere and have a butchers around."

"Fuck you," she said walking past him down the platform to greet Ellie and the others.

"In your dreams luv," Tony said to Matt.

"I'll have a look inside," Matt said, mainly to get away from Tony's big mouth; his fiancée, her lesbian lover and the schoolgirl he'd got pregnant. He carefully placed his hands on the windowsill, avoiding the broken glass and clambered inside to have a look around.

"Is it safe?" Selena asked Brita, as she and Ellie embraced.

"Yes," Brita said over her lover's damp shoulder. "It is basic, but the waiting room is warm and dry, and there are vending machines with food and water."

"Excellent, and well done." Selena patted her on the shoulder as she walked past.

"All I did was look around?"

"I mean for not punching the male chauvinist pig in the mouth," Selena said.

"I'm freezing," Ayesha said, not for the first time. She and Charlie followed Ann up the station where Tony was waiting outside the station buildings for Matt to report back.

Ann reached up and kissed her husband's cold stubbly cheek.

"What's that for?"

"To show my appreciation for you scoping the place out for us girls," she said loudly, aiming a withering look at Selena as she strode by.

Selena gave a dismissive shrug and wandered up to the vending machines. She was grateful to slip the heavy backpack off onto a nearby bench and route through it for her purse. She had enough change to get four bottles of water and crisps and chocolates for all.

"Why don't you just break it open and take the lot?" Ayesha asked coming over with Charlie to help gather up the vending machine booty.

"I'm not like our breaking and entering ape friend over there, I pay for what I take," Selena replied, while the words: *Murdering Hypocrite* flashed up in the frontal lobes of her mind.

"Yet we are already trespassing," Charlie said as they made for the warmth of the waiting room.

"Hmmm, yes." Selena had to concede that point to her.

The offices did not offer up any more comfort than the waiting room and were larger, draughty and mainly empty. Matt had found the keys to the toilets, to everyone's relief and a black bin full of musty lost property clothes. He wasn't suddenly the flavour of the month, but the people that did not know him looked at him with friendlier smiles.

He left the women to it. Neither Eloise nor Hannah wanted him within four metres of them, and his fiancée's surprise lesbian lover gave him frightful stares. He boarded up the office window and stayed in there for the night. Ann and Tony took up residence in the back mail room, using mail sacks for temporary bedding.

Apart from Hannah and Selena, the rest of the women were glad to be able to strip off their wet hospital clothes and crowd around the radiators naked for a time. Selena dished out all the clean undies she had packed and the clothes she could spare. Ayesha, Charlie, Brita, and Ellie, once dried off had to make do with Selena's few spare clothes and the musty smelling clothes from the lost property bin. They looked a right site, but at least they had dry clothes on, a warm, dry room to spend the night in and some food to eat.

Ayesha had found a make-up bag at the bottom of the lost property, next to a prosthetic arm and a single ice skate. She offered to make up Hannah in an effort to cheer the mood and give them something to do. Charlie found some boxes in the offices. She broke them down flat and laid them on benches and the floor so they would not be sleeping directly on cold floors and metal. They locked themselves in for the night.

Selena wanted to talk about their plans for tomorrow, and what they had all experienced since the outbreak; but everyone was too exhausted and emotionally drained to speak. Selena watched them one-by-one, drift off to sleep. Hannah, Charlie, and Ayesha on the benches, while Brita and Ellie cuddled on the cardboard strewn floor.

Selena wanted to talk, find out their background and skills; organise what to do tomorrow and their destination. Maybe even confess to murder? She yawned loudly and kept a nodding watch for all of fifteen minutes before falling asleep.

CHAPTER TWENTY-THREE

WHO STOPS THE RAIN

The light inside the waiting room had gone off after two on some hidden timer system. So Hannah did not know where the light shining into her face was coming from. At first, she panicked thinking it might be a ticket inspector, or member of South Western Trains staff wanting to know why they were all kipping in their waiting room.

Yet it wasn't a torch or the overhead strip lights, it was sharp eye poking natural light.

Sunlight!

Hannah sat up on the uncomfortable bench leaving behind the shard of jagged light that sat where her head lay just a second ago. The sunlight was reflecting off another window on the station and through the waiting room window to land only where she slept. She sprung up, ignoring the urge to pee and her sleeping female companions and hurried over to unlock and open the door.

"Brilliant," she said, waking up Ellie and Brita on the floor as the bright morning light hit where they had been cuddled together.

She hurried from the waiting room to the edge of the platform, past the yellow line to bask in the warm morning sunlight.

"Brita, come on," Ellie urged her sleepy lover up. "Wake up everyone."

The grumbling sleepers awoke, then seeing the sunlight for the first time in ages, stopped to look at it in awe.

Matt, rubbing his bed hair from sleeping in a chair came out onto the platform, parallel with Hannah. She looked at him and smiled wide, forgetting what a low-life he was for the moment as she spun around, her arms raised in the forgiving, warm sunshine.

"Just what the doctor ordered," Charlie said hugging a still sleepy Ayesha as they joined Hannah on the platform.

"What's all the fucking racket," Tony said, with Ann following after. He soon changed his grumpy tune. "Oh, fucking yes. Nice one."

"Oh, that feels so good," Ann said bathing in the sunshine, as it took all the aches and pains from her body for a little while.

Each of the group closed their eyes and raised their faces to the sun and let it flow over them.

"Breakfast is on me," Tony said, smiling. He went inside the station office and came out with a red fire extinguisher and marched up to the food vending machine. He bashed at the locking mechanism only once, to send the glass front juddering open a few inches.

"That's stealing, you know?" Selena said an angry hue to her cheeks as she stormed over to remonstrate with the large man.

"Who are you then, a fucking pig?" Tony said, setting down the fire extinguisher to hand the food inside to Ann. The others were hungrier than fearful of a trip to court over stolen vending machine food. They crowded around Ann to get hold of the crisps and chocolate.

"I'm a high court judge actually," Selena said, realising how haughty she sounded as soon as she spoke. *And a murdering bitch!* Her mind threw into the mix.

"Well then, Judge Judy, don't frigging eat any then," Tony mocked and threw a bag of dry roasted nuts at her. It hit her chest and fell to the platform before she could react.

"Really," she managed to say before turning on her heel and heading back to the sunny part of the station platform.

"Snooty bitch," Ann said, opening a packet of cheese n' onion crisps. The others said nothing in Selena's defence or against, they were too busy stuffing their faces.

"Hey I've got a signal and Wi-Fi on my phone again," Matt suddenly cried. He was away from the group holding his phone with both hands like it was some tiny old religious text.

"Any news on the outbreak?" Selena asked hurrying over. The others followed at a slower pace, some still eating their stolen breakfasts.

"It's bloody slow," Matt remarked. "BBC news site is coming up, says a state of emergency has been called in the South of England. The Red Death plague, they are calling it."

"Does it tell us what to do, where to go to be safe?" Charlie, one of the tallest of the women, asked over a few heads.

"Erm, the whole of the inner ring of the M25 area including London is under martial law. The army and police from the rest of the UK have been drafted in to stop the outbreak that either kills in the majority of cases or turns the victims into homicidal murderers. People are advised to stay indoors or if the flood waters allow, head out of the danger area."

"Tell us something we don't know," Ayesha commented.

"Does it tell us the nearest safe place for us to go?" Selena, the voice of calm reason asked.

"Erm, hang on there is a map." Matt sucked his bottom lip in frustration staring at the screen with the impatient group huddled around him.

"Well?" Tony boomed breathing down on his left ear, with towering menace.

"It's slow alright, downloading," Matt said, trying to be firm, but not too confrontational with the large man. It didn't help that half the group already hated his guts. "Here we go, nearest safe place to go for survivors is Woking."

"We might as well stay on the tracks then," Hannah said.

"Yeah, they lead to Woking, and it seems safer than trying to go by road," Ayesha said.

"Then, when everyone is ready we should carry on down the tracks," Selena said.

"Carry on up the Khyber eh," Tony sniffed and headed off, leading Ann away from the group again.

Ann wanted to stay and talk to the other women, but Tony she knew, would keep her safe, he always did. He had his faults, but he wasn't a coward and would defend her with his dying breath.

The group split up into couples, relatives and factions while they ate. Hannah needed the loo and hoped this wasn't a sign of her life to come; searching for loos or squatting behind bushes every hour. She stared into the dirty toilet mirror afterwards, trying to appraise her appearance. Her cheeks were dirty from overnight tears and her hair a mess. She washed her face in cold water and used her fingers to try and comb her hair into some sort of shape.

"Need this?" Selena appeared at the door with a small towel, toothpaste, toothbrush and hairbrush, like she was in a holiday camp.

"Thanks," Hannah said taking the offered brush.

Selena joined her at the next sink and began to wash her face with pink soap from the wall dispenser. "So, where do you think we should we head today?"

Hannah shrugged, pulling at the tangles in her hair. "Carry on down the tracks I suppose. Woking"

"Get as far away from the infection as we can, you mean."

"Yup."

"We could find a large car or minibus," Selena said idly. "I'm sure that Tony would know how to hotwire one."

"Nah, stick to the tracks, out of harm's way. The roads that ain't been affected by the flood will be chock-a-block with cars and probably Infected."

Selena thought about brushing her teeth, but then stopped and dried her face off instead.

"I was right about you," Selena said, moving to leave.

"What do you mean?" Hannah turned and offered the brush back.

"That you are the brightest of the lot of them out there." Selena smiled at her and opened the toilet door. "You keep it." She nodded at the brush and then left Hannah alone again.

"Too right I'm the cleverest," she said to the mirror as she began to brush her hair again.

"It is very quiet," Brita said to Ellie to break the silence. They led the group along the wide railway tracks, hoping they were leaving danger behind, and that civilisation, control, and safety were ahead.

"Hmmm," Ellie said turning her head back from behind to face the way they were going.

Brita glanced back to see what Ellie had been staring at. She frowned, seeing only Matt following behind the schoolgirl he got pregnant. Brita pursed her thin lips but said nothing. She hoped it was anger or curiosity that made her girlfriend look back at her ex-fiancé and not because she still had feelings for him.

"Do you think he was fucking her, then coming home and making love to me?" Ellie said out of the blue as they left Weybridge station behind.

"You are asking the wrong person." Brita was tight-lipped and clicked in her reply. She tried to swallow down her jealousy and hoped this relationship would not go the way of all her others and die. She tried to put herself in her lover's shoes. Of her coming back from holiday with her, having her first same-sex experience of love, then the confusion and getting back with Matt. The person she had chosen over Brita was sleeping with a student and had got her pregnant. Add to that fact, what had happened to her parents, she decided a little slack was in order.

So instead of jealousy ruining things again in her love-life; she took Ellie's hand in hers and kissed it softly.

"What was that for?" Ellie gave a resemblance of a smile back at her.

"To know that I love you and have your back."

Ellie squeezed her hand tight and leant over and kissed her for three seconds on the lips. It was more than a peck, less of a snog, more of a sign of love and affection. They were leading the group so everyone behind could see, especially Matt.

"Get in there girls," Tony cried out his bawdy encouragement.

"Wow, would you look at that." Selena actually whistled as they left the banks of trees behind to find themselves on a yellow brick built bridge. Normally the River Wey ran twenty feet or so below, but not now. The waters were much higher and the early morning sunlight reflected off two vast flood lakes on either side of their elevated position.

To the right were just trees dotted out of the risen flood water, like some damn had burst over the fields and trees. To the left things were markedly different. The remains of the old Brooklands race tracks were deep underwater. The tall glass buildings of the Mercedes-Benz World buildings were encircled with deep water over head high. Their tracks, the aeroplanes from the museum and the industrial buildings, further along, had become useless modern islands in a biblical flood. Apart from swans, ducks, and geese, nothing moved on the flood lakes on either side for miles around. Apart from the odd island of raised land, the place looked waterlogged as far as the eye could see.

"Bloody hell," Tony exclaimed moving to the side of the bridge to gawp.

"I did a lad's driving day on the track, somewhere under there." Matt pointed past the isolated buildings to where the driving fun day out track should have been.

"Need a friggin motorboat now, mate," Tony replied.

"Guess staying on the tracks was the best idea," Selena said turning to smile at Hannah.

"Top plan," Hannah nodded back with a knowing smile.

The group split into couples or factions to either side of the yellow brick bridge and stared out over the flooded area that was normally water free.

"This won't do us any good standing here gawping at the water, will it?" Ann said to get them moving. Staring at the light reflecting off the water was giving her time to think. And all she could think of was the family she had lost. Sniffing up her tears and wiping her eyes with her palms she trudged on down the tracks. The pain in her thighs and knees a welcome friend now. It gave her mind something else to focus on, beyond the devastating losses she had recently suffered.

She looked back as Tony joined her. Even the big man, was wiping at his eyes. Ayesha was crying openly in Charlie's arms, and that had set off Ellie and even the strong looking Hannah. Matt tried to comfort her but was soon shrugged off short shrift.

"Looks like another station ahead," Ann said aloud, her hand over her eyes as she peered along the straight tracks.

"Maybe we will find help or someplace safe up there?" Charlie said, rubbing the sobbing Ayesha's back as they walked towards it.

"Hersham, Walton, Weybridge, Byfleet and New Haw," Selena chanted, recalling the train station announcement she had heard many times before. Sometimes she had to work at the large courthouses in Guildford and often took the train, as the parking was always a pain. Plus, she enjoyed having to do the commute thing, now and again.

"Guess we just hope for the bloody best eh," Ann said, as she led them on.

Ayesha just about managed to control her sobs, to raw-throated hitches by the time they made it to the next station. She saw the station was small, a little like Hersham had been. It was locked up fast and devoid of life.

She was in a group with Ellie and Brita and Matt, checking the right-hand platform, while the rest took the other. She walked past the station building to the railing beyond. The flood waters were slightly lower here but covered all the roads, pavements, and gardens of the nearby houses. The whole place seemed like a silent post-apocalyptic film set from a movie and not real life in sleepy Surrey. No one was about, and no cars could make it down the deep flooded roads either. She hoped that the people had been evacuated days ago because of the flood warnings and not because the Red Death Infection had decimated all life here too.

"There's nobody fucking here," she wailed in a high frustrated voice.

Charlie had to rush over and comfort her again. She missed her mum so much and her clothes and home and friends, she couldn't cope with any of this, it was too much for her to bear. Even with the sun out, which typically made her happy, just showed up what a terrible world her life had become. Water and death surrounded them all. She sat on the nearby bench and began to sob again.

Ellie brought over a bottle of water from a carrier bag full she had carried from Weybridge station. Charlie took it and offered it to Ayesha. Ayesha was crying so hard, she couldn't even drink or think or control the fear and rising grief in her young body. Charlie held her close and tried not to break down also.

The other side of the tracks were no different. Flood water, like canals, ran around and through the industrial estate nearby.

But there was worst to come ahead.

The group reconvened on the London-bound platform, as Ayesha was a hysterical mess and going nowhere fast. Tony did his usual vending machine thievery, with Ann's aid. Selena tutted but kept any other objections to herself this time.

The group sat in the sunshine and ate. Glad to have at least snacks to keep them going and fair weather for the first time in weeks. Brita wasn't in the mood for sitting, so decided to scout out the tracks ahead. Ellie kissed her and warned her to be careful, but did not join her.

"Can I come too?"

Brita had just reached the end of the platform where it sloped down to the tracks again. She turned to see Hannah hurrying after her. She looked past the schoolgirl to see Matt sit down on the same bench as her Ellie. "Yeah, for sure," she muttered and turned back to her task, not waiting for the girl.

Hannah had to jog to catch up with the pretty, but stern looking Danish woman.

"Had to get away or the crying would set me off again," Hannah said for something to say. She didn't think Brita would break the ice first.

"You have lost people?" Brita asked, trying to be sociable. She kept to the left-hand side of the railway embankment, her eyes over the side and the flooded world below.

"Everyone," Hannah replied, with a hitch in her voice.

"Sorry, I didn't mean to upset you in your condition," Brita said in her emotionless, matter-of-fact voice.

"Nah, it's okay." Hannah stared at her feet for a while.

They walked on in silence, trying to see any signs of the flooding ending or people and life below. There was none they could see.

"Guess this is weird, me being here with you," Hannah finally said, trying to break the ice again after a suitable pause.

"Why?" Brita replied, in her abrupt manner. Hannah was trying to work out if it was her usual voice, losing something in translation or she didn't like her much.

"Because I've got preggers by your girlfriend's fiancé," Hannah tried to add some lightness and a nervous giggle to the one-sided conversation.

"You are young and are allowed to do stupid things, I think. It is Matt as your teacher that is in the wrong, not you. He abused his position as a teacher to have sex with you, which is his fault, not yours. I do not hate you, Hannah, but wish to break in his fucking teeth every time the prickspiller smiles at my Ellie." Brita nodded.

"Join the queue," Hannah said in an amused voice. "Are all men like that, so fucking immature?"

"In my limited experience, yes, for sure." Brita looked down at her and gave her a ghost of a smile that accentuated her high cheekbones and lovely blue eyes.

A sudden squeal of locked brakes and a crash of an impact ahead snapped their focus ahead, down the tracks again. There was debris on the tracks ahead, but they could not see anything from their position, so they broke into a run. Coming to the end of a row of trees that blocked their view, they suddenly saw the problem ahead, and it stopped them in their tracks.

CHAPTER TWENTY-FOUR

THE END OF THE ROAD?

Hannah and Brita could not believe their eyes.

An enormous curved section of the M25 London Orbital Motorway that spanned the railway tracks, the river and canal below had collapsed into the floodwaters. An eight-hundred-yard section built on concrete supports had given way under the raging flood waters. The supports had not been designed to deal with flood waters ten feet high and had folded like a pack of cards sometime before yesterday. Cars, buses, lorries and trucks were mingled with broken up parts of the motorway jutting out of the floodwaters. It had mostly happened off to the right sending cars and people into the deepest part of the river and adjoining canal and to their watery deaths. To the left of the concrete littered railway tracks it stopped just before a red fire engine precariously rocking over the edge. Obviously new on the scene it was the crash they had heard. Most of the tracks were surprisingly debris free, the curved section of the Motorway having fallen to the right in a domino effect and into the deep flood waters over the side of the tracks.

"What the merry fuck!" Hannah used one of her grandfather's favourite garden, out of grandma's earshot swears.

"Look," Brita pointed into the lake of waters that rose above the boundaries of the river and canal that intersected deep below the high water line. A body floated in the water. When they spotted one, then they saw more. All dead, all drowned and floating around the wreckage of the motorway and their sunken vehicles. A few, Brita noticed, were skinless and infected, but thankfully dead.

Hannah gulped in air after forgetting the basic body motion of breathing automatically. She coughed a few times, but could not keep her eyes from the carnage below. She watched transfixed as the upturned body of a girl her age, it seemed, floated into the branches of a half-sunken oak tree and lodged there. The girl's hands still clinging to a soggy grey teddy bear, even in death. It seemed too real and unreal at the same time. Like she was part of a Hollywood CGI disaster film. The scene overwhelmed her, the loss too much for her young mind to comprehend. She felt the world around her turning black at the edges, like beetles biting away at her reality, gnawing the edges of her sane real world. She wanted to run, close her eyes or at least turn away, but she could not. Her whole world was crashing down around her, crushing her, making it harder and harder to breathe.

A long whipping sound saved her from closing down completely. She spun around on survival instinct to see what the noise was and whether it was a threat to her and her baby or not.

Brita had turned first, giving her a place to spot her vision. A cream coloured hose had been spun out from somewhere unseen at the rear end of the fire engine. It was hastily followed by a blond haired young fireman in his protective clothes, but no helmet. An axe head was visible from the back of his jacket as he slid down the hose like a pole, his gloves protecting his hands.

Once he hit the ground, he pulled the axe from his jacket. The two women took a step backwards.

He raised a gloved hand to them. His face was young and handsome but covered with dirt and a little blood. "Stay back," he warned them and turned to look up at his fire engine. Then two things fell down from the broken motorway above.

Two bodies.

One dressed like the young firemen fell headfirst onto a raised concrete sleeper, and its red skinless face exploded with blood, bone, and brains. The other was a woman, in a green floral dress that landed on her feet, before she tumbled over. Her legs, arms and face were gone, just grisly red remnants of the human, wife, and young mother she had once been, remained.

Brita was shocked when growling in her throat she rose from her heavy fall. Her right ankle was broken and twisted inwards at an unhealthy angle. She walked on it anyway, raging against the pain and heading arms outstretched towards the healthy fireman.

"Stay back miss, please," he warned her. Whether she heard, or understood or just ignored him, they did not know. The Infected woman in the bloody green dress hobbled towards him. Brita and Hannah wanted to cry out a warning, but events took precedence. He sidestepped the woman and brought the axe around into the side of her neck, embedding halfway through. She fell onto the track dead, as the fireman warily stepped forwards and rocked the axe head to free it.

"Are you okay?" Brita called over to him, as he stood over the dead infected woman's body, looking down at what he had just done.

"No, not really," he said turning and walking towards them. Hannah and Brita took another involuntary step backwards. Seeing this, the fireman lowered his axe in his left hand and pulled off his glove, clamping it under his armpit. He reached within four feet of them and extended his bare right hand. "I'm Piers Lucas, I'm very pleased to see another healthy normal living person."

Hannah judged the fireman was in his early twenties and hurried to grab Piers' hand before Brita. "I'm Hannah, and this is Brita, and I'm, we are pleased to meet you too."

"Anymore of you up there?" Brita pointed up to the fire engine.

"Not alive, no," Piers looked at his boots and then up. "Are you two alone?"

"No, there are a whole group of us back at the train station, come on I'll introduce you," Hannah said putting her arm through the fireman and leading him off back to the station platforms. She winked at Brita as she passed.

Brita smiled, shook her head and with a quick glance behind

followed after them. He was a very dashing, handsome young man in a uniform she had to admit, just not her type.

The rest of the group were very pleased to see Piers, especially the women. Even Ann and Selena seemed to be drawn to this new handsome addition to their group. Tony was glad to see another bloke, but Matt wandered off to the toilet in a sulk. He had two exs it seemed in the group, and no chance of winning them back with Fireman Sam in the mix.

They made a fuss of him, giving him food and a can of coke to drink as he sat down on a bench to catch his breath. He and the rest of his watch had been tasked with taking the fire engine to safety beyond the exclusion zone outside the M25 area. He and three other crew had been heading for a base set up in Woking. An evacuation centre had been set up for all emergency services to leave the quarantine zone and join up with the British army. He didn't know much more than that, the motorway suddenly disappeared ahead of them, and they had crashed. One of their crew Steve had been taken ill and had gotten worse since they left the station. He attacked Sandra, who was driving the pump engine at the time and instead of slowing down we crashed.

"I was the only one that survived," he said looking down at his boots. "Unless you count Steve who was infected." There was a tired, emotional shudder to his voice as he exhaled. To Hannah's annoyance, Ayesha quickly sat down next to him and put a comforting arm around his shoulders. She saw the smile of thanks Piers gave Ayesha and flushed with jealous anger. She had seen him first. Then she stopped and laughed at herself. Did she, the schoolgirl with a bun in the oven have dibs? Did she have any chance with him above Ayesha? Feeling immature was not her usual game, but seeing what her life had become, she knew growing up wasn't just about having career goals, dressing and talking older or sleeping with your teacher. She wandered away and stared down at the road below, rubbing her belly, wondering what would become of her.

"You okay there?"

Hannah looked up to see Selena standing over her.

"As much as I can be right now, with everything going on."

"I was going to give you a womanly pep talk, but I think we need to move." Selena pointed past Hannah's right ear to the flooded streets and houses below the elevated railway station. Hannah turned to see two obviously Infected figures wading out of a front garden towards the station.

"Come on," Selena said calmly tapping her shoulder. "Let's go tell the others."

"Yep," Hannah said as they went back to the group crowding around Piers. "Thanks, though."

"For the warning or the all so over too soon pep talk, I had rehearsed in my head on the way over?"

"For bothering to check on me."

"Us women of the world need to stick together, more so now than ever before. Things are going to get worse I fear before they get better."

Hannah wanted to ask her what she meant, but they were back at the group already, and Selena was telling everyone about the Infected nearby.

They hurried on past the remains of the M25 overpass, most of the group gawping at the sunken vehicles and corpses in the water. Piers, Hannah, and Brita had seen it before and urged them onwards down the tracks. They were glad to leave the devastation behind them. Yet as they walked towards the next station, the embankment began to gently incline downwards, so the flood waters on either side of the tracks rose higher and higher as they saw the next station in sight. The tracks only fifty feet or so ahead shimmered in the late morning sun.

The entire group felt an unease creeping over them. The high railway embankment had given them some comfort blanket of protection from the world below, but that had been eroded. They were nearly on the same level as their watery surroundings, and they had never felt so vulnerable. As they walked up onto the platform, they could see the local shops and businesses were empty and closed and showed no sign of life at all.

"Where the hell is everybody?" Hannah said, feeling suddenly chilled as the sun dipped behind a bank of white clouds.

"Evacuated?" Piers suggested.

"Could they evacuate so many millions of people from London and the Home Counties so quickly and with these levels of flood water?" Selena put in her two penneth worth.

"The army?" Ann said, as they hurried along, the shops lost behind the station's buildings for a while.

"Could be," Tony said.

"After the chaos of the army medical station, are you so sure?" Brita said grabbing Ellie's hand for comfort.

"It's the British Army luv, not some tin pot fucking part-timers like the Dutch," Tony shot back at her.

"I'm fucking Danish not Dutch," Brita said with venom, squeezing Ellie's poor fingers in anger.

"All the same, blonde, dyke fingering, Volvo driving, clog hoppers to me luv." Tony stopped, turned, and laughed down into her face.

"Fuck you, big fat ugly dick," Brita sneered up at him, unafraid. Ellie tried to pull her from the confrontation, but she held her ground.

"You asking for a dry slap, you little cunt?"

"Hey," Selena tried to intervene, but Tony easily pushed her pinwheeling back. Only Charlie and Matt stopped her from falling off the platform into the water.

"This isn't helping," Matt angrily called over to the toe-to-toe pair.

"That's enough," Piers said, leading with the hand holding the fire axe, he put it as a solid barrier between them.

"Huh, I've pissed bigger gallstones than you luv," Tony said with a grunt and turned back to walking along the platform. Ann tried to show solidarity with her husband, but he pushed her away with a loud, "fuck off."

"What a prick," Ayesha said, following after at a distance to the married couple.

"You okay?" Piers asked Brita, lowering his axe to let her pass.

"Will be when we leave that fucker behind, for sure," Brita almost growled at him and pulled a frightened and embarrassed looking Ellie after her.

"Well that was awkward," Hannah stated, as the group

followed the Gables up the platform at a safe distance.

"And he has the only weapon," Selena whispered at her shoulder. "We will have to watch him."

Hannah's reply was cut short as a woman came flying out of a first floor bay window above a hairdresser's shop down in the sunken U-bend of a road to the left of the platform they were all on. She fell down into muddy waters with an almighty splash, and then came up sputtering for air.

The group froze.

Appearing, by some miracle to be unharmed she began wading through the chest high water in the opposite direction from the station. It was a fatal error of judgement. Three Infected with oozing red sores where their skin had once been came splashing like mad things from an alley at the side of a hairdressers. Hannah, Charlie, and Piers all shouted out a warning to her, but it didn't matter. The three Infected caught her within ten feet of where she had splash-landed and took her down under the murky flood waters as they bit and tore the poor woman to death. Her struggles soon became nothing, as the Infected stepped back from the clouded red water around her floating corpse.

"Bastards!" Tony yelled and fired the L85-A2 at the three murderers.

His shots hit the dead floating woman in the back and peppered the water around the Infected like a fist full of pebbles thrown into the sea, but he missed all of them.

"Give me that you idiot," Brita had left Ellie behind to scream at the loud, stupid Englishman.

"Fuckoff." He dismissed her raising the rifle again at the Infected that had spotted the group. Brita quick as a flash kicked Tony in the soft spot at the back of the knee, He went down quickly as Brita moved forwards to tear the rifle from his grip and back-heeled him in the nuts for good measure.

The Infected were wading through the flood waters, towards the station. Only an easily scalable chest high green fence separated them from the group on the slightly higher platform.

"Come on we need to move," Piers called out as they ran to catch up with Brita, Tony, and Ann.

"What the merry fucking hell have you done to my Tony," Ann wailed at Brita.

"My fucking plums," Tony hissed through clenched teeth, his big hands between his legs as he lay on the platform.

"Shut up," Brita hissed back coldly. She breathed in and then out then fired a single round. It hit the lead Infected man in his chest and sent him down under the water. Only the buoyancy of his body saw him rise above the dirty water. The other two, undaunted by the loss of their fellow, struggled out of the deeper water and up to the fence. Brita shot the next infected dead centre of the head. The Infected woman rocked backwards with an arc of the skull, blood and brain matter hitting the water behind just before her lifeless body.

The last Infected was up over the fence, as Brita calmly adjusted the sight on the top of the rifle. She aimed again, as everyone else in the group screamed for her to hurry up and fire. The infected man scrambled up the wet grass bank and lifted its ruined head. Brita put two rounds into the infected man's head, taking most of it off his shoulders. It fell back and slid down under the water near the fence.

Only then did Brita lower the rifle and click on the safety.

"My rifle now, *bitch*," she spat at the downed Tony and set off down the platform with Ellie after her. Everyone else in the group followed suit, praising her calm, deadly accuracy with the rifle. Only Matt stayed behind with Ann to help the pained Tony to his feet.

"That bitch is going to fucking get hers," Tony grunted hands on his hips, as he tried to get the wind back in his sails.

"I agree," Matt said beside him. Ann didn't like the foreign girl, but the looks her husband and Matt exchanged frightened her to her core.

CHAPTER TWENTY-FIVE

THE WOKING DEAD

The next part of their journey along the tracks was tiring and hard going. They had thought to have rested up at West Byfleet station, but that hadn't been the case. The tracks slowly dipped so embankments of trees and bushes ran up either side of the waist high waterlogged tracks. Matt's phone signal died a quick death, not before he passed on the bad news that the outbreak had spread to Wales, the North-East of England and the first case had turned up in Scotland. They had to keep to the muddy embankments, and most were not used to, nor properly dressed for such a hike. Ann and Tony lagged behind because of their physical limitations, rather than anything else, but it suited the mood of the group. Tony was a loudmouth bully and woman hater, and most thought he deserved to bring up the rear.

Ann didn't like being at the back, for fear of attacks by the Infected from behind. She kept looking behind until Tony pulled her up on this with a slap on her arm. She always bore the brunt of his frustrations. He couldn't hit the Danish girl, so he clipped her one instead. She had years of experience of this. Part of her was glad to have such a brute of a man to protect her, but she also longed for the mostly female community of the leading group ahead.

They kept to the edges and top of the embankment when possible, for the next hour. The trees and lush green foliage kept the hot sun off them, but also limited their surroundings. They could see nothing much beyond the stretching tracks that they followed.

"Hey look," Hannah suddenly cried out pointing ahead.

The side of the embankment on the right was lowering two hundred metres ahead. And the tracks must have risen for the water stopped and became intermittent puddles. They followed the schoolgirl down the left-hand embankment to find that the water on the tracks was only ankle high. The further they traversed it sunk lower and lower until they emerged from the flood waters and could look down to their right through the border of trees. The waterlogged remains of an allotment could be seen below, the crops ruined by the flood water that had subsided from this area.

"What you think?" Ayesha asked moving closer to where Piers stood peering over the hedge down to the allotments.

"That's a good sign, hopefully," he smiled at her.

"So any rings under those manly gloves of yours?" She said, pulling at her hair with her fingers. She knew she must look a sight in scrubs and a dress from Weybridge station's lost property box, but it was all she had to work with.

"Eh?"

"Any Mrs. Piers, waiting at home for you, or a girlfriend?" Ayesha moved closer, her shoulder almost touching his. Her night with H seemed another lifetime ago now, and she desperately needed something to take her mind off her loss, even for five minutes.

"Only me mum," he smiled wider back at her. "Girlfriend dumped me a fortnight ago."

"Silly girl," Ayesha almost purred, touching his arm briefly. He felt solid and full of muscles.

"Come on Ash, time for flirting later dear," Charlie walked past and patted her bottom as she did.

"Yea, better keep moving," Piers smiled at her again and left her on her own.

"I'm so going to do him," Ayesha muttered to herself, just as Hannah walked past her and gave her a knowing look.

"Get in the queue," Hannah smiled back at her.

"Yeah, right," Ayesha put her arm around Hannah and patted her tummy.

The sun and the railway embankment rose a little higher. To their right, they could see an only slightly water covered road running parallel with the tracks heading into Woking and hopefully warm clothes, food, and safety. The road gave way to houses and back gardens, where some grass could be seen on the lawns. They trudged on under a road bridge but heard no sounds of cars or life above them. The trees on the right then blocked their view, or they would have seen the flood waters had returned to cover the lands again. To the left, they passed a shopping complex with big name carpet, electrical and white goods stores. And it seemed that civilisation was not too far away from them, and the horrors of the flood and Infected left behind at last.

They all picked up the pace, without noticing, so eager they were to reach Woking.

The tracks lowered again, and they could see evidence of taller buildings ahead in the town. The flood waters soon returned to ankle then knee level as the train tracks became level with the surrounding area. A metal chain linked fence replaced the trees and high hedges and the tracks could be seen to widen up ahead, opening out into Woking train station. It was the largest one they had seen on their travels down the line and a hub for many London to south coast train services. They could see a long train at a very forward platform and their hopes of finding somewhere safe to stay rose.

Yet with their hopes so did the flood waters rise again. They were up to their knees as they reached the end of the first platform. Everyone was glad to scramble up the sloping side of the platform and walk along it. The train on the platform was dark, empty and powered down. The station was as silent and deserted as Christmas Day. They made their way along the lone platform, glad at least to be out of the water again. They could see a car park to their left with twenty or some cars, but no sign of people at all.

An eerie feeling covered the group as they made their way down to the main platforms and station. The usual orange letters of the train announcement boards were blank, and nothing moved, nor sounds were heard. Selena nodded towards the steps leading to a covered bridge that connected all the plat-forms and exits. Everyone trudged upstairs with a rising feeling of unease.

"Left or right?" Ellie asked as she and Brita made it to the walkway first.

"Left takes us into Woking town centre," Ayesha said, join-ing them. She had had many a shopping trip and night out in most places local and London.

"What's to the right?" Ann asked. She didn't get out much at all by train.

"Mainly houses and shit," Ayesha replied, following Brita and Ellie left.

The collective group mind was made up, with Ann, Tony bringing up the rear as they were the least fit. Matt hung back near them, as he was persona-non-grata. The covered walk-way led down a flight of steps to an exit on platform one. There were a set of closed ticket gates ahead leading to a shuttered exit. Ayesha and Brita hopped over with ease while the others waited. Apart from a sealed shut partial glass doorway, the exit looked a no-go. Brita and Ayesha tried to lift the metal shutter, but it was bolted shut.

"No way we are getting out of here without bolt cutters," Ayesha called back to the disappointed group.

"We will just have to find another way out then," Selena stated from the middle of the group. Everyone dispersed into their pairs, family or cliques to search for another way off the station. Hannah and Selena went down one end of the plat-form, with Matt trailing five feet behind. He tried to avoid their turned gazes, pretending to look for exits or try locked station doors. Anna and Tony were exhausted and sweaty and decided to sit on a bench near the locked exit and wait for a shout on which way to go.

No point expending any more energy than required, she thought to herself. Yet stopping and resting, she closed her eyes and images of her dead family flooded back to her. She began to weep. She got so upset even Tony put his thick arm around her. Her mind raced to that skinless child in the hospital that had once been her grandson. Then of her daughter, son, and granddaughter, and when would this all end so they could give them a decent burial?

Brita, Ellie, and Charlie led the way down the other end of the long platform. Piers was a little way behind, with Ayesha nearly skipping along to keep up with the quiet, handsome fireman. Ayesha was grilling him on his tastes from food to music, to holiday venues, making Charlie smile. It sounded like the old Ayesha. Charlie wiped away a silent tear for their joint loss. Ellie was holding onto Brita's hand tightly. With all the recent loss and Matt's betrayal, she wasn't surprised she didn't want to let her go more than a few feet away. Brita had not lost anyone. She hadn't really known Mr. & Mrs. Chambers that well, so only felt a slight associated loss because of Ellie. It was all about her Ellie now and taking care of her through the grieving period and to keep her safe from any harm. She tapped the side of the rifle without thinking as the long brick wall running parallel with the platform gave way to a shorter iron fence, intertwined with bushes and trees. They had to step back down into ankle high cold water to get to it.

"This might be better," she said, reassuring Ellie with a smile before she let go of her moist hand. There was a three-centimetre gap between the end of the old tall brick wall and the newer grey metal fence. It was pushed a little way in like someone had tried to enter the station this way. "We need to move the fence to make a gap or cut the wire somehow."

"Here let me have a go," Piers moved up behind her hefting his fire axe down from his shoulder.

Brita stepped aside to let the fireman stand in her place.

"You can do it Piers," Ayesha said in an eager loud almost American cheerleader mode.

Piers wedged the axe head through the gap and resting it against the brick wall levered it to the left with all his might. The metal pole that held the chain linked fence in place gave a little. "Everyone grab the fence and pull inwards," Piers suggested.

Ayesha made sure she got the prime place next to him, as the remaining women grabbed the fence in their hands.

"One, two, three," Piers said, and then pulled hard. The fence pole gave a metre and sagged inwards towards them. It was enough for some of the group to slip through, but not all. Piers lowered the axe in the gap and tried again, it gave way more, leaving a V-shape crevice that should let them all through.

"Ayesha, go fetch the others. I think we have our exit point," Piers said without looking back at her.

Charlie saw her crestfallen face she knew so well. "I'll go fetch them," she said patting Ayesha on the shoulder as she went back down the platform to get the others.

"Wait here," Piers said, squeezing through the gap between the brick wall and pulled down metal fence post. His boots splashed through the muddy water onto the submerged pavement below.

"See anything babes?" Ayesha called after him with concern.

"Just empty roads and big buildings," Piers said looking up and down the street. "Not a sign of anyone, though."

"Weird," Ayesha said.

"You would have thought we would hear or see something in a big town like this?" Ellie said, looking timid and frightened like a doe caught in a hunter's sights.

Brita was about to reply, when a car alarm started sounding somewhere far off and unseen from where they were. "Maybe someone is about then." Brita smiled thinly and rubbed Ellie's arm. Yet were they normal healthy people or had the infection spread rapidly bypassing their flight to safety?

She turned to see the others slowly making their way down the platform towards them. Brita hoped this place was safe so she and Ellie could get away from Tony and his fat, weak wife and Matt the ex.

Everyone could squeeze through except Tony and Ann. But Ann's fears of being left behind were soon appeased as Tony pulled down the fence to the floor like it was made of bamboo and not steel and stepped over it. They headed left down the road back to where the main town and shuttered and locked station exit were. Apart from the distant car alarm and the splashing of their feet through the water, the town remained quiet and vacant of life.

They kept to the pavements to be slightly higher out of the flood waters. But it still covered their feet and ankles, and even

those with proper shoes had soggy cold feet. Only Piers escaped
numb wrinkled toes because of his fireman's boots.

"I so need to wash and blow-dry my hair," Ayesha said to
break the near silence.

Tony gave a disapproving grunt, from where he and Ann
lagged behind. It annoyed Hannah so she spoke up in solidarity
for the woman most close to her tender age. "I need a hot bath,
hot meal and then warm fluffy slippers."

"Warm, open fire for me," Selena piped up.

"Hot shower and hot chocolate," Charlie said joining in. It
seemed to raise their spirits as they splashed along.

"How about you two?" Hannah pointed over to Ellie and
Brita.

"I just want my mum and dad," Ellie just managed to get
out before bursting into tears. Brita held her close, ending the
brief happy conversation they had going. Her tears dripped
down her dirt lined face and down into the waters around her
bare ankles. Tony went to speak some unfeeling witty come-
back, but Ann nudged him in the ribs. She had wanted to join in
the conversation, but never had the chance to say what she truly
wanted. They walked on in silence, across the street local shops,
closed and dark, were passed by, one-by-one, as they headed
back towards the train station's shuttered exit.

"What's going on here?" Piers' words woke everyone from
their thoughts of the people they had so recently lost. Most of
the group looked up to see the road ahead between the railway station's high brick wall and the local *Budgens* blocked by
an armoured vehicle and a checkpoint made up of barbed wire
wrapped poles nailed to X crosses of wood on each end. The
water, the barrier, and even the green camouflage armoured car
was covered with dead bodies.

Red, fleshless bodies of the driven mad Infected.

The water was littered with them. The closer they edged
they could see the bodies under the dirty flood waters everywhere. It was carnage and not the enthusiastic welcome they
expected.

"Fuck me," Tony said in his booming voice as he splashed
closer to tower over the rear of the group for a better look.

"So much for being safe in Woking," Ann said, disheartened.

"Maybe it's safer closer in. This might just be an outer defence of the town to keep the uninfected populace safe." Piers tried to be positive.

"We have little choice but to go forwards and look. It is no good going back and retreating," Brita spoke up unslinging the rifle from her shoulder.

"Who is coming with me to scout ahead?" Piers asked, even his brave voice wavering a little. He had seen dead bodies and burnt people many times before, but not on such a bloody scale as this.

"Maybe we should all go this time. As a group. Safety in numbers," Selena suggested.

"Yeah, let's all stick together on this one," Charlie backed her up.

"Okay," Piers said hefting his axe and heading forwards across the road to the other pavement by the shops. This route had less infected dead ahead of them if they hugged the walls of *Budgens*. Hannah swallowed hard as she followed Piers' lead and stepped over an Infected corpse bobbing in the water. The water looked almost a ruddy blood colour around the military checkpoint.

As they neared the barrier, watching all the corpses, just in case they were playing dead.

"I can't," Ayesha said in a loud voice. Selena turned to see her being comforted by Charlie, the first of the submerged Infected corpses in front of her, face down in the water. Charlie took her arm and tried to guide her over. Ayesha's right foot rose up out of the water several times, but then she placed it back where she had started like a horse refusing a water jump at a show jumping event.

"Move your arse girl he's fucking brown bread, he can't hurt ya," Tony splashed past, being his usual sensitive self.

"But what if he ain't dead, maybe they are like zombies like from them films?" Ayesha was getting herself more and more worked up.

Charlie looked down at the corpse whose head bobbed and floated up onto the pavement and half rested there. She was having second thoughts about crossing over the body.

"Fucking birds," Tony splashed over and stomped his wet Croc-covered foot down on the Infected corpse's head five times in quick succession until it at last bobbed up with broken flat skull and red and pink brain leaked out of its eye sockets. Ayesha hopped over the corpse and vomited into the red water by the window of the shop. Charlie gave Tony a withering look and followed after to comfort her.

"Tony," Ann said, in an exasperated voice.

"What you on about, got the fucking job done didn't I? She got over old *deadboy* here," he said, giving the crushed skulled corpse a farewell kick before heading towards the barrier.

"Barbarian," Selena muttered under her breath and joined the front of the group next to Hannah and Matt at the barrier.

Peering over, they could see the bodies of soldiers, some wore ripped open and bloody hazmat suits and others in just regular combat gear and facemasks. All had died defending the barrier.

"Shit," Matt said surveying the scene beyond.

"No safe haven for us then," Ellie stated.

"Let's move this barrier in a bit so we can get past, this might have been an isolated incident. The army and the evacuation centre might be okay," Piers said, using his axe to thump into the wooden side of the barrier and drag it back, to avoid touching the razor sharp barbed wire. He had to pull and then push a few watery corpses out of the way, glad he was wearing gloves. He led them through one-by-one beyond the army checkpoint. The road carried on straight under a large cantilever metal and glass canopy that looked out of place amongst the other older surrounding buildings. It looked like it should be covering the entrance of a spanking new hotel and not an old railway station and taxi rank. Another road curved sharply around to the left. This was totally blocked by an army troop carrier, wedged in at an angle across the way.

Piers took a deep breath and moved head forwards under the roof when a wailing red Infected creature popped up from behind a long concrete planter and ran at the startled fireman.

CHAPTER TWENTY-SIX

NO HOPE

Piers panicked, and in trying to raise his axe to defend himself he ended up fumbling and dropping it beneath the murky floodwaters. Brita was helping Hannah through the barrier and could not get the rifle to her shoulder in time. The Infected man was nearly on him, just as three shots rang out halting the poor creature in its tracks.

Piers spun round, only to see Brita shrug her shoulders. Then the passenger door of the large troop carrier with its window rolled down, blocking the turning, swung fully open to reveal an army officer holding a handgun in his gloved right hand. He was dressed in modern combat gear and wore a black beret on his head.

Piers fished in the water for his axe and joined the group moving closer to the cabin of the vehicle. The officer pointed his handgun at them to stop. "That's far enough," he ordered in a deep Welsh accent.

"Thanks for..." Piers said, pointing back to where the dead Infected floated.

"Well, you thank me now, but you might not in time," the officer replied.

"Who are ya and what happened here?" Ayesha piped up, only feeling half sick now.

"Where's the army and evacuation centre?" Selena asked.

"Overrun and destroyed by the disease and the bloody *Skinners*. Lieutenant-Colonel Howard took a convoy south towards Aldershot with as many healthy people as she could take. I stayed behind to lead the rear-guard action and give them time to get out of Woking. Sorry, I haven't got better news for you all."

"Who the bloody hell are you then, Custer?" Tony boomed over at the soldier in the cab.

"Captain John Burton 32nd Wessex Gunners, Royal Artillery. I wouldn't say it's a pleasure."

"Is there anybody left alive here or anywhere safe?" Charlie asked.

"I'm sure there are some people holed up that aren't dead yet, but they soon will be."

"Why's that?" Selena said.

"Because the bloody Red Death has gotten into the water supply. If you've drunk from a mains tap in the last two days, you are just a walking corpse, I'm afraid. Sorry to be the bringer of such bad news." The Artilleryman's voice was both sombre and jovial at the same time, which made it more terrifying somehow. "Some of my men might still be at the temporary HQ we set up at the Premier Inn down the road, you could try there or maybe head to Aldershot or Farnborough and try and get evacuated before the Red Death melts your skin off and either kills you or turns you into a fearless homicidal maniac. Your life, your choice on how you want to go out I suppose."

"What the fuck," Ayesha exclaimed.

"What's wrong with you, where's your compassion?" Charlie called over to him, hugging Ayesha tight.

"Won't you help us, come with us?" Piers moved towards the cabin, but the Captain raised his handgun and pointed it at the fireman's head.

"Too late for me Fireman Sam," the Captain replied pulling off his left leather glove to reveal most of the skin underneath had been eaten away. "I suggest getting your arses out of here before it reaches my brain. Good luck, you'll need it." He slammed the door of the personnel carrier shut and leant his head on the dashboard, in supplication to his fate.

The group, weary, deflated and soggy from the knees down looked around at each other, wondering what to do next. Woking had been their goal; now that too had been swept away by the Red Death and flood waters.

The group of survivors stared at each other, lost and bemused, until a single shot rang out to break the silence.

To be concluded in:

THE RED DEATH

BOOK TWO OF THE END OF ALL FLESH

ABOUT THE AUTHOR

Peter Mark May is the author of seven horror novels and one novella: *Demon, Kumiho, Inheritance* [P. M. May], *Dark Waters* (novella), *Hedge End, AZ: Anno Zombie, Something More Than Night* and *Forky's House*.

He's had short stories published in genre Canadian & US magazines and UK & US anthologies of horror such as *Creature Feature, Watch*, the British Fantasy Society's *40th Anniversary anthology Full Fathom Forty, Alt-Zombie, Fogbound From 5, Nightfalls, Demons & Devilry, Miseria's Chorale, The Bestiarum Vocabulum, Phobophobias, Kneeling in the Silver Light, Demonology* and *Tales From the Lake Volume 5*.

He also writes historical crime under the name Alexander Arrowsmith. His first two of a series of novels, *The Athens Atrocities* and *The Medousa Murders*, were published in 2019.

He also runs Hersham Horror Books and has published twenty-eight books so far.

Website: http://petermarkmay.weebly.com/

Curious about other Crossroad Press books?
Stop by our site:
http://store.crossroadpress.com
We offer quality writing
in digital, audio, and print formats.

Made in the USA
Lexington, KY
15 November 2019

57104056R00163